I0817808

JACOB CRAWFORD

The Shadows, Book One of the *Dark Sentinels* series

Published by Ravenhart Press, 8635 W. Sahara Avenue, #677, Las Vegas, NV 89117
www.ravenhartpress.com

Cover art by Matt Davis
Interior layout and design by Caitlin Greer
Hard Cover ISBN: 978-0-9996106-2-6
Paperback ISBN: 978-0-9996106-1-9

First Edition

For our beautiful city.
We are all #VegasStrong.

One

Valium, Xanax, Prozac, Lithium, Zyprexa—dozens of bottles, all my mother's best friends and worst enemies, tucked neatly into one little box.

Scratch that. My mother never had any friends, and she was always her own worst enemy.

My father and I had no need for a box of anti-depressants and anti-psychotics. We'd closed that chapter of our lives. With any luck, we'd be able to start over. For a moment, I wondered if he'd packed them on purpose, like some kind of twisted nostalgia. It was probably just a mistake, though; an oversight on the part of the movers. I threw the box away and returned to unpacking.

This house was nice. Quiet. Maybe it was just that I didn't have any terrible memories here. Maybe this was how it felt to be peaceful.

I sat in the spacious living room, all towering, floor-to-ceiling windows facing the greenery of the backyard, the floor a rich, dark wood with ornate rugs rolled out under the sofas. Our furniture was more or less in place, though most of it remained covered in protective plastic sheeting and thick, gray blankets. The moving crew shuffled about upstairs, unloading the last of our belongings.

I found a box of pictures next. My parents' wedding. I sighed and closed the box, carrying it out to the garage where I put all the things I didn't know what to do with. It was impossibly hot in the garage, like stepping into an oven. That would take some getting used to.

The intense Las Vegas summers were brutal, and weirdly different from Los Angeles' muggier heat. Not that hot weather really bothered me. I was always cold, so it was kind of nice. Then again, it was early June; it was only going to get hotter.

I went back into the house and dug around the stacks of boxes until I found my art supplies, which had somehow wound up in the kitchen. I carried the box up to my room and set it by my easel. A collection of old drawings caught my eye, and I got distracted sorting through them. I picked up a rough sketch of my father, serious, hunched over his desk deep in thought. I'd drawn it because, at the time, I'd never really seen him in work-mode. I was used to my warm, inviting father, not the serious lawyer. There was another of my cousins, and some still-life pieces.

I lingered longest on the fantasy drawings—dragons and elves—because they reminded me of a webcomic I'd planned on starting in middle school. It was a pretty blatant rip-off of *The Lord of the Rings,* but it was a project I still wanted to do something with.

I put the sketches on my desk for later. I wanted to get my room at least semi-livable before the day was over, and getting caught up in comic planning was not going to help me reach that goal.

My dad walked in while I was putting my clothes away.

“Hey, you hungry?” he asked, leaning against the doorframe. He’s tall—about six-foot-four—but the doorways in this house were so tall he almost looked like a normal-sized human. His usually-tidy brown hair was a little disheveled after all the moving, and instead of a suit, he wore an old t-shirt and faded jeans; a strangely casual look for my normally professional dad.

“Sure,” I said, kicking aside an empty clothing bag and opening the next. “What’re we having?”

He rubbed the back of his neck and chuckled. “Uh, pizza?”

“You do realize we can’t live off pizza forever, right?” I pointed out.

“We can order veggies on it,” he suggested.

“Why don’t we see what else can be delivered?” I asked with a grin.

He laughed. “Well, how about Thai? Your grandma told me about this great little place.”

“Ooh, yes. Order me some Pad Thai.”

“Okay. I’ll call you when it gets here.”

He headed back downstairs, and I finished hanging my clothes, arranging and rearranging things until they were just the way I liked them. I stepped back and looked at my work. It was good enough for now, at least. There was still more to sort through, but I'd get to that after lunch. I navigated through the boxes and cellophane-wrapped furniture to reach my bedroom door, figuring the food would arrive soon.

My foot caught on a box in the middle of the room and I tripped, stumbling and catching myself against the bed. I turned to nudge the box out of the walkway and stopped mid-motion—it was the box of pictures from my parents' wedding, which I'd already put in the garage.

Had my dad brought it up? I hadn't seen anything in his hands. It was a weird thing to put in my room, anyway. Maybe in his office, or his own room, though I doubted he wanted to remember my mother any more than I did. I huffed and picked up the box, carrying it downstairs.

There was a large mirror hanging in the hall, which I was careful to avoid. I didn't want to see her. I didn't want to see my mother's auburn hair, olive skin, or amber eyes. I didn't want to see her small features or bony build. I was even the same height as her (five-foot-nine *exactly*), and no one had ever missed an opportunity to tell me how much I looked like her. It was worse now that I was sixteen. It seemed the older I got, the more like her I became. I hated it. I didn't want to think about any of the ties I had to her. Carrying my mother's genetic code scared me. Having every aspect of my body serve as a constant reminder that we were related didn't help.

I found my father in the kitchen and perched the box on the counter as he cleared a space for us to eat.

"Hey, where do you want these?" I asked.

"Want what?" he asked, looking up at me.

I lifted the box slightly. The label, WEDDING PIX, was hard to miss.

"Oh. That. Um...just put those in the garage. We can decide what to do with them later."

Confused, I took the box out to the garage again and set it on a stack of other miscellaneous items, right where I'd left it last time.

Back in the kitchen, I helped set the table. The doorbell rang while I was getting us each a bottle of water. My dad lingered at the door, talking to the delivery guy and making him laugh with some joke I couldn't quite make out. He had a gift for connecting with other people, even if he was only around them for a minute.

We sat down at the table and I opened my box of Pad Thai, the smell making my stomach growl. I hadn't realized how hungry I was; moving really worked up an appetite.

Just as he opened his Mongolian beef, my dad's phone started to ring. He glanced at the screen and sighed, looking up apologetically at me.

I tilted my head to one side. "Is it work? It's okay, I don't mind if you answer it," I assured him, twirling some noodles onto my plastic fork.

"I'll just be a second," he said, grabbing his phone and getting up.

I continued to eat, too ravenous to wait for him to come back. He returned after a few minutes, sitting down and opening his plastic-wrapped fork.

"Well, I have some bad news," he said, scooping up a bite of food.

I stopped eating. "What? Is something wrong?"

"Nothing major, but I'm going to have to fly out to Chicago on Thursday."

"Really? We just got here."

"I know, but the case I'm working on needs some special attention. My whole team's flying out for this meeting."

I stirred my food as I considered that. Being a high-profile lawyer had always meant a lot of work for my dad, but he was typically more open about what was going on, at least to me. "The case I'm working on" was code for "the case I'm afraid to give you too many details about." The reasoning behind his hesitation was never good.

I decided to tread carefully. "Special attention? Did something happen?"

He shook his head. "It's just some new details that can't be handled over the phone. I shouldn't be gone long. Two days at the most. Hopefully not even that long," he said, keeping his eyes on his food.

I nodded. Clearly, I wasn't going to get anything else out of him this time. "Are you going to make it back in time for Aunt Celia's party?" I asked. Technically, it was a party for her daughter Leah's first birthday, and it was looking to be a big event. From what I could tell, it had transformed and was now part birthday party, part family/friend reunion. The guest list had expanded far beyond the group you'd usually invite to an infant's first birthday.

"I'll make sure I'm back in time," he assured me.

"Okay, because I'm not explaining your absence to anyone," I said, my tone mockingly grave.

He chuckled. "Oh, no. I wouldn't want to face your grandmother's wrath."

"We'd have to move again," I agreed.

We finished eating and cleaned up, heading out to the garage to sort through all the stuff we weren't sure where to put. As I stepped through the door, I could see the box of wedding photos was once again out of place. It had fallen off the stack I'd placed it on, scattering the pictures on the floor of the garage.

"Oh, jeez, how did this fall over?" I knelt down to scoop up the albums and framed snapshots. There were several little booklets of pictures, and a few smaller boxes of loose images spread all across the concrete.

"Huh. It must've been on an uneven box or something," my dad said as he started sorting through bags.

"Maybe...but I was sure I put it down right..." I muttered. There was a brown journal or planner with some kind of faded symbol on the front mixed in with all the pictures. It seemed to be stuffed full of pages and post-it notes, probably my mother meticulously chronicling wedding plans, like she did everything else in her life. I'd seen her scribbling like mad for as long as I could remember, documenting all sorts of things. I supposed those notes must have ended up somewhere. I threw it back in the box and closed the lid. I didn't want to see anything of hers.

My dad opened a box of files and started rifling through it. "Hey, honey, can you go check the mail? It's probably full by now. I started forwarding things here last week."

"Sure," I said, kicking the box of wedding pictures out of my way as I passed.

Outside, the sun was blazing. I squinted around at my new neighborhood; I was still getting a feel for this place. My house sat toward the end of a vast cul-de-sac. Our street was relatively quiet, and I hadn't seen a single other car on it all day.

We were in a gated community, in a section full of large, custom homes built on vast spreads of land. It left our street without a sense of uniformity, which honestly, I liked. Our house, for instance, had a kind of 1930s *avant-garde* feel to it, like you'd see in the old movies. Next door was a house with a completely different style. It was all angles and edges, very modern, with a big glass dome perched on top, which looked like a cross between a workshop and a greenhouse. Across the street a large house with a kind of neoclassical chateau look stood, huge and regal, overlooking the cul-de-sac. It went on like that, with each house having its own style. They all seemed to have a similar color scheme, though, and that tied it all together a bit. I took my phone out of my pocket and took a few pictures. I would see it every day, but if I wanted to draw it, I'd like reference pictures. Besides, most of my drawing happened in the middle of the night.

As my father had predicted, the mailbox was stuffed, full of papers and envelopes of all sizes. I ended up dropping a bunch of magazines and advertisements.

"Dammit." I stooped over to pick them up. When I rose, I let out a little yelp. A tall, rail-thin woman in a bright orange dress stood before me, a bit too close for comfort.

I gathered my fallen papers. "Sorry, you surprised me."

"Apologies. I didn't mean to startle you," she replied. Her voice had a musical quality to it—high and light. "Just checking my mail."

I nodded. I had no idea how she'd managed to get so close before I noticed her. It gave me the creeps.

She was older, probably around my grandmother's age, but with dramatic makeup, and short, platinum-blonde hair that stuck up at odd angles. Her dress—a brilliant, prison-inmate orange—seemed to be made entirely of sheer scarves layered one over another, until they collectively became opaque. There was a floaty quality about her, like she wasn't quite walking, but gliding.

"I'm Joanne Königin. Welcome to the neighborhood," she said, holding her hand out to me.

I shook it hesitantly, still a little on edge.

"Rosalind Weissmandl," I said. "And, um, thank you," I added, remembering my manners.

She smiled. She was alarmingly pale, and her eyes were such a light blue that they almost seemed colorless. Women aren't usually taller than I am, but she was, significantly so. In fact, she was almost as tall as my dad. I wanted to check if she was wearing heels, but I couldn't tear my eyes away from hers.

"It's nice to meet you. I suppose I'll see you around," she said.

"Yeah, good to meet you, too."

With that, she drifted off, back to her house. I had seen it when we'd first arrived and thought it odd. It was the modern, angular house with the glass dome on top. I peered more closely now, seeing furniture and some other things within the dome, though with the glare from the sun, I couldn't quite tell what was up there.

Shaking off the weird feeling she'd given me, I turned and headed back toward my house. I told myself I was feeling out of sorts because of the move. I told myself nothing was wrong. But as I looked up at my own home, squinting against the brilliant sunlight. A flash of movement in my bedroom window caught my eye, like a fast-moving shadow.

I blinked to clear my vision as a cloud drifted over the sun, casting shadows across the house and making me shiver.

I shook my head. Joanne really had thrown me off, because I could've sworn someone was in my room.

Two

The following afternoon found me sitting cross-legged in front of my bookshelf, trying to decide how best to arrange my collections. In my lap was a book called *Between Worlds* by Rowan Fallon, this celebrity scientist my dad had met on one of his business trips. He'd gotten me a signed copy, and I was now distractedly thumbing through it. Something about the mathematical probability of alternate dimensions that was way over my head. Might make a good premise for a comic, though, if I could get versed enough with the scientific principles to understand it. My phone rang and I jumped. I'd been uneasy all day.

It was my cousin, Hazel. I answered the phone and held it between my ear and my shoulder as I continued to sort books.

"Hey, Haze."

"Rosalind! You're finally here! How's your new house? When do I get to see it?"

I chuckled. "Yup. I'm here. Unpacking, in fact. I can show it to you now. Wanna come over and help?"

"No way. *But,* I do have a much more exciting proposition for you."

"Oh? And what would that be?" I asked, putting a stack of books on my shelf.

"My friend Samantha is having a little get-together tonight..."

I suppressed a groan. "Hazel..."

"No! No! Listen, it'll be fun! Please come with me?"

"Hazel, I'm dirty and sweaty and gross, and my house is still more boxes than furniture..."

"*Please?* I've missed you and this would be a lot of fun! And I could introduce you to some of my friends!"

I sighed, then laughed. She knew I could never turn her down, and she used that liberally. "Okay, all right, I have to check with my dad first, but fine. What time is it?"

"Yes! Thank you! I promise we'll have fun. It's at six. I'll pick you up around a quarter to, okay?"

"Yeah, sure. See you then."

I went downstairs and found my dad setting up his office. There were framed pictures of me when I was little, and a snapshot of us together. He even had some of my old drawings framed and ready to hang.

"Hey—oh, sorry," I said, realizing he was on the phone.

"It's all right, I'm on hold. What's up?"

"Just wanted to check if we're doing anything tonight," I said.

"Uh, no. Why?" he asked.

"Hazel wants me to go with her to a party."

My dad looked surprised, then happy. "Really? A party? That sounds fun. Who's going to be there?" he asked.

I shrugged. "Hazel said it was at her friend Samantha's house. I guess it's some kind of end-of-the-school-year thing?"

"Are her parents going to be there? I don't know this family," my dad said. I couldn't help but smile at his protectiveness. We'd had a rough year; we both worried more than we should about the other.

"Yeah. I think so. I can give you the address. Hazel texted it to me."

He smiled and nodded. "Sure. Anyway, sweetie, I think you should go. It'd be good for you to start meeting some people your age out here."

I thanked him and left, feeling a little awkward. I hadn't been to a party in a long time. I didn't really go out much; so little, in fact, that my dad was happy whenever I *did* decide to socialize in any capacity.

I decided it was a good thing that I was going. It would make Hazel happy, it would make my dad happy, and most of all, it would make me feel like I was at least semi-competent at being a teenager. Besides, it wouldn't hurt to get to know some of the people I'd be going to school with in the fall; I might even make a few friends.

That's setting the bar a little high, Roz. Baby steps. I ignored the pressure of "making friends" and distracted myself with getting ready.

When Hazel texted to let me know she was outside, I gathered up my things and went to say goodbye to my dad, who was busy messing with the TV.

I found Hazel standing on my doorstep. "Ready to par-tay?" she asked, grinning at me.

I rolled my eyes. "Ugh. Don't say 'par-tay'. If you're going to say things like 'par-tay,' I can't be around you," I teased, moving to step outside.

"Wait!" she said. "I want to see your house."

"Now?" I asked, glancing over my shoulder at the mess of furniture and boxes behind me.

She ignored my concern, looking past me and finding my dad. "Hi, Uncle Geoff!"

"Hello, Hazel. Would you like the grand tour?" he called back.

"Yeah!" she said, bouncing past me and looking around.

I let my father lead the tour while I trailed behind them, looking around, having the weird experience of my own home still being relatively new to me. My father even pointed out things I had missed, like the pretty little windows all along the top of our dining room, or the woodwork on the walls in his office.

Upstairs, I caught sight of a leather-bound book that looked vaguely familiar. It sat on the stack of books I hadn't finished sorting out, but it wasn't one of mine. I was puzzled, but Hazel asked me a question about how I was going to arrange my room and I forgot about it, telling her where the lighting was best (at least, based on what I'd seen so far) and where my art would hang.

"Oh! We'd better go!" Hazel said suddenly, glancing at her phone. It had chirped and whistled several times since she'd arrived, but unchecked notifications didn't seem to stress her out like they did for me.

My dad gave us each a hug and told us to have fun, then returned to fiddling with the TV. I promised him I wouldn't be home too late, then followed Hazel out to her car. She grabbed me as I was buckling in and pulled me over so my face was smushed up against hers.

"Smile, Roz!" Hazel said, holding her phone out before us and snapping a few pictures before releasing me. She scanned through them until she found one she liked, my phone chimed with an Instagram notification.

I checked her post and saw a filtered image of the two of us, Hazel smiling like a model and me looking slightly confused but mostly content. I was almost surprised that I managed to look relaxed in the picture, but I shouldn't have been. Hazel always managed to draw the laughter out of me.

"Okay, let's go!" Hazel started reversing the car, and I braced myself. Hazel wasn't a *dangerous* driver, per se, but she drove...enthusiastically. We flew out of my subdivision and out into traffic. I tried not to look like I had a death grip on my seat.

I should've just driven myself, I thought as we wove between cars that were *only* going the speed limit.

"Oh, my turn!" Hazel chirped, and I closed my eyes as she made a very abrupt right-turn.

I didn't feel secure until I once again stood on solid ground, waiting for Hazel while she adjusted her long, raven hair. She was all copper skin and dark eyes and ridiculously long, shiny hair. Despite being cousins, Hazel and I don't look remotely related. Her mother might by my biological aunt, but her father is Indian, and

Hazel inherited his features. She stood a little shorter than me, curvier, generally looking more like a woman and less like a scrawny boy than I did. Add to that her fashion sense and flair for being fabulous, and you had someone who always looked great. I fidgeted with my outfit, wondering if I looked all right.

Samantha's house was huge and wide open. It looked like a good chunk of the school was there, and adding the caterers, entertainers, and wait staff to the mix made the house pretty packed. *Only in Vegas*, I thought. It was an extravagant party, bigger than I'd expected, and my anxiety immediately spiked.

I grabbed myself a bottle of water and held onto that, unsure what other drinks might contain. I didn't like anything that inhibited my judgment, and I was already nervous, being around so many strangers. I wasn't going to risk drinking anything that would take down my guard.

Hazel, much more at ease in such environments, led me around and introduced me to a bunch of people from her school—our school, come the fall—and I did my best to remember everyone's names and faces. A few of them I knew from past visits, but most of them were new to me. They all seemed nice, at least, and I was able to make decent conversation with them. Maybe starting at this school wouldn't end up being so bad—new beginnings and all that.

I was talking to the party's host, Samantha, about her work on the school paper when Hazel dug her nails into my skin.

"Ow, *why*?" I asked, prying her fingers off my arm.

"It's him! The guy I told you about," she said, squeaking excitedly as she spoke, fixing her gaze on a guy sitting in the backyard by the pool. He had stylishly messy blond hair and was tossing a football in the air repeatedly, talking with a friend and laughing loudly.

"Oh...um...Sean?" I asked, searching my memory for the name.

She nodded, bouncing slightly.

"Why don't you go talk to him?" Samantha said with a grin, glancing over at the two boys.

"Yeah," I agreed, finally managing to free my arm. I didn't really want to talk to the guy, but it seemed like the logical thing for Hazel to do.

"What? I can't do that!" she said in some strange combination of a whisper and a shriek.

"Why not?" I asked in unison with Samantha, both of us genuinely confused.

"Because!"

Samantha laughed, then turned when someone called her, excusing herself to tend to whatever she was needed for.

I rolled my eyes, turning my attention back to my suddenly shy cousin. "Hazel, you've talked to at least twenty guys since we got here."

"Yeah, but none of them are *him*."

"Uh-huh, and how are you ever going to get anywhere with *him,* if you don't start talking to *him*?"

Hazel fidgeted uncertainly. "I don't know...he's got his friends with him...I'll be too nervous."

I really had to work to keep from laughing; I'd never seen my confident, cheery, happy-go-lucky cousin like this before. It was kind of cute. It was also ammunition.

I could tease her about this for a long time if I played my cards right. Talking to people I didn't know made me uncomfortable, but to hold this over Hazel's head? That might be worth it. I took her arm and gave it an encouraging little squeeze.

"Come on, he's only got one friend. And you have me. It's evenly matched. Let's just go see what happens."

She nodded and I steered her out the back door and around the pool. I wasn't usually the outgoing type, but Hazel was so helpless, I had to do something. She was always the one guiding me through social situations like a lost puppy, and now she was lost. I decided to try channeling my father's charisma. I put on the easy smile that I'd seen him wear a thousand times, thought of that confident way he had with people, and ignored the way my stomach was twisting into a knot.

"Hey," I said as we approached the boys. My knee wobbled a little when they both looked up at me, but I pressed on. Now was not the time to let my social anxiety win out.

I introduced myself and used the pretext that I was new to Las Vegas to strike up a conversation. I sat down at the edge of one of the lounge chairs around the pool, giving Hazel license to do the same. She took a seat beside Sean, smiling nervously.

Beside me was Sean's friend. He held out his hand for me to shake.

"I'm Ford," he said. He had light, brown-blond hair and blue eyes, but most notable was his impish grin, like he was in on some hilarious joke.

I shook his hand. "Rosalind. Rosalind Weissmandl. What kind of a name is Ford?" I asked. I couldn't help myself.

He laughed. "It's a nick-name. My full name is Rutherford Nicholas Kristof Abramovich the third. It's kind of a mouthful."

I snickered at that and glanced over at Hazel, who seemed to have hit a stride. She caught my eye and grinned, then returned her attention to Sean, talking about the coming school year.

"That is...quite a name," I said, fighting back laughter.

"Right. Hence, 'Ford'."

"Not Ruth?" I asked.

"No. Ford. And you're...Rosin?" he said, raising his eyebrows and grinning.

"Rosalind," I corrected. "Or 'Roz', if you must."

"Oh, I absolutely must. And...Weiss...what's it?"

I chuckled. "*Weissmandl.* It's Jewish."

"Oh. Are *you* Jewish?"

"Yeah. Though...well, I always say I'm 'Jew-*ish*' since, you know, I'm not exactly orthodox or anything."

Ford chuckled. "I get that. Anyway, that's a funky last name," he added with a taunting kind of grin.

"Uh-huh. Big talk from Rutherford...what, Nickelodeon Christmas Arrowsmith?"

"Excuse you, madam. That's *Rutherford Nicholas Kristof Abramovich. The third,*" he said pointedly.

I snickered at his expression. "So, do you drive a Ford?"

He grinned. "You're really stuck on that, aren't you?"

"Are you related to Henry Ford?" I pressed.

He laughed a little. “No. But I do have a Ford van.”

“Wait, you drive a *van*?” I asked.

Sean broke away from his conversation with Hazel to say, “Classic, creepy, kidnapper van.”

“You’re just jealous of my excellent van,” Ford said, gravely serious.

“Why do you drive a van?” I asked.

Ford shrugged. “Seats a lot of people, it’s old so it’s easy to repair, and no one wants to borrow it *ever*, so that’s nice.”

Things got quiet between us then. I drummed my fingers on my lap, starting to feel the awkwardness of having nothing much else to say to a complete stranger. Hazel, however, was doing pretty well with Sean, and I didn’t want to disrupt her progress by lingering in uncomfortable silence.

Thankfully, Ford rescued me from that by saying, “So, you’re new to town? Where’d you move from?”

“Los Angeles. I was born in Vegas, actually, and we lived here till I was five, but then my mom wanted to get into acting, so we moved.”

“Oh, would I know her from anything?”

I shook my head. “Just some random commercials, a couple soap opera appearances, nothing really noteworthy,” I admitted.

He nodded. “So, did she give up and you guys came back?”

My stomach knotted a bit as I spoke, but I pressed on. Hazel gave me a little sideways glance. I ignored it.

“You could say that. We mostly moved for my dad’s work. And because the rest of my family’s here. It was just...time for a change of pace.”

"That's cool," he said. "Do you live close?"

I shook my head. "Not so much, we're in Queensridge."

He laughed. "That's where I live."

"Oh, really?"

"Yeah...actually, I seem to remember seeing a moving truck across the street from me yesterday," he remarked.

"Wait. What's your address?"

"Thirteen-twenty Harrington Avenue," he said.

I laughed. "I'm thirteen-seventeen Harrington Avenue."

"Well, it's nice to meet you, neighbor," he said. "It'll be nice to have someone rational on my street."

"Oh? Lot of crazies around?" The strange woman I'd bumped into at the mailbox came to mind.

"A few, yeah. And by that I mean *me*," he said with a chuckle.

I nodded. "I thought I was getting that vibe from you."

"The woman next door to you, in particular, though. Her name's Joanne and she's completely nuts," he said.

"Hey, I met her! Yeah, she did seem pretty weird."

He leaned forward and said, very seriously, "I think she's a witch."

That was a little much for me. Though Ford did seem to sound the most serious when he was joking. This time I just couldn't tell.

I raised my eyebrows. "Really? And do you have any reasoning behind this?"

"Um, *yes*, absolutely."

"All right, let's hear it. Back up your claims."

Ford sat up straighter. "Okay. First off," he said, holding up one finger, "She stays up most of the night, and I almost never see her during the day."

"I saw her during the day. And anyway, isn't that vampires?"

"Creatures of the night. It's all the same category."

I chuckled. "Okay, fine. What else?"

"She's always having the weirdest people over. And they come over late, late at night."

"Maybe she just has weird friends. This is Vegas, after all."

He held up a third finger. "She dresses really weird."

"Weird how?" I asked.

"I dunno. Colorful, lots of shiny stuff."

"I'll give you that one. Eccentricity?"

"I don't know, maybe. Anyway, she also hates water—definite witch sign."

"What?" I asked with a laugh.

"Whenever sprinklers go off or it starts raining, she runs for cover like she's under attack."

"Well, her clothes are probably all dry-clean only. I bet she's just afraid to ruin them," I reasoned.

"No, it's because she'll melt," he went on, undeterred. "I've heard her speaking in tongues."

"You do know there are other languages besides English, right?" I shot back.

"She has this creepy ability to make people do whatever she wants."

I grinned. "Maybe she just seduces them into doing her bidding."

Ford shuddered and I burst out laughing.

"Whoa, hey, Rosalind, that's over the line. She's old and creepy, that's just wrong," he said, making me laugh harder.

"All right, all right. What else have you got?"

"Well...she has a black cat."

"Oh, come on, that means *nothing*."

"No, but listen! I've never seen her and the cat at the same time, so I don't actually think she *has* a black cat. I think she *turns into it* so she can spy on people."

That cracked me up all over again.

"I'm serious, though. She's been that way for years. Her husband even left her over it, though I think she killed him. Everyone thinks so."

I made a face. "That's kinda twisted."

"It's true. Growing up, my friends and I would watch her. We have a theory that she killed her husband and ate him."

I wrinkled my nose. "That's really gross. What's wrong with you?"

"I'm not kidding!" he insisted. "You just don't get it because you haven't witnessed it yourself. I swear, it's hard to explain, but she's...freaky," he said with an overly-solemn nod.

"Right..." I said, snickering.

"Seriously, I think she might have even put a curse on the people who used to live at your house."

"What, really?"

"Yeah. They were having this big dispute over some trees they planted in their yard, and she went berserk, wanted them removed, said they were hanging into her yard. I don't really know what her problem was, but they wouldn't take the trees down, and she was furious.

Anyway, after that, things started getting really bad for them. They lost their business and had to move."

"Couldn't that be chalked up to the bad economy?"

"Not just that. It was a couple and their kids. Their oldest son got really sick. I remember an ambulance being there one day; then I never saw the kid again. The official story is that they moved to get him better treatment, but I dunno. He was perfectly healthy before, so it's pretty suspicious. It was also weird how they just left one day, and had never talked to anyone else in the neighborhood about what happened. All we knew was that one day they were gone."

"That's...really sad, and a little weird, but you can't assume Joanne did all that."

"I don't know; it was pretty unusual. It happened so fast. And then as soon as they were gone, those trees were gone. I don't even know how she did it—they just disappeared one day."

I nodded, still grinning a bit. "Well, you've made an...interesting argument."

He laughed. "I'm serious. You don't believe me, but I swear, something's up with that woman."

We talked for a while longer, and I eventually mentioned my Instagram account where I posted various drawings or things that inspired me. He followed me, laughing at my username, @_RozAlGhul. When my phone chimed to notify me of a new follower, I swiped across the screen and rolled my eyes.

"@NotHarrisonTho, huh?" I asked.

"Just so no one's confused," he answered.

Ford then started scanning through my uploads, which made me a little anxious. You never think much about what you're posting online until someone looks at your account in front of you, then suddenly everything seems dumb and you're wondering why you ever felt like sharing it in the first place.

"Wow, you're a great artist," he said.

My cheeks flushed a little and I looked away. "Thanks."

"How long have you been drawing?"

I shrugged. "Since I can remember. I got serious about it when I was around eight, I guess."

He looked through the entirety of my Instagram, commenting on the drawings and the pictures alike. I had a few of myself and Hazel, one from Halloween with painted faces and elaborate costumes that he loved. I also had a bunch of character sketches and even a couple extremely embarrassing attempts at comics. Whenever he laughed at a joke or complimented a sketch I wanted to sink into the floor. He kept liking things, and every time he did my phone buzzed in my palm, physically jolting me with his attention.

I was surprised when I realized how late it was. The party was dwindling down, and Hazel checked her phone, announcing it was time to leave. It didn't seem that dark out, but it was Las Vegas, and like Los Angeles, it never got truly dark. Regardless of all the light blaring from the city, though, my eyelids were feeling a bit heavy. We said our goodbyes and headed out.

I discreetly scrolled through Ford's pictures on the drive home while Hazel happily chattered about her talk with Sean. They were having lunch later in the week. I listened, but she didn't need many responses when she got going like this. So I was free to scan through the various uploads—a few of him and his friends, a couple of family members, but mostly, his account consisted of cars and engines and other mechanical components.

Miraculously, we didn't crash on the way home. I gave her a hug and thanked her for a fun night. I had genuinely, and unexpectedly, enjoyed myself.

My dad had fallen asleep watching TV on the couch. I found him there when I got home. I considered waking him, but decided not to. Instead, I covered him with a blanket and left a little note saying I was home. I didn't want him to wake up and worry.

I took a quick shower and changed into my pajamas, then collapsed into bed, still feeling a little odd about my unfamiliar surroundings. It would take some time before I'd be used to this house. For now, though, I just needed some sleep.

As I checked my phone one last time to make sure Hazel had gotten home okay, the dim light from the little screen illuminated my nightstand just enough for me to spot the outline of an unfamiliar book. I pointed my phone's light at it.

On my nightstand was the journal from the box of wedding photos.

Three

I sat up in bed and looked around the dark room, the hair on the back of my neck standing up. My pulse quickened, and I was completely alert. It didn't make any sense, but I had the feeling that there were eyes on me.

I turned on the light on my nightstand and surveyed the room again, without all the shadows. It was a mess of still-packed boxes and furniture that hadn't quite found its place yet.

I picked up the journal, running my finger over the faded insignia on the front. It looked like a bird in flight, wings spread wide, encased in a circle and a triangle. It reminded me vaguely of the Vitruvian Man, but with fowl instead of a human.

And suddenly, I remembered the out-of-place book on the stack by the shelves. I'd seen it while giving Hazel the tour, but forgotten about it in our rush to get to the party.

A nervous flutter filled my stomach for no real reason other than I couldn't figure out how the journal had gotten there. I moved to undo the latch, then stopped, hesitating. I didn't want to read anything she'd written. I wasn't interested in the ramblings of someone who could just leave her husband and daughter behind without a second thought.

I still felt like I was being watched. I kept turning around, expecting to see someone there, but no, I was alone. I got up, fighting the childish fear that something was going to grab me from under my bed. I ended up closing my curtains and checking the dark corners.

Snatching up the journal, I marched into my bathroom and opened the cupboard under the sink. Angry beyond reason, I threw the book into the empty little garbage can. I shivered again, pressing my fingers to my temples and trying to massage away the flair of pain.

A noise in the hall caught my attention. My father must be coming up. Maybe he had put the journal in my room earlier. I stepped out of my room to ask him.

In the hall, though, I was alone. The house was eerily silent, and strangely dark. There was no sign of anyone else. When I turned to go back to bed, I caught sight of my open door swinging slowly. Then it slammed.

I shuddered, my mouth going dry. Goosebumps raced up my arm as a chill drifted down the hall. It was impossible to see in the darkness. Despite the large window overlooking the open stairway, the house was shockingly dark. I should have been able to see the brilliant lights of the Strip and its many resorts, but everything was shrouded in blackness, like power was out to the entire city.

Inside my skull, the pressure from before intensified. I grimaced, taking a deep breath to steady myself. I opened my mouth to call out for my dad, to see if maybe he had gone into my room for some reason. It didn't seem plausible, but what else could it be? The words never made it out, though. Before I could say anything, frantic whispering floated down the hall, from near the guest room.

"Dad?" I said, barely managing to speak.

No one answered, but the whispering continued.

"Hello? Dad?" I asked, feeling along the wall for the light switch. It was disarmingly dark.

The whispering grew louder. It reminded me of a panicked prayer, but I couldn't understand the words.

"Dad?" I said more loudly. I found the switch and turned on the light. "Dad is that you?"

"*Pomóż mi—*"

I froze completely, staring into the now-lit hall, trembling slightly. I wanted to do something, but I couldn't move. I felt rooted to the spot, paralyzed.

The whispering resumed, eerie and disjointed, floating down the hall toward me.

"Hello?" I asked. My voice shook. I shivered again in the cold.

From the guest room came a soft sob.

"Dad?" I said more loudly, almost panicky now.

"Roz?" my dad called from far off, sounding sleepy.

"Dad!" I cried in relief. I tried to reign in the terror. "Hey, Dad? Were you talking to me?"

He appeared at the bottom of the stairs, looking like I'd woken him. "No, I was asleep. Are you all right?"

I swallowed hard and forced myself to nod. "Yeah. I just...thought I heard something. Um...Dad?"

"Yeah?"

I glanced over at my closed bedroom door.

"Roz?" he asked.

"It's nothing. I just...I heard..." my throat caught as I tried to steady my breathing. "You. I thought I heard you up here. But I guess it was nothing," I said, trying to sound calm, even though my breathing was still shaky and my heart was hammering painfully.

He frowned, still concerned. He was fully awake now, studying my face. "What did you hear?" he asked, making his way up the stairs to me.

"Uh...just some creaking. It's probably just my imagination. I'm still a little unfamiliar with this house." I forced a laugh, "You know how I can get."

He looked around before checking the alarm panel on the wall by his bedroom door. Everything was in order.

"Where'd you hear the sound coming from?" he asked.

I gestured to the unassuming hall before us. "Down there."

There were two other bedrooms down the hall. My father went into each, turning on the lights and shuffling around. I moved closer, my steps dragging a bit, unwilling to go down the hallway. It appeared non-threatening now, and my father was with me, but my hands still trembled.

My dad went back down the hall and checked my room, then his. Finally, he came to stand beside me at the top of the stairs.

"I can't find anything," he said.

I laughed, despite myself. "Well, of course not. Of course, there's no one here, Dad. It's just me being jittery. I haven't slept well lately. It's probably getting to me."

He nodded, but he still looked dissatisfied. "Are you going to sleep now?"

I nodded. "Yeah. I'm tired."

"Well, goodnight, sweetie," he said, giving me a hug and a kiss on top of my head.

"Night, Dad."

I went back to my room, certain that I would not be able to sleep anytime soon. A thorough search of every corner turned up absolutely nothing unusual, which was exactly what I had expected. Of course there was nothing out of the ordinary for me to find. There had been nothing for my dad to find, because there was nothing for *anyone* to find.

While checking behind my curtains, I spotted a little orb of light floating in the darkness. It took me a moment to realize that it was the glass dome perched on top of Joanne's house. I could see her moving around within it, dressed in a flowy red outfit. She was painting with wild motions and exaggerated gestures, flinging paint at the canvas.

Ford's witch, I thought. I watched her for a moment before closing the curtains again.

Trying to convince myself that the air conditioner closed my bedroom door, I lay down in my bed and pulled my covers tightly around myself. I wasn't cold, but I rolled myself into a little cocoon, feeling comforted by the hug of the blankets. I thought about what Joanne might be painting, and the party with Hazel, Ford's wild theories, and anything else to keep my mind off the night's inexplicable events.

"Do you really have to go? Isn't this something you can deal with from home?" I asked, hating how nervous I sounded. I just didn't like the idea of staying alone in this house overnight. Today was the first day for our cook and housekeeper, Dalisay, but she would be leaving at five, and then I'd have to brave the house alone as it got dark. This place was still new to me, and I hadn't gotten over whatever had happened the night before.

"I'm sorry, kiddo, I can't get out of this one. I'll be home well before the party," my dad said, shuffling his paperwork together and sliding it into his briefcase. "Do you want to come with me? It would be pretty boring, but we could grab dinner when I'm done with my meeting."

I shook my head. He was flying to Chicago and back, returning tomorrow or the next day. That was far too much travel for me with my fear of flying. It was even less appealing to me than staying in this house alone.

"No, it's okay," I assured him. "Hazel wants to come by, anyway. Maybe she'll sleep over."

He smiled. "That sounds fun. I'm glad you're getting to spend more time with her," he said, closing his briefcase.

"Me too. Well, have a safe flight," I said, as I followed him out to his car. "And text me when you land," I added.

He promised he would and drove off, and I sighed as I watched him disappear around the corner.

Inside the house, I felt strange, like I didn't quite belong. Part of it was exhaustion; I hadn't slept well after my eerie encounters, though I kept trying to convince myself that I'd imagined the whole thing. Even with Dalisay—who was very sweet and easy to get along with—I was uneasy. Honestly, I think she was, too. I caught her peeking nervously into a room, and wondered if she was experiencing something odd, too.

I went up to my room, looking for something to do. I didn't feel like unpacking anymore, but I was still restless. From my open window, I caught sight of Joanne in her backyard. She was watering plants with a little pail, wearing layers that seemed like they'd be uncomfortably warm on this hot summer's day. When I looked closer, it seemed like she was talking, though I couldn't see a headset or phone anywhere near her.

That's not witch-level weird, though. I rolled my eyes at my own internal dialogue. She could be singing, she could be reminding herself of something, she could have a tiny Bluetooth in her ear. Why was I even thinking of what Ford had said? I sent Hazel a text, hoping she could distract me.

Hey, do you still want to come over?

Yeah! But I can't now :(at the Apothecary w/mom.

Hazel worked part-time at the Apothecary, a little shop her mother owned. It was cool, even if I didn't really believe in all the stuff she sold there. Crystals and books about positive healing energy or whatever. Plus a bunch of ancient herbal remedies and stuff. But I liked it nonetheless, and it was really important to Hazel.

OK. When do you guys close? I sent back.

6:30. I'll come by right after :D

K, see you then!

"Rosalind?"

I looked up to see Dalisay's nervous face. I frowned at her expression.

"I just...was wondering if there's anyone else here," Dalisay said, her brow furrowed.

"No. No, just us," I said.

She nodded, looking troubled.

"Why? Did you see...something?" I asked, eyes narrowing.

"I...no...," she said, her voice soft.

I watched her. "Did you hear something?" I pressed gently.

Dalisay's eyes went a little wide at that.

"No," she lied. "No, no, it's fine," she forced a smile. "I just wanted to let you know that I'm done for the day, and there's dinner on the stove if you're hungry."

"Oh," I said, caught between disappointment and relief. "Okay. Thank you, Dalisay. Let me walk you out."

I said goodbye to her, and she scurried into her car, driving away a little faster than necessary.

I wondered what she'd seen or heard that scared her. *Something* had happened, and after last night, I had a pretty good idea what it might be.

But she hadn't wanted to tell me. To be honest, I couldn't really blame her. I reluctantly went back inside, alone and a little unsettled. I didn't know what to do with myself, so I went to the kitchen and looked for that dinner she'd mentioned. I'd have to tell Hazel that I had plenty of food. Dalisay had left me soup, salad, steak, rice, and green beans.

I did a few little things—reading, scrolling through amusing posts on my phone, listening to music. I put on one of my favorite movies, *The Red Shoes*, for background noise. I'd developed my love of old movies thanks to my mother. It was one of the few things about her I hadn't rejected in the last year. I loved the movies too much. But even with all those distractions, I was restless. Usually, time by myself was fun, but I felt strange; like I didn't quite know how to behave.

My phone chimed, and I checked the text. Hazel was letting me know that she'd be free in half an hour. I wrote back, letting her know I'd be expecting her. It would get dark in a few hours, and I would be more relaxed if she was around. I was developing another headache, which was one of my reactions to stress.

While I was typing, a door closed somewhere in the house. I froze, my pulse quickening. For a few seconds that seemed like an eternity, I sat perfectly still, straining to hear any more sounds. I tried to tell myself I was being silly, that I was just imagining things, but I was sure I'd heard a door shut, and my mind was racing for an explanation. Then I heard footsteps making their way down the hall.

I stopped breathing. There was someone in the house. But no, there couldn't be anyone here. The alarm was set, and everything was locked. I could feel my heart hammering as I stood up, my mind racing for an answer.

I heard footsteps again. My logic was sounding pretty flimsy. Another door opened and slammed shut, and the light beside me flickered, threatening to go out. I clutched my phone, my fingers shaking as I dialed 9-1-1.

"Nine-one-one. What is your emergency?" a woman asked.

"There's someone in my house," I whispered, afraid whoever had broken in might hear me.

"What's your address?"

"Thirteen-seventeen Harrington Avenue," I whispered, my mind still racing.

A weapon—I needed a weapon in case the police didn't arrive in time. I cast around the room and spotted the wooden yardstick serving as a window lock until we could get the latch repaired. I darted across the room and snatched it up, clutching it tightly in both my hands, phone squeezed between my ear and my shoulder. My palms were sweaty. I held the stick like a baseball bat, wishing I'd stayed in softball longer, staring down the hall where the noise was coming from.

"Miss, can you see the intruder?" the 9-1-1 operator asked.

"No. No, but I hear them."

"Can you get out of the house?"

I considered this. I probably could, but the idea scared me. The idea of staying inside scared me more, though.

"I think so," I answered, swallowing the lump in my throat.

With her guiding me, I walked slowly toward the front door, trying to figure out where the sound had come from. I stepped cautiously into the hall, looking around for the intruder. No one was there. My father's office door was closed, but I *knew* it had been left open. I was certain of it.

"Are you out of the house yet?" the 9-1-1 operator asked.

"No," I whispered. "Almost."

The hall light snapped on by itself and I dropped, biting back a scream. Legs shaking, I hurried toward the door, looking all around.

Before leaving my house, I went to turn the light off. I didn't want it signaling to the intruder where I'd gone. I swung my arm out at the switch as I hurried into the entryway.

The second I did, my pulse skyrocketed again, because just before the light went out, I saw the figure of a man standing before me in the gloomy hall.

And then I was plunged into darkness.

FOUR

My breath caught in my throat as I fumbled along the wall, desperately searching for the light switch. I couldn't feel it, and the seconds of almost absolute darkness felt so long and heavy with the threat of the unknown. The light from the living room wasn't strong enough here for me to see the intruder.

"Miss? Are you there? What's wrong?" The operator's voice sounded far away, obscured by static.

I couldn't speak. When my shaking fingers found the switch, I clumsily flicked it on, illuminating the entryway.

The light spilled into the hall, revealing the man, still hidden by shadows.

"*Kwiaty,*" he said.

I screamed and swung my stick, but he stepped back, disappearing into the darkness.

Living room and entryway lights both snapped off at that moment, and I went tearing toward the front door, blind in the complete lack of light. As I burst out the door, the alarm went off, cutting through the warm evening air and panicking me even more. I tripped and sprawled across the walkway, scrambling to my feet and stumbling out into the street. I bolted across the asphalt and stood on the lawn of a house across the cul-de-sac from mine.

Gasping for breath, I stared back at my house in confusion and terror. The outside lights were on, but everything inside was dark, the front door opening to a black hole. The alarm still blared, the sound invading the entire street as people peeked out of their windows.

For a moment, I just stood there, shaking so badly I could barely think. I sank down onto the curb and put my head in my hands. The adrenaline started wearing off, leaving me with a trembling, dizzying exhaustion. I had forgotten I had 9-1-1 on the line. I raised the phone to my ear to find the operator demanding to know if I was all right. I apologized, letting her know what had happened.

It was surprisingly light outside. I peered at my house's windows, wondering why the interior had been so incredibly dark if there was still a decent amount of light from the sun. It had sunk behind the mountains, but cast enough rays to illuminate the evening. Yet even when I'd had lights on inside, it had been dark. I kept my eyes on the door, waiting for someone to come out, but nothing happened.

That's because he wasn't an intruder, part of my mind nagged. I pushed that thought aside and blew absently at the hair that had fallen in my face.

"I'm okay," I told the operator. "I'm outside. Whoever's in my house didn't follow me."

"Roz?"

I started, looking around. Ford was standing behind me, holding an oily rag. How had I missed him? I was really out of it.

"Are you okay?" he asked, coming closer.

"I—I don't..."

"Excuse me, but are you hurt, dear?" another voice cut in.

I spun around and found myself face to face with Joanne.

"I..." I looked at my house, then back at Ford. How could I ever explain this?

Joanne came closer, watching me with concern. "What happened? You look like you saw a ghost."

I gave a nervous, panicky laugh. "I don't know. I mean, no, I think there was someone in my house," I told them.

"What, seriously?" Ford asked.

"Oh, my goodness, are you hurt?" Joanne said, putting her hand to her heart. Out of it as I was, I noticed how Ford tensed around her.

I shook my head, eyes drawn back to the front door. I was clutching my yardstick tightly, and my whole body was shaking.

"Well, I'm glad you're all right," Joanne said, looking toward my house. "I was on my evening walk, and I saw you looking absolutely terrified. I just had to check on you."

"Thanks," I said, still a little breathless.

"So," Ford said, eyes darting between Joanne and my house, "what happened? Did you call the police?"

I nodded, holding up my phone.

"Miss?" the 9-1-1 operator sounded almost agitated.

"I'm sorry," I said to her. "I'm talking to a couple of my neighbors."

I got a call-waiting notification and told the operator I had to go; my dad was calling. The police were on the way, so she reluctantly let me hang up.

I walked away from Joanne and Ford to answer. The security company had called him when our alarm went off, and naturally, he'd panicked. I had to tell him several times that I was fine. I switched off the alarm from the app in my phone and told him the police were already on the way. He stayed on the line with me until they arrived, and I had to hang up to talk with the officers. I pointed out my house, watching as they stepped carefully inside. Joanne and Ford were still with me. We stood on the curb and waited, expecting them to drag someone out at any minute.

In the calm of the evening air, my sense returned enough to make me wonder why Ford had been outside. I turned to him, curious.

"What are you doing out here?"

Ford grinned. "Doing some repairs on my van. Upgrades, really. Stronger engine."

I nodded, still distracted. That explained the rag in his hands, at least.

Hazel got there while the cops were still inside. I had forgotten to text her, so she pulled up to my house, looked confused, then spotted me and drove over to Ford's.

"Hey, what's going on?" she asked, stepping out of her car.

I told her about the break-in and she joined us on the sidewalk, greeting Ford and Joanne with a vague hello. We all focused on my house, watching the police from a distance.

"Did they catch him?" Hazel asked.

I shook my head. "They haven't found anything yet..."

All the lights were on in my house now, and they'd been inside for some time, though I hadn't seen or heard anything to give me a clue.

The police came out after a while and crossed the cul-de-sac to reach me.

"Well, Miss," one of the officers said, "We searched the whole house, but we didn't find anyone. No signs of forced entry, either." He looked annoyed.

"Are you sure? I saw a man—he was in my hall. Do you think he could have run off?" I asked.

"Listen, unless you saw someone come out the front door, I can guarantee that no one is in there, or *was* in there. That house is empty."

I shook my head. "No, no, I *saw* someone," I insisted.

The officer clicked his tongue in annoyance.

"Well, maybe you need to get your vision checked. In the meantime, keep in mind that calling the police for non-emergencies is a serious offense. Consider this your warning."

I had to bite down on my tongue to keep from saying something that would get me in even more trouble. I couldn't believe that, after all this, he was accusing me of making it up.

What if I am?

"Well, I know what I saw," I said, sounding more certain than I felt.

He nodded. "Well, if there's a *real* problem in the future, call us then."

With that, he turned back to his patrol car. They drove off, leaving me to face my supposedly empty house alone.

I sighed and rubbed my temples, my head light as the pain dissipated, though it was still nagging at the back of my skull.

Hazel looked toward my house. "So...I'm guessing you'd prefer to come to *my* house tonight?"

"Yes. Definitely. I...there's no way I can be in my house alone."

She nodded. "Okay, let's go."

I thanked Ford and Joanne for staying with me until Hazel arrived, and then I mustered up all the courage I had left and went inside. We turned off most of the lights, leaving a few on just because I couldn't stand the darkness. I replaced the yardstick that kept our living room window shut, a little reluctantly, as I had grown accustomed to clutching it. Hazel joined me in my room while I got some clothes, and then we hurried out. I was desperate to get away from the house.

I spent the whole ride over to Hazel's trying to sort out what I was feeling. I couldn't decide if the man in my house was real or not. And I couldn't decide which of those options scared me more.

I was also having a hard time determining how much to say to Hazel. I didn't want to sound crazy, but, at the same time, I wanted to get some feedback on what I'd seen.

In the privacy of her room, I decided I needed to tell her everything. Hazel listened attentively, eyes wide, as I recounted the events of that evening. Saying it out loud made it sound completely insane, but I'd committed to giving her the whole story, and so I did.

When I was done, I watched her nervously, waiting for her to tell me that she thought I was losing my mind.

"It sounds like your house is haunted," Hazel said in a whisper.

I stared at her, but she was dead serious.

"You...you think I have a ghost?" I asked, stunned.

"Well, what else could it be? I mean, the journal, the lights going on and off, voices, whispers, that guy who just disappeared into thin air? Sounds like ghosts to me."

I shook my head. "Hazel, that's insane."

"Didn't you say the people who lived there before you left in a big hurry? Maybe something happened that made them scared to be in that house anymore."

I wanted to argue, but that possibility hadn't occurred to me, and now that Hazel had brought it up, I was curious.

"I don't...really believe in ghosts," I said, but it sounded weak. I have never been one for outlandish theories or unscientific beliefs, but after tonight, I was having a hard time rationalizing things.

"Well, *something* weird happened," Hazel said.

I considered protesting this, but as much as I didn't want to admit it, the thought of ghosts had me both intrigued and terrified—too terrified to dismiss it outright.

Hazel gasped and waved her arms. "Oh! Oh! I know what to do!" she said, leaping up and grabbing her phone.

"What?" I asked. I was alarmed by her enthusiasm, which was stupid, because Hazel was always enthusiastic.

She sat down next to me, typing quickly on her phone.

"Emily," she said, not looking up from the screen.

"Who?"

Hazel looked up, grinning. "This girl I know, Emily. MacNeil, I think. I met her in drama class or calculus or something."

"Drama class *or* calculus? How do you mix those up?" I asked.

"Shush! Focus!"

I snickered. "Okay. Okay. Why is Emily relevant?"

"*Because*. She's a paranormal investigator. Well, kind of. She wants to be one. I think Samantha has her number, hold on."

I watched Hazel text, going through her network of friends to see who knew how to get ahold of Emily.

Finally, Hazel gave a triumphant little "Hah!"

I looked up from my own phone. I was texting with my dad, assuring him that I was at Hazel's and everything was okay.

"Got her. I'm going to set up a meeting, soon. She'll know how to tell if it's ghosts," Hazel assured me.

I didn't know what to say to that. I was so tired, and still fighting off a stress headache.

"Yeah, sounds good," I said, not sure if I actually wanted to meet this Emily girl or find out what her opinion was.

I listened to Hazel go on about her ghost theories, but it just made me even more freaked out than I already was. Finally, I told her how tired I was, and we went to bed.

Sleep was no relief, though. I spent half the night in unsettling dreams. One dream was just a replay of the...whatever it had been. I still didn't understand what had happened. Another dream—somehow more disturbing than the last—was simple: I was standing in a clearing in the woods. No grass or trees grew in the clearing. When I looked up, I saw that the birds were even making it a point to fly around it, rather than through it. I looked in all directions. I was standing in the center of the strange little space, surrounded by aspen trees at the edge of the dead patch.

"Rosalind."

I woke with a start, and was unable to get to sleep again. I spent the rest of the night lying awake, trying to decide if I preferred ghosts or insanity to be the explanation for all this trouble.

Neither option sounded appealing.

Five

"I still can't figure out what you must have seen," my dad said as he drove.

"Dad, I'm telling you, there was someone there," I said.

He looked over at me and sighed. I could tell he didn't want to say outright that I was imagining things, but that's what he thought. For a horrible moment, I wondered if I was reminding him of my mother.

"Well, just let me know if you see anything else...unusual, okay?"

I nodded. I didn't blame my dad for doubting me, but it still hurt a little.

While my father didn't see it as a related event, I was acutely aware of the fact that Dalisay had refused to continue working at our house. On Friday, a new girl, Beth, had been sent in her place.

Beth, too, had lasted only a day. Today, the housekeeping service sent Hilda. So far, she was all right, but the day was still young, and we'd left her alone in the house. I was betting she wouldn't be back.

My dad was a little perplexed by all this, but took it in stride, as he did most things. I kept thinking of that look in Dalisay's eyes as she'd gazed up at me. She had been scared.

It was the day of my little cousin Leah's birthday party. I was actually excited to go, not only because it would be fun, but also because it gave me an excuse to get out of my house. This was very contrary to my natural response to leaving the house, but things were different now.

The party had grown massive enough to warrant changing venues, so rather than meet at my Aunt Celia and Uncle Mitch's house, we gathered in a beautiful, landscaped courtyard at some golf club, decorated with delicate lights in the trees and a canopy made of thin, soft cloth that looked like something out of a dream. We'd definitely moved past "Leah's First Birthday".

Hazel hurried over to me, looking around like we were conspirators in some grand scheme. "Any more paranormal activity?" she asked in a whisper.

"No, not since Thursday," I answered. I was trying to be discreet while I greeted the rest of my family.

"Well, guess what?"

"What?" I asked.

Hazel leaned closer and said very quietly, "You're meeting Emily today."

"What? You brought her here?" I hissed.

"No, no, but she's free later on. We can go after the party, meet up with her, and tell her about what's been going on with you."

I sighed. "Hazel, I've been thinking about this and, I don't really think..."

"Okay, look, Rosalind? You're going through some kind of weird paranormal denial or something, and I'm totally here for you through that, but..."

"What? 'Paranormal denial'? What are you even talking about?" I demanded in a whisper.

"*But,*" she said, ignoring me, "something supernatural definitely happened to you the other night, and I think she can help. Let's just talk to her, okay? If it doesn't help, then fine, it doesn't help. But it can't hurt."

I was about to argue, but just then, my grandmother appeared and drew me into a tight hug.

"Rosalind! It's so good to see you!" She held me at arm's length and looked me over. "You got taller again," she commented with a smile.

"Hi, Grandma," I said. My grandmother was five and a half feet of pure elegance. She wore her salt-and-pepper hair in a neat bob, framing her heart-shaped face. I look nothing like her, and in a lot of ways, I think that's a shame, because my grandmother is beautiful and strong and stable, and that's much more the person I'd like to emulate. Those are the genetics I'd like to pass on.

"How's the new house?" she asked.

My stomach twisted and it took effort not to look at Hazel, who I knew must be laughing at me now. "It's great. You should come over for dinner."

"Try and keep me away," she said with a wink. She kissed my cheek and patted my arm. "I'm so glad to have you back home."

I smiled, feeling oddly weak. My grandmother turned to Hazel then, hugging her close and discussing something I couldn't focus on. My thoughts returned to the house, and to this new girl named Emily that I would soon be meeting.

"Rosalind, dear, where's your father?" Grandma asked.

I nodded to the other side of the courtyard. "He's saying hi to Aunt Celia."

We all made our way across the quickly-filling space to greet the rest of our family—Hazel's parents, my Aunt Fiona and Uncle Naagesh, her younger brother, Haldi, and my Aunt Celia and Uncle Mitch, along with Mitch's brother and his husband. I was hugged and kissed and punched in the shoulder (courtesy of Haldi) until finally, everyone had gotten the we're-so-glad-you're-back-in-town itch out of their systems.

The birthday girl, Leah, had recently learned to walk. Or at least, she could take a few awkward steps before falling over. Everyone was very impressed, and soon their attention turned completely to the one-year-old in pink frills. I watched her take tentative steps on chubby baby legs and smiled, unable to stay anxious in the face of her cute babbling.

The party had filled up, and there was cake, a pile of presents, and more people than my introvertedness knew what to do with. I knew I'd eventually have to greet many of these people, but for the moment, I hung back, talking with my cousins, watching my father play host, so to speak. Haldi didn't know about any alleged ghosts, and I enjoyed his carefree discussions about skateboards and upcoming movies and other safe, stress-free topics.

After a while, I broke away from them, making the rounds myself. I said hello to various extended family members, some of whom I hadn't seen in years. I had lost sight of my father, so I got a plate of food and scanned the crowd. I found him and headed in his direction, but as I drew closer, I realized he was talking to a tall, blonde woman. A strikingly beautiful woman. She had the long, slim form of an actress. Her face, too, made her look like she should be in movies. There was something cold and appraising about her beautiful features—she was lovely, but sharp, angular. Her exposed arms were toned, and her shoulder-length blonde hair was pulled back into a stylishly-casual ponytail. She turned, noticing me before my father did. Her clear blue eyes swept over me, as if analyzing me. I faltered under her gaze. I'd never encountered such a piercing stare before.

My Dad still hadn't noticed me; he was smiling broadly, a weirdly dopey expression on his face. When the tall blonde woman's eyes scanned over me, he followed her gaze, realizing I was there. "Oh, Roz. Hey, come here. I want you to meet Veronica."

"Oh, hello," I said, shaking her hand.

"Veronica, this is my daughter, Rosalind."

She smiled at me. "It's nice to meet you, Rosalind. Geoff's told me so much about you," she said. Her voice was lower than I expected, more serious. It seemed too strong for how beautiful she was.

"I went to high school with her brother," my dad explained. "You remember Victor? Anyway, I haven't seen her since I left for college."

"I was hoping I'd see you here, actually," she said with a smile. "I was thrilled when Celia invited Victor and I. It's been too long."

"Where is Vic, anyway?" my dad asked. "I haven't seen him yet."

Veronica gestured toward the buffet. "Eating. Naturally."

They both laughed like that was incredibly hilarious.

I nodded, feeling out of place. "Well, that's...nice," I said stupidly, fumbling for an answer that would sound like I was at all interested. "Anyway, um, I'm going to keep saying hi to everyone. It was nice meeting you," I said to Veronica before slipping away. I wasn't sure why, but I had not been pleased to meet Veronica, and the way my dad was acting around her left me irritated.

Rather than continuing to socialize, I found Hazel again. She was with my grandmother and my aunts, so I sat at a table with them and ate my lunch while they chatted. It was calm, and generally nice, and I tried to just enjoy the moment, but the harder I tried, the more I failed.

After the party (which had to end before two so that Leah could go down for her nap), I went home with Hazel. We were meeting Emily that afternoon, and Hazel had promised to drive carefully so I didn't have to figure out Vegas navigation on a deadline.

It turned out that we were meeting Emily at a hotel-casino not far from her neighborhood. It seemed kind of strange to me, but Hazel acted like it was perfectly normal to head to a casino to meet up with friends. Las Vegas was familiar to me, but there were still some elements of living here I'd have to get used to.

Despite my reservations, the casino was nice. One of the better spots, I guess, with the added bonus of never closing. She led me inside to a restaurant called the Grand Café.

"There's Emily!" Hazel said happily.

There was a small girl with long hair that faded stylishly from black to a gorgeous purple. She had on dark, dramatic makeup and black nail polish. She wore a deep purple, almost black, dress and an assortment of bracelets. She was finishing off a cheeseburger as we approached. She surprised me when I saw her. From her name, I had expected someone Scottish or Irish, but this girl looked to be of Asian descent.

"Hey, Em," Hazel said, sitting down across from Emily at the table and gesturing for me to do the same. I did, feeling awkward, like maybe I was under investigation.

"This is my cousin, Rosalind," Hazel said. "She'll be going to school with us in the fall."

Emily looked at me and smiled. I fidgeted in my seat as I contemplated the conversation we were about to have.

"So, you're the one with the ghosts," she said.

There we go. I flushed lightly. "Uh...well, I don't really think so, but Hazel seems to."

"Emily knows everything about the paranormal," Hazel said.

Emily laughed. “Well, I wouldn’t say that, but I do spend a lot of time studying unexplained events. And I do some paranormal investigation.”

“And you think you can help me?” I asked.

Emily shrugged. “I’m hoping I can. Now, full disclosure: I *am* looking for a good haunting to use for a case study. I have a grant proposal to prepare, and I really think this would be perfect for that.”

“A grant?” I asked. “What kind of grant?”

“Paranormal studies,” Emily said with a grin. “I’m applying to the Edinburgh College of Parapsychology. Well, that and some other universities with paranormal programs, but that’s my dream school. Anyway, the Society for Paranormal Research, Investigation, and Training gives three grants every year, and they’re basically a guarantee on your college application if you get one. So, that’s what I’m aiming for.”

I didn’t know what to say to that. I had no idea that there were paranormal societies or grants for paranormal research, let alone colleges that actually taught the supernatural as a serious subject.

“So...will you be able to help me?” I asked, fidgeting.

“Oh, yeah,” Emily said, nodding enthusiastically and munching on a fry. “I’ve gotten rid of ghosts before. So I help you get rid of ghosts, and you become my research project. From what Hazel’s told me, your situation might be perfect for this. I’ve been looking all over, but there’s nothing all that active showing up on my radar. Nothing *noteworthy*, you know? I want my project to stand out. So, you know, I’d love to work with you on this and help clear up your house—that is, if you’re comfortable with me documenting it.”

"All right. And, I'm just making sure here, but...how does this involve getting rid of ghosts?" I asked, eyeing her uncertainly.

"It involves helping the ghosts to move on," she answered.

I nodded. "Well, I guess you can change my name or something if you do end up using it."

Emily clapped her hands. "Yes! Absolutely. Whatever you want."

"And you'll help me get rid of my ghosts? If...that's what's actually going on?"

"I will do everything in my power to get you completely ghost-free," she promised.

I gnawed on my lip as I considered this. "And you've gotten rid of ghosts before?"

"A few times," she said, and I wondered if she was being entirely honest. I almost didn't care. She knew more about this than I did, and that was enough to help me. At least, it would be if it really did end up being a ghost problem.

"Okay. All right. Yeah, I'd love your help...you know, if you can."

Emily nodded. "Great, let's get down to business, then. When did you have your first encounter?"

I recounted my various "ghost" experiences to her. Emily's eyes glittered with excitement as I spoke. The strange dream about the clearing came to mind, but I didn't bring it up. It probably didn't mean anything. When I mentioned throwing the journal away, Emily cut me off.

"Wait, you threw it out?" she demanded.

I fidgeted. "Well, yes..."

"Why? It's important. There's something in that journal that the ghost is trying to communicate about to you," she said.

I stammered, caught off guard. I played it off with clearing my throat, giving myself a moment to recover before saying, "But what would some...*ghost*...guy want with my mother's journal?"

"I don't know," Emily said. "But what I *do* know is that there's something in there that's important to the ghost. Maybe it's just a clue or a statement he relates to. An image. Anything, really. Either way, that's your ticket to helping this ghost," she said, pointing sternly at me with a French fry.

"Wait, helping him? I just want him to leave me alone," I said, my voice rising slightly. My mind flashed to the symbol on the cover of the journal. Was it relevant?

Emily shook her head and popped the fry into her mouth. "You have to help the ghost resolve his unfinished business, then he'll be free, and you'll get your house back."

I sighed. "Look, I don't even know if there really *is* a ghost."

"What about Thursday?" Emily asked.

I turned and looked at Hazel, who shrugged and gave me a guilty smile.

"Sorry, I was telling her about it, and I got kinda carried away..."

"Did you tell her anything else?" I asked, a little more sharply than I'd intended.

Hazel's eyes went wide. "No. I promise. Just the stuff you told me about the house."

"If what Hazel told me is true, then you are dealing with a serious haunting," Emily said.

I nodded slowly, my stomach knotting. I kept trying to tell myself that I didn't believe in ghosts, but I wasn't as convinced as I had been before. We were silent for a moment as Emily sipped at her milkshake and Hazel watched me carefully.

"This is a lot to take in," I finally said.

"I know, Roz. Emily, tell her how we can fix it," Hazel said, too excited to contain herself. She was actually bouncing slightly.

Emily glanced at Hazel, then back at me, like she was trying to decide if I could handle what she was about to say.

"What? What is it?" I asked.

She smiled. "Rosalind, how would you feel about hosting a séance?"

I stared at her.

"Are you serious? A séance? Are we in a B-movie now?"

Emily laughed. "I know, I know, it sounds crazy, but I'm not kidding. Séances can be really effective."

I was starting to feel sick. I glanced at Hazel, who was watching me, looking a little nervous, like she was afraid I was mad at her.

Hazel was excited, and Emily too, but neither of them had been there. Neither of them had been scared out of their minds, afraid that maybe something terrible was going to happen.

They didn't have to live in a house with the threat of the unknown hanging over them at every minute of every day. They thought it was great, because they weren't there. But I couldn't take a shower, or make myself breakfast, or go to sleep, or even walk from one room to another without wondering if something was going to jump out at me—and wondering if this time, it would hurt or even kill me.

My throat tightened when I thought about the intruder from Thursday night. Everything pointed to the house being empty. My dad had changed all the locks and updated our security system, but it didn't make me feel any safer. Was a séance going to help, or make it worse? Nothing had happened for almost two days. Maybe it would go away on its own. Or maybe I was just going insane.

"Guys, I don't know if I can do this," I finally said.

Hazel looked disappointed, but Emily nodded.

"I understand. This stuff can be pretty freaky."

"Right. And I don't...I don't even know what happened, I just..."

Emily shook her head. "You don't have to explain yourself to me. But I *do* think I can help you; so, when you're ready..." she opened her purse and pulled out a little black card, handing it to me.

I took it and read the stark white letters: *Emily MacNeil, Paranormal Investigator.*

Well, damn, I turned the card over in my hands. *I don't have any business cards.*

Emily tapped the card. "In case you change your mind, or just want to ask some questions, I'm free for most of the summer, and Derek works, but we can sort out the schedule. Whenever you need help or want to move things forward, just call or text me."

"Who?"

"My friend. We work on all this stuff together."

I put the card into my pocket. "All right. Thanks. I will."

Hazel took me home after that. I didn't really want to be in my house, but I didn't have anywhere else to go. I had already stayed over at Hazel's twice this week. People were going to start thinking I was crazy. I was already suspecting as much.

I puttered around the house, careful not to go up to my room. I went outside to work on some sketches and saw several extra cars parked outside Joanne's house. I peered at them, watching a collection of people in brightly colored outfits laughing and chattering as they made their way up her footpath.

I raised my eyebrows, glancing across the street at Ford's house. He had mentioned colorful characters, I just hadn't realized he'd meant it so literally. Finding a relatively secluded spot where they couldn't see me, I sat on one of our patio chairs, watching more of Joanne's guests arrive for what I could only guess was a costume party. Some had really gone all-out, with feathers and sequins and ornate headdresses. I took a few discreet pictures for my Instagram, and character designs. I always found coming up with unique outfits kind of challenging, but this would be great inspiration.

My dad came home not long after me, sitting with me for a bit. When the sun set, and the party was in full swing with no more guests arriving, we headed back inside. I forced down some dinner and went through my evening routine until I couldn't reasonably put off sleep anymore. As I did every night, I turned all the lights on and checked over my whole room. I knew it was useless—

even if I found something, what was I going to do? Fight? Cry? Scream until it killed me?

I reminded myself that things had been uneventful for the past couple of days. Most likely, I would have another quiet night, unworthy of all this anxiety.

Telling myself all this trouble was behind me, I climbed into bed and shut off the light. My room was cool as I lay down, tugging the blankets around myself and closing my eyes. I was tired and ready to sink into dreams, hoping that tonight they would be peaceful.

Just as I was drifting off, someone sat down on the edge of my bed.

Six

I sat up, wide-awake. The air in my room had become so cold that I could see my breath.

There was no one sitting on my bed, but before I could take comfort in that fact, I heard slow, ragged breathing.

The hair on the back of my neck stood on end as I tried to think what to do.

"Wh-who's there?" I asked, my voice weak. I shivered in the cold and drew the covers more tightly around myself.

The breathing moved, coming closer to me.

"What do you want?" I demanded.

There was no answer, but the breathing was louder than ever, and right beside me.

"Stop it...stay away from me..." I said.

I started to climb out of bed, but something pushed

me back. I was slammed down, my head striking a hard surface, sending my vision spinning. I was not laying among the soft sheets and pillows of my bed, but on a cold, metal table that almost seemed to hum. The sound stabbed like a knife into my temples, and a headache erupted behind my eyes.

Bindings, cold and humming with that same energy that made my head throb, coiled around my arms and legs, snaking across my torso, holding me in place. I screamed, thrashing and calling for help. Tears and pain blurred my vision, but I could make out several figures hovering over me.

Another thing making it hard for me to see was the blinding light, which had overtaken the once-dark room. It shone from everywhere, so intense that it burned my eyes. I squinted, trying to see the beings hovering over me. Pale, thin, tall, with no discernable features. There was a lit-up quality to them, as well, as if perhaps the light wasn't behind them, but within them.

The electric hum grew louder as the beings over me came into clearer focus. I struggled, and as I screamed, another bind slid over my mouth, holding my head immobile.

I went into a full-blown panic then. The bindings cut my skin as the beings tried to restrain me. I opened my eyes in time to see what looked an awful lot like a syringe held in one of their hands.

Tears slipped from my eyes as I fought to breathe around the crushing grip of the contracting bindings.

"Rosalind!"

As inexplicably as it had started, everything stopped. I gasped for air and just lay there shaking as my father rushed to my side. He looked down at me with bleary eyes and disheveled hair.

"Rosalind? Sweetheart, what happened? Are you okay?"

I opened my mouth to speak, but started crying instead. He sat on the edge of my bed and hugged me until I was composed enough to talk. I clutched at him like a frightened toddler and tried to make sense of my reeling mind.

"Did you have another nightmare?" he asked.

"No! No, Dad, it wasn't a nightmare! There were...it was..."

I looked up at him, expecting to see doubt. Instead, I saw concern, then fear.

"Rosalind, what happened?" he asked. "You're bleeding."

Confused, I climbed out of bed and went to the mirror hanging by my closet. My hair and clothes were a mess, but that wasn't what caught my eye. Along my face, neck, and arms were cuts, blood oozing out in little droplets.

They were marks from the bindings, cutting angry red lines across my skin.

I called Emily as soon as I was alone. It took a while. There was a lot of panicking and fretting from my dad. He'd searched the whole house, twice. He'd bandaged my wounds—I refused to go to the hospital, though that was his first instinct— and made me run through what had happened a total of three times. He'd asked a million questions, none of which I could answer. I wasn't being secretive, I just genuinely didn't know what was going on.

I couldn't wait for morning, so I grabbed my phone while my dad was downstairs searching the house yet again and dialed the number on her card.

"Hello?" she asked, sounding a bit groggy.

"Hey, it's Rosalind. I'm...sorry to call you so late...um...look, I changed my mind. You're right. We have to do something. We need to do the séance. Soon. As soon as we can."

"Did something else happen?" she asked around a yawn.

I glanced over at my bed. "Uh...yeah..."

"What was it this time?"

I took a deep breath and went over the details of the night as quickly as I could. I didn't really want to talk about it again—just thinking about it made me shake.

Emily let out a slow breath. She sounded completely awake now. "Incredible. Are you all right?"

"Mostly. I have a few cuts and scrapes..."

"Wow. Okay, no, we definitely have to do this soon. Um...how about Monday? Would that work for you?"

I didn't answer. I was standing, rooted to the spot, staring at something on my nightstand.

"Rosalind?"

My mother's journal. The old one, from her wedding. The one I'd thrown away.

"Rosalind? Are you there?"

"I...yeah...sorry."

"What's going on now?" she demanded.

"The journal. It's back."

"*What?* I thought you threw that away!"

"I did."

We were both silent for a while.

"Have you read it yet?" she finally asked.

"No!" I said, shrieking a bit. I took a breath to steady myself. "I mean...I'm too tired to get into all that now. I think...maybe in the morning?" I started pacing, twisting a lock of hair between my fingers. "Anyway, I just wanted to tell you that I think you're right...this is...not normal. Something's going on, ghosts or...I don't know what. But we need to do this soon."

"Definitely. I'll call Derek and start getting everything ready."

She had said Monday. It was Saturday, technically Sunday. I glanced nervously at my bed again. I wasn't sure I could last that long.

"Yeah, that'd be great," I said as steadily as I could.

We hung up and I sat heavily on my desk chair, watching my bed. I wasn't sure how I'd ever sleep in it again.

Something about this encounter nagged at me. It had been different from the others. Scarier, somehow. I hadn't felt the way I had when seeing the other...apparitions. I was still hesitant to call them ghosts, but what else could they be?

These things didn't seem like ghosts, I thought, remembering the eerie appearance of whatever had attacked me.

I decided to text Hazel and let her know what had happened. Odds were she was asleep, but I felt bad telling Emily and leaving Hazel out of the loop.

Part of me still reeled against it all. I didn't like the "ghost" explanation, and now I felt like I'd seen something else entirely. Maybe I was having night terrors. Or some other weird sleep disorder. There had to be some kind of logical explanation.

"Here, honey," my dad said as he returned to my room, handing me a steaming mug. He'd made me cocoa. I smiled—it was what he'd always done when I was little and had a bad dream.

My room was warm again, but I gripped the mug, clutching the heat of it between my hands, holding on to its familiarity.

My dad leaned against the desk, looking tired and strained.

We were silent for a few seconds, neither of us knowing what to say. He got up and started searching through my room again, though he must have known it was pointless.

"Dad, I know it sounds insane, but..."

My father stopped looking behind furniture and curtains and turned to me, watching me intently.

I took a sip of cocoa to buy myself some time. I didn't want to have this conversation, but I wasn't sure how to wave off his concern anymore.

"Dad?"

"Yeah, kiddo?"

"I think the house is haunted."

He stared at me, but I couldn't read anything more in his reaction than the worry that had already been there.

"Do you think I'm crazy?" I asked when the silence had dragged on too long.

"No, Roz...I..." he sighed and raked his hand back through his hair. "I'm just worried. I don't understand what's happening here. You..."

He looked at the cuts on my face and neck. He

couldn't explain those away as a nightmare.

"I don't know what to do," he said, sounding frustrated.

I looked down at my cocoa. "Me either...but...do you believe me?"

My dad sighed and rubbed the back of his neck. "I believe...that something strange is happening here."

I nodded and took another sip of cocoa. He thought I was crazy.

We were silent as he looked around the room, like he didn't want to leave me alone.

"Come on. Let's go downstairs," he said standing up straighter.

"What?"

"I..." he looked around my room again. "Roz, I don't want you sleeping alone in here. We can each take one of the sofas."

"Dad..."

"It would make me feel better. I'm worried about..." he gestured with his arms. "I'm worried about whatever happened in here tonight."

I didn't really want to sleep on the sofa, but I didn't want to sleep in my room, either. Honestly, I just didn't really want to sleep at all. But if it would make my dad feel better, then maybe at least one of us would be able to rest tonight.

We went downstairs and made up beds on the two large, plush sofas there. My dad did yet another check of the alarm system and the doors, but everything was as it should be, so we settled in to try and get some sleep.

Worried as he was, my father didn't fall asleep very fast, but he did eventually drift off. I wasn't able to get to sleep, though, and just being awake started to stress me out, even without any unusual activity.

I kept thinking of the journal, unsure if I should read it or burn it. I didn't know why some ghost-man who didn't speak English kept trying to give me an old journal from my mother, but apparently it was important.

I had brought my headphones with me, so I put them on and listened to some music, trying to drown the terror out with something familiar.

But I still couldn't sleep. I sat awake all night, despite how tired I was. The buzzing, frantic energy that had come from my last encounter kept me wired. My house wasn't safe. That thought plagued me.

Joanne's party was still in full swing. With our house completely silent, the softest hum of activity from her and her guests floated over to where I sat. Not enough to disturb anyone's sleep, but enough to make me wonder what everyone was up to. I tried to peek from the living room windows toward her house, but trees and the angle of the house obscured my view enough that all I could see were some lights. The dome atop her house was dark and silent, glinting in the moonlight.

Finally, too bored to sit still, I crept up to my room and retrieved my computer. I pulled Emily's card from my purse and took it downstairs with me. Back on the sofa, I situated myself so the light of my screen wouldn't disturb my snoring father.

Emily had a website where she wrote about and posted videos on the strange and supernatural. I clicked around for a while, reading about ghosts and Bigfoot and other inexplicable phenomena. She had posted a lot of information, none of which made me feel better.

I saw a button in the top corner of her site that read *East/West*. Curious, I clicked it.

This led me to a different site. Dark, with a pair of glowing red eyes staring out at me from the side of the page. I clicked the "About" tab and read. It was a podcast, centered completely around paranormal activity and unexplained events. Everything from UFOs to "lizard people" who apparently lived in underground tunnels. No wonder Emily liked it.

The show broadcasted on an AM channel, but was also available for streaming online, and download as a podcast.

Lower on the "About" page, there was a picture of a guy wearing sunglasses. "Chad," the show's host. I scanned the rest of the site. The red "ON AIR" sign in the banner was on, and the listed show times said it was playing now. On the right hand side, there was an archive of past episodes.

I plugged my headphones in and clicked the "listen now" button at the top of the page.

"...caller says her daughter has a disturbing imaginary friend. Janice, you're on the line."

"Hi Chad, thanks for having me," a nervous sounding woman said.

"Thank you for calling in, Janice," Chad said. He had a kind voice.

Janice told a story of her daughter's imaginary friend, whom at first she'd thought nothing of, but was now quite unnerved by. The imaginary friend's name was Eleanor, and she apparently told Janice's daughter all kinds of things about how she'd died, and how life had been for her. It sounded like Eleanor had grown up in the fifties.

I listened for a long time. Callers talked about finding strange animals they couldn't identify in their basements, or hearing talking in the night. One caller claimed to have made a friend of her ghost, who helped the caller by telling her if certain people had malicious intentions or not.

There weren't many answers, though. Just people calling in and sharing their stories. I felt like I'd gone to a group therapy session, with how much their experiences resonated with my own, though none had mentioned anything that sounded like my experiences tonight.

Still, I didn't want to call in myself. I wasn't ready to discuss whatever was happening in my house in such an open forum.

While I listened, I searched online for any information on the things I'd seen in my room. Even thinking about it made my heart race and my throat tighten, but I pressed on. I needed to know more. I searched "tall white figure" and got everything from Slender Man to aliens. Slender Man didn't fit, but the entries about aliens almost seemed to. The feel of the table, multiple presences. I didn't remember what attire, if any, they'd been wearing, but I had been half-blind from the light and the pain. There were a lot of pages about "tall white figures"—forum threads, articles, wiki entries, accounts and research papers, even photos and videos. I wasn't enough of a detective to tell which things were faked and which were real, but most of it seemed pretty legitimate. Either way, kidnapping and torture were game for the various mythical or extraterrestrial creatures that fit the physical description of what I'd seen around my bed.

I closed those pages, shuddering at the memories. Looking for something safer to read about, I searched sleep disorders. The only thing that seemed at all close to what I was experiencing was something called "sleep paralysis", where people woke up paralyzed, in pain, and experiencing intense fear. Hallucinations often went hand in hand with this disorder, many of which seemed to try to attack or kill the sleeper. I looked at my arms. Unless I was imagining the stinging welts covered by bandages, sleep paralysis probably wasn't my answer.

"Tomorrow, we'll have special guest Rowan Fallon on with us to discuss the likelihood of aliens, other dimensions, and how we might travel to these other worlds."

I paused. The name caught my attention. *Rowan Fallon*, where had I heard that before?

The book! I got up and ran to my room, hesitating as I reached the top of the steps. I didn't want to return to my room, but I was suddenly incredibly curious what was in that book. If she was on that show...and she was a renowned scientist—a *real* scientist—then she might have some answers.

Creeping into my room like I was on some secret mission, I darted to the shelf, found the book, and hurried back downstairs. As I reached my little nest of blankets on the sofa, I realized I should have also grabbed my mother's journal. The way my stomach twisted at the thought of it reminded me that there's no way I would have been able to read it just yet, though, so I shrugged it off and settled back into my seat.

Skimming the table of contents as I put my earbuds back in, I saw that the book was extremely scientific. One of the chapter titles wasn't even in English—it was some mathematical equation.

How pretentious, I thought, but for some reason, I turned to that chapter and looked it over. It opened with a description of some sensor she used to pick up frequencies that apparently indicated the existence of other dimensions. I rubbed the bridge of my nose as I read, realizing that three in the morning after a terrifying ordeal was probably not the time to try and process high-level mathematics and engineering.

I flipped back to the beginning of the book and read the forward, which was by Stephen Hawking. I was surprised, but he seemed impressed by Dr. Fallon's research, theories, and findings. She had won awards and been offered prestigious fellowships I'd never heard of. He wrapped up the forward by calling her "one of the greatest scientific minds of our time" and promising that this book could change the course of scientific advancement.

The show was still playing in the background, and I mentally tuned back into it, listening to the callers' stories as I flipped through Rowan's book. Before, I'd have shrugged all of this off as a bunch of conspiracy theorists egging each other on, but now I felt a kind of kinship with these people. That worried me. I wasn't ready to be part of the group who believed in government conspiracies to cover up alien activity or whatever, but the show was at least partially legitimate.

It ended, and I closed my laptop, feeling more alone than ever.

Seven

I sat awake for the rest of the night with my sketchpad, drawing. I drew people I'd seen going into Joanne's party, or whatever that had been. The outfits were beautiful and outlandish, the faces were smiling...it soothed me. I could concentrate on the lines, on the shading, on capturing the expressions and emotions and unique energy of each person.

When the sun started to rise, I got up and dressed quickly, eager to go do...something. I wasn't sure what. I didn't feel like being in the house. I was still anxious from the night before, and the journal was nagging at the back of my mind. If I wasn't there, I couldn't read it, and if I didn't read it, I didn't have to deal with whatever it said.

I didn't want to go far; my dad was still asleep, and he'd be worried if he woke to find me missing, especially after last night. So I just went out and sat on our porch, sipping a mug of coffee and enjoying the quiet of the early morning air.

I spotted Joanne strolling around the block. It struck me as odd that she was up so early, as her party had gone on well into the night. She was sauntering down the road, wearing a baby blue jogging suit that looked like it was made of silk.

For some reason, I wanted to talk to her. I got up and made my way to the sidewalk to meet her.

"Hi, Ms. Königin," I said as she came nearer.

She turned her wide, pale eyes to me, looking like I'd pulled her out of deep thoughts.

"Oh, Rosalind, how are you, dear?" she asked, smiling as she came to a stop beside me. Standing near her like this, I saw that she was even taller than I'd realized—almost as tall as my father.

She spotted the bandages on my arms and frowned. "What happened?"

"Oh, just got a couple scrapes moving stuff around. I'm good," I lied.

"Getting settled in? Any more strange occurrences?"

"No, not since Thursday, thankfully," I said. "Oh, I saw you painting the other night. I like that glass dome you've got on your house."

She smiled. "Do you? I love it. I love seeing the stars when I work at night, not that you see many with the Strip. But that can be lovely to look at, too. I also enjoy seeing the trees and houses from high up when I work during the day."

"Are you a professional painter?" I asked.

She chuckled. "I am, yes. I don't know how much someone your age would know about the world of painting, but I am rather well known among art aficionados."

"Wait, I can't believe I didn't realize this before...your name is *Joanne Königin*?"

"Yes..." she said, sounding a bit perplexed.

I laughed and clapped my hands. "Oh, my God! You're *the* Joanne Königin! The one who painted *The Watchers*! I can't believe it. I love your work! I have a book of some of your early pieces, I—wow. That's incredible!"

Joanne laughed. "I knew I liked you. Now, what's a girl your age doing reading about old painters?"

"I want to be a painter. I mean, not professionally, I don't know if I could ever do that, but I love painting. I'm not too good at it yet but I'm always doing sketches that I hope to eventually turn into paintings."

"Oh, really? That's wonderful. You know, if you ever wanted some pointers, I'd be happy to have you over and share some of my knowledge."

"Really? Are you serious?" I asked.

"I'd love it. To be honest, I don't get much good, art-appreciating company these days, and I'd be happy to have someone to share my craft with."

I paused. What about all the things Ford had said about her, did they have any merit? After all, if there were ghosts in my house, why not a witch next door? She *did* give me a strange sense, though it wasn't really a bad feeling. Just...different.

But the rational part of me balked at all that. Joanne was a little odd, definitely, but I wasn't going to pass up the chance to learn from a master over some childish rumors.

“Yes, absolutely, whenever you’re free.”

“Oh, that sounds fun. Maybe you could come by tomorrow?”

“I have some...stuff to take care of tomorrow, but maybe. Here, can I get your number? I can call you when I know what’s going on so we can make plans.”

We exchanged information and she sauntered off, waving and smiling.

My phone started ringing as Joanne disappeared into her house.

“Hi, Hazel,” I answered.

“Rosalind! I got your text, what happened? Are you all right? Do you need me to come over?”

“No, it’s okay. I mean, it’s not...not really. But...I called Emily last night. We’re on for the séance. I guess. Tomorrow, I think.”

“Just tell me when I need to be there and what I need to do and I’m there,” she said. She sounded so determined I almost started laughing, only I couldn’t, because I was getting shaky again just talking about it. Speaking with Joanne, I’d been fine, like none of this terrible stuff was happening. I’d been thinking about painting and getting to know a person whose work I admired. Now I felt like I was being dragged down into a cold abyss.

“I don’t know what you have to do or bring or...or any of that. You can ask Emily, she’ll know what to tell you.”

“Right, I’ll do that. Anyway, I’m so sorry, Rosalind, that text you sent will probably give me nightmares. I don’t know how you manage to stay in that house.”

“Me either,” I said, glancing at my new home.

“So this is definitely a ghost thing?”

"I-I think so..."

"You're being visited by the dead..."

"Yeah, that's kinda what living in a haunted house is all about."

She laughed. "Have you read that journal yet?"

My stomach knotted at the mention of it. "No, I don't know when I'm going to."

"Rosalind...I think you should read it. I think it's probably important."

"No, it's not," I snapped, pacing back and forth on the sidewalk.

"Well...can I ask you something?"

I sighed. "Sure."

"Do you think...maybe...you should try to get a hold of your mom?"

"What?" I stopped pacing. "Why would I want to do that?"

My tone was harsh, and it must have startled Hazel, because when she answered, she sounded shocked. "I-I...don't know...I was thinking that maybe she could help you with this...I mean, she—"

I barked out a laugh. "Hazel, I understand what you're trying to say here, but you seem to be forgetting something: It doesn't matter if my mom can help me with this or not, it doesn't matter if she wants to help me, *she is the last person I would ever want to talk to*."

I resumed my pacing, too jittery to stand still any longer. "I wouldn't want to hear what she has to say. Just like I don't want to read her stupid journal. I told you before that I didn't want to talk about her and I *definitely* don't want to talk *to* her, no matter what's going on. Not now. Not ever."

My voice rose as I spoke, my palms sweaty. I was jumpy, like I was under attack, but nothing was happening. I was just standing outside, having a fit on the sidewalk.

On the other end, Hazel was silent.

I sighed and stopped pacing, sitting down on the curb and putting my head in my hands.

"I'm sorry, Hazel...I shouldn't take this out on you."

"It's okay, Roz," she said, her voice soft. "I shouldn't have brought it up. I know you don't like to...talk about this stuff."

"Still. I shouldn't snap at you. I just...I didn't sleep last night after that whole...thing."

"Well, how *could* you sleep after that?"

I shook my head. "Either way. I just...I don't want to talk to her, or about her, okay?"

"All right, Roz. I won't bring it up again. It's completely up to you."

"Thank you." I sighed, rubbing a hand over my face. "Um...what about you, what's new with you?"

"Uh, nothing as exciting as late-night bed intruders."

I made a face. "Oh, God, is that what we're calling this incident?"

"It's official," she said with a laugh. "But...nothing, really. Oh! I do have a date with Sean, though!"

"*Really?* You waste no time, do you?"

"Since we're not in the same place, please punch yourself in the arm for that remark, courtesy of me," she said.

We both laughed. I had her tell me a little more about Sean, and this upcoming date. It was nice to listen to something normal and fun, and Hazel was so excited, which always made me happy.

"Roz!"

I turned and saw my father standing in the doorway, his face drawn with worry.

Waving, I gestured to my phone and mouthed, "I'll be right there."

He nodded and went back inside.

"You okay?" Hazel asked.

"Yeah. Yeah, just, my dad. Anyway, um, I should go."

"Okay. I have to get to breakfast, anyway. Keep me posted on whatever's going on, and let me know what time the séance or whatever is."

"Will do."

We hung up and I stood to go back inside.

I found my father in the kitchen, making a cup of coffee.

"You're up early," he said when he saw me.

"Yeah. This room is bright." I put my empty mug in the sink. I wasn't about to bring up the previous night's attack.

"I was thinking we could go out for breakfast," he said.

"Oh, sure, that sounds fun."

"Okay. Let me just get dressed," he said, taking his coffee upstairs with him.

He was ready a few minutes later and we left. In the car, I finally started to feel tired. Maybe it was the heat of the day, but the jittery energy that had kept me awake so far had given way to a strange weariness. I just wanted to lie down, but I didn't want my dad to worry, so I made it a point to keep the conversation going. I considered suggesting we go up to the mountain, but I didn't say anything.

My dad drove us to a restaurant that I was barely aware of and I followed him inside, trying to pay attention to things like the menu and the very enthusiastic man who'd introduced himself as our waiter. It was hard to focus.

"I was thinking we should go have lunch on Monday," I said after the waiter had delivered our food, trying to make conversation despite my exhaustion. "Hazel was telling me about this great Greek place. I haven't had decent hummus in forever."

"Sounds great. Not Monday, though. I'm meeting..." he stopped, looking awkward.

I watched him, confused.

"I'm...having lunch with someone," he finally said.

"Oh. Who?"

"Just, Veronica. You remember her, from Leah's birthday? Monday's the only day she had free to meet."

"Oh. So, you're...what...going on a date with her?" I asked, trying to sound casual while my throat tightened.

"No, no, not a date, just catching up with an old friend." He read the concern on my face and set his fork down. "Rosalind, it's nothing, we're just meeting for lunch tomorrow," my dad said, almost apologetically.

I felt bad. My dad didn't have to justify going to lunch with someone, and I knew that, but part of me couldn't stand the thought of him going out with her. I hated the idea that he might be moving on, even though no part of me missed my parents' marriage. Besides, he had a right to move on if he wanted to. It had been almost a year, and he deserved to be happy more than anyone else I knew. My father had worked so hard, and for so long, and always gave so much to others. I *wanted* him to be happy. I just...didn't like the thought of that woman.

"Right, it's fine. Have fun," I said. I wanted to sound sincere, but I mostly sounded sarcastic. I tried to correct my tone, but it didn't seem to be working.

Thankfully, my dad is understanding. He reached out and squeezed my hand, "Roz, your mom..."

First Hazel, now him, what's up with everyone today?

"She abandoned us," I finished the thought for him before he could soften it up or make it sound less pathetic. He made excuses for her, but she didn't deserve it. "She left us, that's it, and neither of us should have to sit around, wallowing in sadness and missing her. She ditched us, no explanation, just poof! Gone. We can move on," I said, more harshly than I'd intended.

My dad looked sad, but he'd learned since she'd left us behind that I was completely unsympathetic toward my mother. He seemed tired, and I winced, guilty—it had hurt him, too. I needed to remember that.

I cleared my throat and took a sip of water. I wanted to regain my composure before I spoke next.

Let's try this again. "So. Veronica. I met her, but only for a minute. What's she like?"

"She's very nice. I knew her when we were kids, her brother and I were best friends, but I haven't seen her since I left for college. It was good to see her again; I'm looking forward to catching up a bit, hearing what her family's been up to, that sort of thing."

There was part of me that was immediately suspicious. In my mind, I had pegged this girl as a conniving, greedy gold-digger, despite having exactly zero information about her. My dad makes a lot of money doing what he does, and he was single now. There are plenty of women who'd love to swoop in, ship me off to a boarding school, and live the lavish life of a spoiled, rich wife. He'd certainly had enough admirers back in Los Angeles.

I pushed my food around my plate. My dad wouldn't do that to me.

"What does she do?" I asked as casually as I could.

"Apparently she's a model. I was surprised by that—last I heard, she wanted to be a cop, but then again, it has been a long time, so I suppose change is to be expected," he said with a little chuckle.

Ugh. Model. Gold-digger: Check.

"Sounds exciting," I said, trying, for my dad's sake, to feign interest.

We made nicer, safer chit-chat through the rest of breakfast, but idea of my dad possibly becoming interested in another woman still bothered me. Not even just this woman, specifically, but any woman. Not that I was longing for the old days with him and my mom together. She'd made him miserable for a long time before delivering the final blow; I wanted my dad to be happy. I just...didn't want to deal with another person in my life right now.

It was a complicated emotion. I forced down what I could of my food and tried to keep conversation light. As long as I could keep us off ghosts, Veronica, and my mother, I'd be fine.

I was about to breathe a sigh of relief that we'd made it through the meal without talking about the whole ghost incident when my dad cleared his throat, glancing over at me uncertainly.

"Um, Roz," he started. I had to suppress a groan. I wasn't emotionally prepared for this conversation.

"Look, about last night," he went on when I didn't respond. "You said...you think the house is haunted?"

I couldn't meet his gaze. I didn't know what to say, and I couldn't remember why in the world I'd thought it would be a good idea to tell my father there were ghosts in our house.

"I was scared," I said lamely. "I had a nightmare. I mean...you saw what happened."

"Well, that's the thing: I *didn't* see what happened, honey. I heard you screaming and ran into the room. I have no idea what is actually going on."

My eyes were still down, fixated on my hands folded in my lap.

"Was someone in our house? Did someone hurt you?" he asked, leaning closer.

I shook my head. The guilt and fear in his voice broke my heart. I could only imagine how much this was scaring him; it was scaring me, and I knew more than he did.

"I...I don't know, Dad. I really don't know. No one was there...it was just..." I shuddered and stopped talking. I didn't want to lie to him, but I didn't really want to tell him the truth, either, even though I'd already made the mistake of saying the word "haunted" to him.

He sighed. "Sweetie. If...if you feel like the house is haunted, then..."

I glanced up at him, thrown off by his tone.

"Then what?" I asked.

"Then...I don't know. What do you do about...about ghosts?" he asked, his voice sounding disbelieving and confused.

I shrugged. "Exorcist?" I realized, a little to my own annoyance, that I didn't know if exorcisms were a strictly Catholic thing. Could Jewish people even hire exorcists? I doubted the ghosts cared about my heritage, and honestly, I'd turn to anything if it would solve this.

My dad didn't seem concerned with any of these details, though. He was probably more focused on calming down what must've appeared to be his mentally unstable daughter.

"Right. Of course," he said carefully. "Well. How do we get one of those?"

"I...have no idea," I admitted.

We both laughed at that, and I wondered if he really believed me, or if he was just trying to pacify me. I'd watched him with my mother for years, and I knew that while he meant well, my father didn't really believe in anything mystical.

"Do you think the house is safe?" he asked.

"I think so. I hope so." It wasn't true, but what were we going to do, move again?

"Is that what you think happened while I was out of town?" he asked.

I shifted and looked down as I nodded.

He sighed and rubbed his hand across his face.

"If this has been going on for a while, we need to do something."

I glanced up at him. "Are you really thinking about calling an exorcist?"

“Maybe,” he said. “We could do that. I mean, I think we can. You might have to be Catholic for that...” he mused, looking contemplative while he echoed my own curiosity. After a second, he shook his head, looking back at me. He looked uncomfortable.

“What?” I asked.

“I’m just wondering if, maybe, it wouldn’t be a bad idea for you to go back to therapy. Just for a little while, to help you adjust.”

My stomach clenched. I had grudgingly agreed to therapy after my mother ditched us, but I had never liked the idea of it, and with me already questioning my mental stability, it felt more like a slap in the face than a potential solution.

“I...don’t know...” I said.

My dad nodded and returned to his breakfast, though I knew this wasn’t the last I’d hear on the topic.

After that, we didn’t talk about ghosts anymore. I told him about meeting Joanne that morning, and how she had offered me painting lessons. We talked about art, and the various exhibits in town that we might like to see. It felt almost normal, and I did my best not to dwell on ghosts and therapists and other uncomfortable things.

We went home and my dad went into his office to make a few calls. I puttered around the house for a while, restless, uneasy. The doorbell rang and I was actually relieved—my need for a distraction had surpassed my desire to avoid contact with most people.

The woman at the door wrote a cheery smile that made her blue eyes scrunch up. She had abnormally bouncy blonde curls, and a high-pitched voice.

"Hi! I'm Jessa Lee! Is this the Weissmandl residence? I'm from Housekeepers Las Vegas!"

"Yeah, come on in," I said, stepping aside to let her in. My father had decided it should be my job to oversee the housekeeper and get her situated, so after poking my head into his office to let him know she'd arrived, I led Jessa Lee though the house.

There wasn't really much to explain, and I'd done this three times already, so it felt rather routine. With just my dad and I, the house stayed pretty clean. My dad's a bit of a germaphobe, so Jessa Lee wouldn't run out of things to do, but it was all rather self-explanatory.

Her biggest task would be cooking. Neither my dad nor I were very proficient in the kitchen, so we were counting on her to produce something healthier than takeout and restaurant food.

"Ooh, cooking's my specialty," Jessa Lee said as I told her about our culinary needs. "The agency told me about that. I just *love* to cook! And this kitchen is fabulous!"

"We've got everything you should need," I told her. "You can move things around if you want to, just let us know so we don't get lost."

"You got it, doll."

"Okay, well, do you have any more questions?" I asked.

She shook her head. "Not now. I'm going to get started cooking, then I'll do the laundry. You guys said you're good with leftovers, yeah? I like to cook for the week so you've got all your meals ready to go."

"That's perfect. Thanks, Jessa Lee. I've got some work to do upstairs. Just call me if you need me," I said, indicating the intercom.

"Thanks, Roz! I'll let you know when lunch is ready!"

My dad left shortly after, heading to his office to pick up some paperwork. I sat on the floor in my room, listening to music and researching how to get rid of ghosts. There were an alarming number of "How to Exorcise Your House" articles, but none of them seemed legitimate.

I kept wondering if "exorcists" were actually a real thing. I'd kind of thought that the whole notion was something Hollywood made up. Actually, I'd never considered it at all until a few days ago. I kept searching, and eventually learned that a rabbi could perform an exorcism, which made sense, if anything made sense anymore. I couldn't really tell.

Even after finding out that exorcism was a real thing for which real people would show up and do real work, I was reluctant. I closed the pages and sat on my bed, drumming my fingers on my lap.

Downstairs, I heard a yelp and shattering glass. I leapt to my feet and rushed over to the stairs.

"Jessa Lee?" I called. "Are you okay?"

She didn't answer, and I hurried to the kitchen, hoping she hadn't gotten hurt.

"Hey, are you all right?" I asked as I rounded the corner.

Jessa Lee stood pressed against the fridge, eyes wide.

"What happened?" I asked, my stomach was already sinking.

"I..." she shook her head. She was even paler than before. "I don't know...I thought I saw..."

I watched Jessa Lee carefully.

After a few seconds of ragged breathing, she let out a shaky chuckle and shook her head.

"I'm sorry for startling you. I must've gone and spooked myself," she said, forcing another laugh.

"What did you think you saw?" I asked. I was trying to keep my tone light, but Jessa Lee's head snapped around at my question and we just stood there, analyzing each other.

"Nothing," she finally answered, holding my gaze. "I didn't see anything. It was probably just a shadow. Something out of the corner of my eye."

I nodded. I couldn't keep asking, and she didn't want to talk about whatever it was, so I decided to drop it.

Jessa Lee hurried over to the broken mug on the floor and started cleaning it up.

"Sorry about that," she muttered to me, keeping her eyes averted.

"It's okay," I assured her. Her demeanor had completely changed, and I didn't know what to do. As far as I knew, my dad had never seen the ghosts. Why had she? Why had any of the housekeepers?

If other people are seeing them, then I'm not crazy.

I almost laughed. No need to go jumping to conclusions.

Jessa Lee plastered a smile on her face and shooed me away in what was probably meant to be a joking, light-hearted manner. She kept assuring me she had everything under control. Not knowing what else to say, I left.

Once I'd walked out of the kitchen, though, I didn't know what to do with myself. I didn't want to be in the house. I didn't want to keep reading about ghosts. I *really* didn't want to try to sleep, despite how tired I was.

I needed to get all of this craziness off my mind. Almost without thinking, I pulled my phone from my pocket and called Joanne.

Eight

I was surprised that Joanne was willing to have me over so soon, but not an hour later, I stood in the front room of her house, completely speechless. It was amazing. There was art *everywhere*. Every available space on the wall bore a painting. Pedestals held little sculptures, and in spot-lit corners were statues.

Some paintings were small: little three-by-three-inch canvases. Others were enormous, dominating entire walls. One, in particular, caught my eye; a painting done all in tan and brown and deep, rich red. It was a medium-sized canvas hanging over the landing along her vast stairway. I could just make out a mutilated face in the chaos of the painting. It looked like how I imagined pain would be embodied. Just staring into the eyes of the distorted, tormented face gave me chills. I turned away—something about it was just too intense for me.

"All these pieces are originals," Joanne said as she led me through the house. "Many of the painters are my close friends. I do have some older, more well-known works of art, but they're in my gallery downtown."

"Your collection is incredible."

"Thank you. I've been gathering them for a long, long time," she said, admiring a beautiful painting of sunshine peeking through clouds.

A big, circular table of photographs with a colorful flower arrangement in the center drew my attention. I spotted an old, black-and-white snapshot of a woman who looked very much like Joanne, but younger and with long, dark hair.

"Who's she?" I asked.

Joanne smiled fondly at the photograph. "My mother. She was in Germany during World War II. She escaped, but only barely. I heard many stories about what she went through when I was a girl. Some, I didn't hear till I was much older."

"Wow," I said, studying the picture. Joanne had the same uncanny resemblance to her mother that I did. I wondered if it was a blessing or a curse to her.

"Were you born in Germany?"

"I was, yes. We moved here when I was very young, though. My parents were farmers."

The other pictures on the table drew my eye. Joanne with various movie stars and celebrities, posing with friends who were every bit as eccentric and wild as she was. There were none of the husband Ford had mentioned, but I didn't think that was terribly unusual; I, after all, had gotten rid of many pictures as of late.

"This way, my studio's right up here."

She started up the stairs and I followed, gazing up again at the unusual, intense painting. Closer up, I saw that the artist had layered texture onto the canvas, even creating the appearance of stitches running along the canvas' surface.

"Who painted this?" I asked, tempted to reach out and feel it.

She glanced over and chuckled. "Oh, that's my own. I painted that during a dark time."

"Oh, wow. I'm sorry. It shows. It looks...painful."

She continued up the steps and to a little spiraling metal staircase that led to the glass dome. I followed her up.

"I was in pain. My husband, Jacek, had just left me. We were fighting constantly, it was a dreadful time. That painting is actually the only work of art from that period that I still have. I destroyed most of the things I made around then...I wish I hadn't, some were very good."

I looked around the wide, clear dome. It was like being outside, or maybe in an aquarium. The sun was brilliant, high in the sky, lighting and warming the whole room, though not to an unbearable heat. I could feel cool air moving through the dome, keeping it from getting stuffy.

Joanne went on, "Anyway, that one survived, so I keep it as a reminder of what I've endured."

The prominently hung painting was a bit eccentric, but I respected the gesture. Joanne wasn't exactly a subtle person, anyway—I could see why Ford, as a child, had thought her so unusual: She wore tons of makeup, strange clothing, and was thin almost to the point of being unhealthy. She was, truthfully, kind of scary looking at first, but I was quickly beginning to see past that. I could tell that she had once been very beautiful. And more than that, she was kind. She was incredibly welcoming and hospitable, with a generosity of spirit and zest for life I envied. I hoped the neighborhood kids hadn't given her too hard of a time—the idea of her ever being harassed made me sad.

"It's really hard when people just...leave," I said.

"Have you had your heart broken recently, Rosalind?"

I shook my head. "Not how you're thinking. My mother—she," there it was again; the catch in my throat. The wobble in my voice. I swallowed hard. "She abandoned us. It's been pretty hard on my dad."

"And you?"

I looked down, focusing intently on some paintbrushes. "Yeah," I whispered.

Joanne smiled sadly. She reached out and squeezed my shoulder.

"Well," Joanne said softly, "then you have something very real to work with. Some of my greatest work comes from my pain. Use it; it's actually one of the best ways to heal."

I nodded, awkward. Joanne seemed to sense this, because she clapped her hands and said, "Okay, let's start painting. Did you bring brushes?"

She gave me a seat before a blank canvas and an assortment of paints.

"I didn't know what paints you prefer, so there are several kinds. That canvas is best for oil-based, but if you want to work with acrylics or watercolors, I have everything for that, too."

"Oh, no, oil paints are fine," I said, still taking in the view. I could see all around from so high—my house, my closed bedroom window, Ford's house, with Ford himself in the open garage, still working on his van. And in the distance, the Strip with its unique skyline. The towering spire of the Stratosphere, the gleaming black face of the Luxor's pyramid, the brilliant golden surfaces of the Wynn and Encore, and the wide circle of a ludicrously tall Ferris wheel all shimmered in the sun.

"The view up here is awesome," I said as I unpacked my brushes.

"Oh, isn't it? I love it. It's inspiring. Not as nice as my cabin, but it's still wonderful."

I laid out my supplies in a neat little row. "You have a cabin? Where?"

"Not far from here. Up in the mountains, about an hour outside the city."

I stopped, remembering my dream. I glanced at Joanne, scrambling for something normal to say. It seemed that she still thought I was sane; I wanted to preserve that.

"That's right," I said quickly. "My aunt and uncle took me hiking up there once."

"It's lovely. I try to visit at least once a month, more when it's hot like this."

"It sounds great," I said.

"You should visit sometime. It's beautiful this time of year—all wildflowers and butterflies," she said wistfully.

I had little experience with painting, despite my many attempts in the past, but Joanne was patient and good at explaining the technical details. She started at the beginning, and walked me through, demonstrating on her canvas; she the picture of grace, and me the poster-child for uncoordinated clumsiness.

Despite my uncertainty, I kept my mind focused on my canvas. I didn't want to think about the ghosts or my dreams. I painted and tried to push it all away. Weirdly, it worked.

"You have a good eye for color balance. That's wonderful, because it's hard to learn."

"Yeah, but my proportions are all off," I said, surveying my painting. It was a puppy. It seemed like a silly thing to paint, but I had no ideas, so Joanne gave me some reference photos.

"Proportions can be practiced and improved; you just need to keep painting."

"Does it take a long time to master?" I asked.

"Not terribly," Joanne assured me. "You'll learn fast, I think. Faster than I did, anyway."

"How long did it take you to get...well...good enough to be professional?"

Joanne laughed. "Honey, you don't want to know."

That made me laugh, too.

"When did you start painting?" I went on.

"Years and years ago, when I was a little girl. At first, I just helped my father on our farm—painting sheds, water tanks, the barn, the house, just mundane things like that. If he'd let me, I'd paint flowers or landscapes. I loved it. When I was ten, I saw a painting set in town. I saved up a little money and started painting and, well, the rest is history, as they say."

"Did you teach yourself?"

"At first, yes. I bought a few books as I got older, and worked with some professionals, but I never had the chance to go to a university or do any real formal training. By the time I could afford it, I was so successful, it seemed pointless," she said with a laugh.

"That's kinda cool," I said, trying to get the shading right. "How long did it take you to get successful?" I was almost interrogating her, but Joanne didn't seem to mind.

"Before I gained any notoriety, it felt like an eternity. Looking back, I can see it was still a long time, but not nearly as long as it felt. I struggled to get by for years. But it was worth it," she smiled at her own painting. She'd chosen a goldfish from the reference photos. Hers was completely effortless *and* better than mine.

"Tell me, what calls *you* to it?" she asked as she added a shimmer effect to the water.

I shrugged. "I've just always loved it. I like to draw, and I like art. I usually just sketch, but I've been teaching myself to paint lately. Trying to, anyway."

"Well, you're off to a good start."

I laughed and stepped back, holding out my arms.

"What do you think?"

"It's lovely. Far better than my first attempts at painting."

"You're just saying that to be nice," I said.

Joanne winked. "Oh, but I'm not nice. At least, that's what my ex-husband used to say."

"I'm serious! You're just flattering me."

"You think so? I still have some of my early pieces. I'll get them out for your next lesson."

"You should, because I need proof."

She laughed and carried her brushes to the sink. I helped her clean up and listened to her talk about her greatest failures in painting a bit more. When we were done, Joanne walked me down and I thanked her for the lesson. She even suggested I come back on Wednesday, which I excitedly agreed to.

It felt later in the day, because it was so bright and hot, and because I'd been awake so long, but when I checked the time, it was just a little past eleven in the morning.

"Hey! Rosalind!"

I turned around and saw Ford pulling up in the most beat-up van I've ever seen. It was old—probably older than either of us—and the faded paint was white and blue. It had dings and scrapes, and I was pretty sure I spotted a patch of duct tape on the back bumper. A trailer full of tools was hitched to the back, rumbling along behind the creaky old van.

"Ford?" I asked. "Hey, what...is all this?"

He parked and climbed out, making his way across the cul-de-sac toward me.

"I run this kinda lawn-service type company. Just finished working. I'm usually not done till a little later, but today was slow."

"You work?" I asked, glancing at his house. From the looks of it, Ford would probably inherit enough to never work a day in his life. The idea surprised me.

"Yeah. Builds character. At least, that's what my dad says. But it also makes money, and I'm far more interested in that," he said with a grin. "What are you up to today?"

"I—" I glanced back at Joanne's house, trying to think of a clever way to tell him I'd just infiltrated the witch's lair.

Before I could come up with anything, Ford tilted his head to one side, studying me.

"What happened to your arms?"

I glanced at my bandages. "Oh, um...it's a long story."

"Yeah? Are you okay? It looks like something's wrong."

I looked up at him, then back toward my house.

"No...but...hey, I have a question."

"Shoot."

"You said the people who lived in my house before...you said they moved out in a hurry. You mentioned a curse. Do you know...if anything weird was going on there? Or if anyone died there in the past?"

Ford looked surprised. "Well, yeah, there was some weird stuff going on with them. I don't know much—I didn't know them very well or anything—but I remember things being kind of off before they left. Why do you ask?"

I shook my head. "Nothing, it's crazy...just. Okay, you said some weird stuff happened. Like what?"

"Well," he considered that. Then he looked at his van. "Hey, I need to work on this. Mind if we move this conversation to my garage?"

"Didn't you just work on it, like, two days ago?"

He patted the hood. "My baby needs a lot of love."

I laughed and we relocated, Ford pulling the beat-up old van into his driveway and opening a single-car garage door. The walls were meticulously lined with tools, and rolling toolboxes stood to the side, holding even more stuff, none of which I had any idea how to use. My dad wasn't a mechanical guy, no one in my family really was, so it all looked a little mad-scientisty to me.

The aesthetic was helped by Ford using a big, Dr. Frankenstein-style switch to turn on the lights.

"Really?" I asked.

He just grinned.

"Anyway," I said, eager to hear more about the family. "You were saying? About the people who lived in my house?"

"Right. Yeah. So I told you before how their kid suddenly got sick," he opened the hood of his van and propped it up on a little built-in rod. The van was old, but the engine looked pretty new.

I took a seat on a nearby stool.

"They didn't live here long. They had the house built, moved in, and moved out a few years later. Kept to themselves. I mean, a lot. Between Sean and I—he used to spend his summers hanging out at my house a bunch. Now he does this counselor thing at a camp in California," Ford said, interrupting himself. He grabbed a bottle of green liquid and opened something on the engine. I watched, intrigued.

"Anyway," he went on, "the two of us ran all around this neighborhood during the summers, met everyone, but weirdly we only encountered them a handful of times. The mom was always tense whenever I saw her. After the ambulance thing, we didn't see them again. Movers came, packed everything up, and the house was empty. A realtor sold the house and she was really perky and kept insisting things were great, which was actually kind of creepy. Made me wonder about the whole thing. Took a long time before you guys moved in. I think it's been over a year."

"Didn't the neighbors talk about it?" I asked.

Ford laughed, pouring some of the liquid into the opening. "Yeah, a little, but this is Vegas. You don't know your neighbors in Vegas. I mean, I know who they are, and I have a general sense of their existence, but it's normal not to have any clue what your neighbors are doing. They kept to themselves. They didn't make friends with any of us, so..." he shrugged apologetically.

I nodded, gnawing on my lip. My knuckles were white, gripping my seat tightly, turning the little stool from side to side. I stopped with great effort and tried to act a little more relaxed.

Ford glanced over at my house, then gave me a sidelong glance. "Why do you ask?"

I shifted my weight. I didn't want to tell him, not really. I didn't know Ford very well. He seemed nice, but most people do when you first meet them. Most people know how to pretend at niceness long enough to fool you.

"No reason," I muttered.

"Come on," he said lightly.

I looked at him, then glanced at my bandaged arms wordlessly.

"What?" he asked, all humor gone from his tone.

"It's just that..." I took a deep breath and looked at him very seriously. My dad thought I was crazy. So far, Hazel didn't, but I wasn't sure how long that would hold out. Emily wanted to study my life like a scientist. What would he think?

I sighed. "Fine, I'll tell you, but you have to promise not to think I'm insane, okay?"

He held up his left hand. "Scout's honor," he said. Then he realized he had the wrong hand up and switched to his right, grinning at me.

I chuckled in spite of myself.

"I'm not using the word 'insane' lightly, here," I added. "I mean *literally* insane. If I tell you, you can't think I'm mentally ill, because I'm not." I wasn't actually sure about that last part, but I wasn't going to let him know that.

Ford was still smiling. "Hey, I made a promise. I'm a man of my word here."

I sighed. "All right, so...I think my house is haunted," I said.

"What? No, seriously?" he asked.

I held out my bandaged arms.

"Wait...*ghosts* did that?" He seemed to have completely forgotten about his van.

"I sure as hell didn't."

I told him about the supposed hauntings, and the upcoming séance.

He, like Emily and Hazel, was far too excited about it.

"Wow...think I could sit in on it?" he asked.

I sighed and shook my head.

"Oh, no, that's fine," Ford said quickly. "I shouldn't have asked."

"No, no, I wasn't saying that. You can come, heck, it would probably be better if you were there," I said with a laugh. "I just can't figure out why you guys are all so fascinated by this."

He chuckled and shrugged, almost apologetically. "I guess everyone's just looking for an adventure."

"Yeah, well, you guys can have it. I'm not much for adventure," I muttered.

He laughed. "I'm sorry. You sound really freaked out. But yeah, I'll be there if you want."

"Sure, just come over when you see the purple-haired chick and her friend," I said.

He returned to his van and I stayed a while, discussing the specifics of a séance and what it would entail. Neither of us knew much about mystical things, but we'd seen enough movies to piece together an irrational, Hollywood-esque idea of what was going to happen.

"What if it's not ghosts? That...whatever...from last night almost sounds more like some kind of freaky scientific experiment. What if it's aliens?"

I made a face. Ghosts were one thing—aliens were a whole different problem.

"It's not aliens," I muttered.

"It could be aliens."

"It's *not* aliens!" I shouted, but I was laughing for some reason, and Ford started to laugh, too.

"You don't know that. What if the aliens *want* you to think it's ghosts so you don't suspect their true, nefarious motives?"

"How would that help them?" I asked, crossing my arms and waiting for his explanation.

"Uh...because then you can't stop them?"

"Uh-huh. And if I *did* realize it was these aliens, what, pray tell, would I do to stop them? Because I don't really think I have the means to pull that off."

Ford rolled his eyes at me. "Pray tell? Okay, Shakespeare, here's what you'd do. Two words: Tinfoil. Hat."

That just made me laugh harder. The worst part was I couldn't tell if he was serious or not.

"I should get home," I finally said. "I need to get my house ready for a séance...however one goes about doing that."

"Okay. I'll see you tomorrow, then. My first séance...this should be fun.," he said with a grin.

I laughed. "At least you'll be able to make it funny somehow."

"It's my gift: Making light of very serious situations. It drives my parents crazy."

We exchanged numbers so I could keep him posted on the séance, and then I left. I was feeling good after that, but the elevated mood wore off as I drew nearer to my house. By the time I reached the front door, my stomach had twisted up into a sickening knot, all joy from time spent with Joanne and Ford evaporating on my doorstep.

I forced myself inside. It was still sunny out; not that that mattered much, but silly as it was, that made me feel better.

My exhaustion returned to me as I entered the house, but I didn't even consider trying to sleep. Jessa Lee was just finishing up dinner when I arrived, so I listened as she explained everything she'd cooked and told me how to best heat it up.

I asked her if she'd been able to find everything all right, and she assured me she had. I walked with her as she headed toward the front door, trying not to let it bother me how much her behavior had shifted since she'd first arrived. She feigned cheerfulness now, and it was clear she wanted to get out as fast as she could.

Once she was gone, I didn't really know what to do. I went to the kitchen to check out dinner. Jessa Lee had left a lasagna for us to warm in the oven, and even some pudding for dessert. It was all safe...until I stepped out of the kitchen for one minute, only to return to find all the drawers and cabinets open.

I almost dropped the teapot I'd gone to fetch. Forcing in a few deep breaths, I set the teapot down on the counter and started closing cabinets. My hands were already shaking, my mouth dry. I shivered, wondering if it would help if I turned the heat up. Probably not.

There was a loud smash and I jumped, whirling around. The teapot had crashed on the ground.

I closed my eyes. For some reason, I was angry. I felt betrayed by the bright, warm sunlight streaming into the house. It was still daytime. Shouldn't I be safe?

I cleaned up the broken pieces and threw them away.

After that, things were normal, but I was jittery, my good mood obliterated. My dad came home, and I heated up the lasagna for dinner. I served our food and we sat down to eat, my dad smiling down at his plate.

"This smells great. I hope she sticks around."

"Yeah..." I paused, unsure if I wanted to start the conversation I was about to start.

"Something wrong?" my dad asked, sensing my mood.

I decided to play it off as lightly as I could. I shook my head and laughed. "Yeah, it's just...isn't it so weird how the housekeepers keep leaving?"

"It is, isn't it?" he asked, setting his fork down and looking at me.

"Do you...have any theories as to why? Did the agency mention anything?"

He shook his head and returned to his dinner. “No. Apparently all of them like us well enough, they just...what I’m getting is that they’re afraid to come back. Something about the house giving them the creeps.”

Everything about me felt heavy. Tired. He was glancing at me out of the corner of his eyes, like he was waiting for me to say something. I *had* told him the house was haunted just last night, and my bandages were still in place, reminding him of the terror we’d both felt.

“Roz? Do you have any ideas what it might be?” he asked carefully. His tone reminded me of when you’re speaking to a small animal that you don’t want to spook.

I considered my words carefully. I didn’t want to scare him, either.

“Well, if I had to guess, I’d say whatever happened to me last night is probably related to whatever’s scaring off all our housekeepers,” I said, my tone measured and even.

My dad nodded slowly.

“You mentioned...a haunting...” he said.

I shrugged. “Well, I mean, I’m not sure. I was scared last night, you know?” It sounded pathetic, but I couldn’t think what else to say, so I just ran us in circles like I had at breakfast.

“We both were. And...” my dad pushed his food around his plate with his fork. “I don’t want to ignore this. I want to do something about...whatever’s happening.”

I was quiet. I wanted to do something, too, but, like him, I didn’t even know where to begin.

That wasn't true, actually: I had something of a plan. If you could call "having a séance with some amateur paranormal investigators" a plan.

We finished eating and cleaned up the kitchen together, talking about normal things. When his work came up, he mentioned having to work late the next day.

"What for?" I asked.

"Meeting with the team. There's a lot to go over in this case. It's kind of a mess."

"The one you keep telling me you can't talk about?" I asked raising my eyebrows. I was hoping I could joke my way into more information, but it was probably a lost cause.

He sighed and nodded, growing serious again. "Roz, it's for your own protection. And mine. And the whole team. This sort of thing can get ugly, and so the fewer people who know about it, the better off everyone involved is," he explained for the hundredth time. He was patient, though. He must have read the worry on my face.

That strained my already shaky mood. How dangerous was this case? Was it possible that my dad was dealing with something really scary? I knew he'd had cases where people threatened—even attempted—to kill him in the past, but wouldn't he at least tell me if something like that was going on now that I was older?

Probably not, actually, seeing as my reaction to a couple weird incidents was to charge around the house clutching a yardstick, having panic attacks at every sound. If there were legitimate death threats on the table, I'd probably just keel over.

My phone beeped, pulling me out of my thoughts. The battery was dying. I sighed and hoped it would hold out. I was expecting a call from Hazel about this whole séance thing.

I went upstairs to shower and change, and when I came back down, I realized that in all my nervousness, I had forgotten my phone on the counter. It was dead. I decided not to worry about it. For now, I just wanted to spend some time with my father. Put his mind at ease about my mental stability. Hazel could leave a message.

We watched a movie, and my dad dozed off on the couch, as he often did.

I got up and went to the kitchen to prepare a cup of tea. As I switched on the electric kettle, the air grew cold in what was becoming a familiar occurrence. Like one of Pavlov's dogs, my reaction was immediate and overwhelming. I was conditioned. The fear swept over me.

I listened, but this time, there was no sound. The lights flickered. On, then off, then on, but weak, wavering uncertainly. I froze in place, then began edging out of the kitchen, trying to get away from whatever was causing this.

Back in the living room, I went to my father's side.

"Dad," I said, shaking him slightly. The lights in the room flickered. "Dad," I was more insistent now, yanking at his arm.

"Wh-what?" he muttered, opening his eyes.

The TV screen flared for a second, then switched back off. The lights were steady.

I sighed.

"What is it, kiddo?" he asked, rubbing his face.

"Nothing. Just...didn't want you to get a backache, sleeping down here."

He smiled and got up. "Well, thanks."

We said goodnight and he went to bed. I remained sitting on the sofa, unwilling to go up to my room. Not that anywhere in this house was safe.

Just as I was working up the courage to go upstairs, my pocket began to buzz. At first, I was confused, but then I remembered that that I'd put my phone there.

Hands shaking, I pulled it from my pocket.

I was getting a call. On my phone. Which had died hours ago.

The call was strange, though. There was no name or number. It didn't even say "unknown" it was just blank. The screen was also missing the *answer* and *ignore* buttons. It was a black screen with a ringing phone symbol in the middle, buzzing lightly in my palm.

I stared at my phone for a long time, wondering what to do. I couldn't answer it, and even if I could, I wasn't sure if I wanted to.

Finally, it stopped ringing and my screen returned to normal.

I stared at the "Missed Call" message, wondering what was going on. At the top of the screen, an announcement popped up.

1 new voicemail.

A little whimper escaped me and my phone went dark. When I tried to wake it, nothing happened. It was dead.

Nine

"I'll be right there!" I called, racing to the door.

Emily greeted me with a smile. "Ready to talk to some ghosts?"

"Yeah, I guess," I said, standing aside so she could come in. Hazel was already inside, and I had texted Ford, so he would be over any minute.

I wasn't in the best mood. I'd only gotten a couple of hours of nightmare-plagued, paranormally disrupted sleep. I still hadn't had the courage to check the message from the previous night. When I'd asked Hazel, hoping it was somehow her, she told me she'd gone to the movies with her brother and forgotten to call. This only made me more unsettled.

"Rosalind, this is Derek," Emily said, motioning to the boy who had followed her in. He was lugging a big case and had a backpack on his shoulder.

"Hi, it's nice to meet you. Thanks for, you know, this," I said.

"Sure thing," he said with a nod. "Wouldn't miss it."

Derek was about my height, but that wasn't unusual for me. He had olive skin and wavy black hair, with eyes so dark I couldn't tell where his pupils ended and his irises began. He smiled, but it didn't reach his eyes, which were too serious for someone our age. My therapist back in LA had once told me I appeared that way. I wondered what it meant.

"All right, first things first, I have some paperwork," Emily said, unslinging her messenger bag and digging through it.

"Paperwork?" I asked.

Derek rolled his eyes. "Emily makes everyone she works with sign contracts."

"I don't *make* anyone sign contracts I just *request* an official acknowledgment of what's about to go down," Emily said, elbowing him. She turned to me and added. "Just your standard release forms. It's a precaution."

I raised my eyebrows at her. "You do realize we're all under eighteen, right?"

Derek held his hand out in a kind of presenting gesture towards me. "Thank you!" He looked at Emily and added, "See? It's all pointless. No one here can legally agree to anything without parental consent. Your contracts are all void."

Emily stuck her tongue out at him and handed Hazel and I contracts. I skimmed mine, but couldn't take it seriously after the line, "...not to be held responsible for damages caused by vengeful spirits."

Hazel signed hers with a smile, and I followed suit, if a bit less enthusiastically.

"Great, thank you!" Emily said, filing our contracts away. "Now that that's taken care of, where are we starting?"

"Um, my room," I said. "It's where there's been the most activity. Plus, we have a new housekeeper over today and I'd rather not have her first impression of me be that I'm a séance-having weirdo."

"*Another* housekeeper?" Emily asked.

"Yup. Another one."

Emily nodded. "Okay, let's get started then."

I led them up to my room, feeling a little awkward. I didn't usually let *anyone* in my room, let alone people I'd just met who were planning to conduct a séance.

Hazel and I sat on my sofa while Emily and Derek set up on the floor and started unpacking their equipment.

"Roz, can you get me that journal that keeps showing up?" Emily asked.

"Oh, sure." I went to my nightstand to retrieve it, nervous about what this whole reading-séance thing might reveal. More than anything, I was afraid it would reveal nothing at all; that nothing would come up and I'd have confirmation that I was simply losing my mind. Maybe *I* was scaring off all the housekeepers by being incredibly unstable.

I pushed those thoughts aside and handed the journal to Emily.

"Thank you," she said, turning it over in her hands, but leaving it closed. I appreciated that.

"What's this symbol on the front?" she asked.

I shrugged and sat down while they started unpacking, and Emily didn't push the topic. I felt guilty for not helping, but I didn't really know what to do. Besides, my head was throbbing again, and I was tired. The dream of the clearing had kept me up last night. Nothing scary had happened in it—it was exactly the same as before. It just left me with such a strange, twisting nervousness. I didn't know why, but it gave me the creeps. Almost worse than the ghosts did. Or...whatever these things were.

"Are you okay?" Hazel asked.

I forced myself to stop wincing and relaxed my face. "Yeah. Just...tired."

Emily glanced up from putting together a microphone. "Did something else happen last night?"

I shook my head. "No, just...this weird dream."

"Oh?" Emily asked, eyebrow raised.

Derek glanced at me. "Anything to do with the ghosts?"

I opened my mouth to say no, but somehow, that felt wrong. Before I could answer, the doorbell rang.

"Oh, that's probably Ford. I'll be right back."

When I returned with Ford, Emily and Derek were setting up cameras around a table.

I made some quick introductions, even though, technically, they all went to the same school and I was the new girl. Emily made him sign a contract as well, which Ford seemed deeply amused by. He stood there reading through the whole thing, asking questions.

"Who wrote this?" Ford asked.

Derek raised his hand, looking up momentarily from his work.

Ford nodded. "This is pretty solid."

"Derek's pre-law," Emily said.

He rolled his eyes. "I am not."

"Not *yet*. But *soon*. So *yes*. Or at least...pre-pre-law," Emily said.

Derek chuckled and shook his head. "Emily logic."

"The *best* logic," Emily said, booting up some program on her computer.

"I have some questions before I sign," Ford said, going back to his contract. "Such as: Why is there a section on property destruction?"

"Poltergeists. They'll mess you up," Derek answered around the wires he was holding in his teeth.

"And this part about physical harm? Has that actually happened with you guys?" Ford went on.

Derek pulled up his pant leg to reveal a scar on his shin. "Everyone thinks it's from baseball, but I got it early on when we still didn't know what we were doing."

"Nice," Ford remarked.

"Yeah," Derek said.

Hazel and I exchanged confused looks.

Ford flipped another page, reading quickly. I watched his blue eyes flick back and forth as he made his way through the contract, his brow scrunching up in concentration. He kind of reminded me of a puppy.

"Okay, what about this. 'All participants agree to comply with the rules and protocols of the séance, as laid out by the Organizers'?"

Derek shrugged. "You don't listen to us, you could end up in trouble. Or you could end up ruining the séance, having no ghosts show up. Which is very disappointing."

"Well, we can't have that," Ford said gravely.

After a little more of this, he signed it, and we got back to work setting up.

"Okay, let's get these windows covered," Emily instructed, looking around at the light filtering into the room. "I need to take some pictures."

Hazel, Ford, and I went around closing the curtains and blinds until the room was dark.

Hazel looked at Ford as we worked and asked, "Aren't you the one who put dish soap in the fountain at school? And it filled the whole quad with bubbles?"

He grinned. "My reputation precedes me!"

"You put dish soap in a fountain?" I asked.

"Yeah, it was awesome," he said happily. Hazel snapped her fingers. "Wait! Isn't your dad the one who owns—?"

"Yeah, yeah, no one wants to hear about that," Ford said quickly, looking embarrassed. I raised my eyebrows at him but he was staring intently at the séance table.

I watched Emily and Derek set up camcorders on tripods, digital recorders, cameras, microphones hooked up to laptops, and little hand-held devices; some with digital screens, and others with little needles. I moved closer, examining the instruments. Derek was laying out a compass and some flashlights.

"What is all this stuff?" I asked.

"All means of measuring supernatural presences," he explained. "These guys," he indicated the digital and analog instruments, "are electromagnetic field detectors. All this stuff will help us determine if there are any ghosts present.

He said it so seriously, it was strange.

"Have you guys seen or...detected ghosts before?" I asked.

"A few times," Derek said, pulling a notebook from his bag.

"There are a lot of haunted locations in Vegas," Emily elaborated. "We've gone to a few of them, plus done some investigations of our own. We've even gotten to present our findings at a couple events!"

I took a deep breath. This was happening, no turning back now. I had paranormal investigators traipsing around my room, taking "readings", whatever that meant.

I was kind of hoping they were just wannabes, silly high school kids looking for a kick, but every second it was becoming more evident to me how serious they were. The sheer volume of equipment they had with them was intimidating.

With the room dark, Emily turned on a little battery-operated lantern and settled in among her many devices. I watched her tapping on her computer and writing things in her notebook while Derek took pictures, seemingly at random.

At first, it didn't seem like anything was happening. The two of them were doing something, but I couldn't make sense of it, so I started to feel almost bored. I propped my chin in my hand and tried not to drift off.

"All right, let's call some spirits," Emily said.

We gathered on the floor, around a low little table Emily and Derek had brought. Emily pulled out a strange-looking deck of cards. They had the appearance of tarot cards, but I couldn't be sure. I'd only ever seen tarot cards in movies. Again, I was reminded how little I understood about the occult, or whatever this all was.

"What are the cards for?" Hazel asked, picking one up.

Emily gently took it and placed it carefully back into the deck, spreading the cards out face-up on the table in a long line. I could see now that they were lettered cards, all white featuring one big, black letter in the center.

"They're for channeling the spirits' energies. If we don't have some kind of tool, it will come directly through a person, and that can be dangerous. Besides, they can spell things out this way."

I glanced at Ford and he grinned. I figured he was thinking the same thing I was; that this was all completely ridiculous and, frankly, a bit dumb.

I pushed my hair back and caught sight of my bandaged arm. Maybe it wasn't so ridiculous after all.

Derek finished lighting candles and returned to sit with us, notepad at the ready. We joined hands and Emily instructed us to be silent for a moment. It seemed like nothing was happening, but I noticed that Emily's breathing was getting deep and even.

After a minute of this, Emily started to speak, her voice soft and calm.

"Spirits, we call to you. Make yourself known to us. Show your presence."

As expected, nothing happened. I opened my eyes and peeked at the alphabet cards. They were still, and I wondered what was supposed to happen now.

For a moment, we sat there in our little circle, lit only by candlelight. Emily repeated her request for the spirits to contact us.

"What brings you here, spirits?" Emily pressed gently.

I had my eyes closed, wondering idly how it would feel to have a ghost join us in this little séance. The idea scared me, but also intrigued me. I was tired enough from lack of sleep that I was starting to drift off when a beep sounded. My eyes snapped open.

Ford, who had my right hand, gave a little jolt.

A card was pulled from the deck. I tilted my head to see it better in the gloom.

P.

"What was that?" Hazel asked.

"The motion detector," Emily said in an excited whisper.

"Did anyone move?" Ford asked, looking around.

"Nope," Derek said, writing quickly. "That was a really fast response, though—they usually take a lot longer to answer."

"What does that mean?" I asked, eyes still stuck on the card.

"I don't know," he admitted. "Your house *is* pretty infested. We'll have to wait and see. They might spell something out."

We waited for a moment, but nothing more happened. About five minutes into this, Derek picked up his notepad again and started writing something down. Emily pulled her computer closer.

"Getting some readings on the EMF detector," Emily said, and I noticed the needle on one of the devices twitching.

The motion detector beeped again, more insistently this time, and a chill ran through the room.

"Temperature drop, five degrees," Emily noted, her voice high with excitement.

I was no longer sleepy. I was sitting up, goose bumps spreading along my arms. I glanced at Ford and Hazel, who were both watching with intrigue.

Derek had gotten up, moving around my room slowly, snapping pictures.

"Can we do anything to help?" Ford asked.

"For the moment, no...just stay still," Emily said. She was jotting down the readings on the compass, which was spinning around.

A sharp exhale echoed through the room and the lantern and candlelight flickered and wavered.

Emily looked at the light, then at us.

"Looks like we have company," she whispered.

Derek snapped a few more pictures with his phone, then jerked back, staring at a blank section of wall in alarm.

"What is it?" Hazel asked.

"I thought I saw..." he looked through the screen again, then back at the wall, seeming perplexed.

"Derek," Emily hissed.

He turned to Emily, who was looking at me.

She gestured toward me. "Take some pictures of Rosalind."

My mouth went dry. There were cameras recording several parts of the room, including the spot where I was sitting.

Derek pointed the camera at me and took a few pictures. Like I was a specimen under observation.

Another card slid forward, stopping beside the first. Hazel, Ford, and I all recoiled.

O.

"Em," Derek said. When she looked at him, he pointed at the screen of a tablet they had propped on my desk. It was hooked up to a microphone, and there was some kind of recording program open. I watched the waveform. Despite the fact that no one was speaking, the lines bobbed up and down, like it was picking up sounds.

I could feel the hairs on the back of my neck standing up.

Emily put a finger to her lips and started to get up, but stopped when she noticed the cards on the table moving.

"What's that? What's that?" Hazel said.

Emily pointed one of the cameras at the moving cards and we watched them slide from the deck. *R* scooted across the table, then *T*...

The cards stopped and one of the tripods toppled over, sending the camera clattering across the floor.

Hazel yelped. My throat was tight. Beside me, I could feel Ford tensing.

Emily's voice was steady. "It's okay, sometimes the spirits will—"

Another camera fell, and the tablet on my desk crashed to the floor.

The lantern light wavered, going in and out, dimming the room. The letter cards flew around, barely visible in the dark. One hit me across the face. I raised my arms to shield myself, though I barely noticed it against the sudden throbbing in my temples.

I saw the journal from my mother slide across the table, inching its way toward me.

The air seemed to shift and move, and a chant began to pick up as the word—just one word, repeated over and over in a frantic whisper—became clearer.

"*Gateway.*"

The journal reached me and I scooted back, scrambling away from it.

Stop, stop, stop, I prayed silently.

The lantern sparked and went out. Hazel and I both screamed.

"Whoa!" Emily shouted.

For a few horrible seconds, we all bumbled around in the dark. Then the light snapped on. I saw Ford standing by the wall, hands still on the switch panel. He looked pale, his eyes wide. We sat in silence for a long time.

Finally, Emily cleared her throat and got up, collecting the scattered cards and fallen cameras.

Hazel was watching me closely with wide eyes, looking like she was unable to speak.

"That was *insane*," Ford said breathlessly.

"Was that..." Hazel looked back and forth between Derek and Emily. "Does that kind of thing happen a lot?"

"Pretty standard ghost stuff," Derek said. "Mostly," he added, so softly I almost missed it.

"Rosalind?"

I looked up at Emily.

"Are you okay?" she asked.

I nodded shakily. "Yeah. Yeah, I'm fine...just...we didn't learn much, did we?"

"Are you kidding?" she asked, grinning and looking around the room. "We saw your ghosts, Roz."

Ten

We went down to the living room and Emily set up with Derek to review what they'd recorded. I found refuge in the kitchen and decided to make something for us all to eat. I was pretty sure we had some Pizza Rolls in the freezer. The housekeeper of the day, Dana, was in the laundry room, and she worked with headphones on, so I wasn't too worried about her noticing what we were doing.

While I switched on the oven, Hazel left to get us all sodas from the garage fridge. Ford sat down at the island and drummed his fingers against the counter, an unusually serious look on his face.

"You know what I've been thinking?" Ford said after a moment.

"It's not aliens, Ford. That was definitely a ghost thing up there. I mean..." I looked up at him, nervous. "It was, right?"

Ford laughed. "That wasn't what I was going to say."

I raised my eyebrows, not sure how much I believed him. "Okay," I said. "What *were* you going to say?"

"There..." he chuckled, then looked up at me, eyes twinkling intently. "There *has* to be some kind of scientific explanation to all this, right?"

I shrugged. "I guess...I don't know. I used to think so, but with all this..." I waved my hand. "Seems like there's something else, doesn't it? Something...more. Inexplicable."

He shook his head. "I get that. And yeah, it does. But it has to be based in science. Nothing is really 'inexplicable'."

"Nothing I saw up there seemed very scientific, Ford," I pointed out.

"No, not to us," he said. "But think about it: A thousand years ago, pretty much everything in our lives today would have seemed like magic. The science of the time couldn't explain it. They'd have thought we were all demons or witches or gods."

"Their science barely passed for science," I said, moving closer to him and leaning on the counter.

"Yeah," Ford admitted. "But I bet to a sufficiently advanced race, *our* science would barely pass for science. Just because we don't know the answer, that doesn't mean there isn't one."

"Right. Okay. And yet...aren't *you* the one who told me my next door neighbor is a witch?" I countered.

Ford grinned. "And how are you feeling about that?"

I rolled my eyes. "She's weird, sure, but I don't know about 'witch'. She's just...her own person," I said with a shrug.

"Oh, whatever. She had some Satan-worshiping party the other day!" he said.

"I'm pretty sure that was just a costume party—"

"*And*," he cut me off, "You haven't even been here for a week. You haven't had ample time to observe her crazy."

"Oh yeah? Well, I've been here long enough to be in her house," I countered.

Ford balked. "You *what*?"

"Yup. Had painting lessons with her Sunday. Saw the dome and everything."

"Well I'll be damned," Ford said, laughing.

"Anyway, I maintain that she's not a witch and I don't have an alien problem."

He chuckled. "Yeah, but in all seriousness...there's something real, scientific, and quantifiable going on here...we just don't have the means to measure it. Or Joanne's witch-ness. Just because she's weird and potentially evil, it doesn't mean there's not some kind of scientific explanation behind it all."

I nodded, chuckling. "Okay. I can agree to that. Not the Joanne being evil bit, but the rest of it."

"Right. And so, if we *did* have the ability to measure it and make sense of it, it wouldn't seem mystical at all. I mean, in ancient China, they thought a dragon was eating the sun during an eclipse. They'd make a bunch of noise to try and scare it away. Now, nobody panics, it's just a celestial event. We understand it. We enjoy it. It doesn't surprise or scare us."

I laughed. "Wow, Ford, I didn't realize you were so academic."

He shrugged. "I like science."

"I can tell." I sighed. "I guess you're right, but...what can we do? We *don't* have the means of measuring this like scientists. I mean, not beyond their...whatsit-thingies." I said, waving my hand toward Emily and Derek.

"Well, I'd like to figure out a way to quantify all this...supernatural stuff. Because *nothing* is actually 'supernatural'. Nothing can be outside nature. *Everything* is part of nature. They're just...elements of nature we don't understand yet."

"Hey. Are you hatin' on the paranormal?" Emily demanded from the other room.

"Not at all, my good lady. Just hypothesizing," Ford called back. I snickered as Emily narrowed her eyes in suspicion.

He turned back to me and raised his eyebrows, grinning.

"So, Mr. Scientist, do you think we ever *will* have the technology to understand ghosts the way we understand lunar cycles?"

"Maybe," Ford said. "I'd be willing to bet we could get there. Probably not even that far in the future."

"What do you think ghosts are, then?" I asked.

Ford considered this. "My theory is simple: Energy. Everything is energy, right?"

"I guess so. I was never all that good with science, truth be told."

"Well, that's what I think," he said with a decisive nod.

I laughed. "Okay, then." I pushed away from the counter, getting back to work.

"Oh, one more thing," he said, growing serious again.

"Yeah?" I said, looking up from my hunt for a baking sheet.

He considered whatever he was going to say for a moment. "Did you know there are sites where you can look up a house's history? And find out if anything...uh...weird happened in them?"

I watched him as I worked. "No..."

"Well, there are." He pulled a folded sheet of paper from his back pocket and spread it out on the counter.

"What's that?"

"A report on your house. After we spoke yesterday..." he shrugged. "I was curious. Anyway, turns out—"

"I didn't know what everyone wanted so I brought one of each for all of us," Hazel interrupted, setting the cans out on the counter.

"I wanted one of each, so that's perfect," Ford said. He folded the paper up and slipped it back into his pocket. Apparently, he didn't want to discuss this in front of Hazel.

Hazel rolled her eyes. "You don't even know what the choices are."

"Doesn't matter, I know I want them all. Preferably mixed together in a giant cup with a twisty straw."

I glanced at Ford. "You were that kid who got a little of everything at the soda fountain, weren't you?"

"You say that as if I've stopped," Ford said.

I snickered as I opened the bag of pizza rolls. Emily and Derek were sitting on the couch, each with their computers out, working diligently. Their faces were serious and full of concentration, which made me a little worried. What were they seeing?

I decided to stay in the kitchen with Hazel and Ford until someone came for me. No sense in bothering them before they were ready when I could just have pointless and amusing conversations that didn't involve ghosts. Hazel had taken a picture of our séance and posted it on Instagram. I wanted to be annoyed by this, but it had come out really beautiful, and I secretly was glad she'd taken it, as I figured I could use it for a sketch or comic. The hashtag "#GhostHunting" made me laugh.

"I can't wait to take you to my favorite pizza place, it wasn't here last time you were in town. And you've got to see the new Cirque show," Hazel said as we sipped our sodas.

"You know where I miss going? Mount Charleston," I said, surprising myself.

"We should go. It's great this time of year," Ford said. He was taking our old soda cans and snapping their pop-tops across the kitchen.

"I want to head up there. Grandma has that cabin," I said to Hazel.

She nodded. "We should ask if we can get the keys."

"I have a question," Ford said, and I could tell by his tone that he was dragging me back into the world of ghosts and the paranormal.

"Yes?" I asked, trying to sound nonchalant.

He took a sip of his soda and frowned contemplatively, making me worried again. Finally, he spoke: "I'm still trying to figure out what you saw the other day in your room."

My stomach dropped. Did we have to talk about this now?

"I don't know," I said. Dismissing it entirely seemed

easier than considering the possibilities.

"I'm serious," he went on, either not noticing my desire to move on, or ignoring it. "I've been reading a lot about the paranormal—"

"What, on Creepypasta?" I asked.

"*—from reputable sources*, and—"

"Reddit is not a reputable source."

"*—And*, there's nothing in that encounter to suggest that you saw ghosts the other day. That's definitely more of an abduction scenario."

"Yeah, okay, but there was no spaceship. I wasn't *taken*, I was just...suddenly...*there*."

"Maybe you don't *remember* being taken. Maybe they transported you and you were knocked out, and somehow you woke up before you were supposed to..."

I shook my head. "But my dad came in and turned the light on and everything stopped!"

"Again. Maybe you were knocked out. Maybe..." he snapped his fingers. "Maybe you were *remembering* an encounter!"

I rolled my eyes. "Okay, so that was the *memory* of a past abduction?"

"Yes!"

"Then why am I all scratched up?"

Ford frowned. He opened his mouth to speak, then closed it again, drumming his fingers on the counter in frustration. I snickered at the determination on his face, and his utter lack of a good explanation.

"Hey. Hey, Roz?" Emily called. "Could you come here for a sec?"

I went to her side, followed closely by Ford and Hazel.

"What's up?" I asked.

"Look," she said, turning her computer to me.

On the screen was a still from the video recording. I could see myself with Ford and Hazel. And around me, hovering in darkness, was the figure of a man. It wasn't clear. He hid in shadows, his body not fully visible, but I recognized him. He was the ghost who'd been in my hall the other night.

I glanced at Emily.

"It gets weirder. Look."

She clicked a few times and brought me to a new image. There were several ghostly apparitions hovering around the edges of the shot, but that wasn't what caught my eye.

There was something in the picture, standing just behind me. It was simple, but that simplicity was what made it horrifying.

The figure was tall, much taller than a person, with a humanoid body. But it was too sharp and angular to be anything human. Its head was a kind of jagged triangle.

What made it really unusual, though, was the way that no light seemed to touch it. I'd seen illustrations of black holes, where all the light just got swallowed up, leaving a...well, a black hole. An absence of everything. Complete darkness.

That was how this creature looked. It looked like it *was* a black hole.

I stopped breathing. My heart faltered, then raced.

"What...what is that?" I whispered.

There was a long silence before Emily turned to me, uncertain.

"Something that's trying to...make contact, get through...I don't really know what or why, but..."

She trailed off, then looked up at me.

"I've never seen anything like it," Derek said. "It's...I don't know. I wouldn't call it a *ghost*. It's something else...something..."

"Scary? Horrible? Sent from Hell?" Hazel supplied.

"Definitely that last one," Derek muttered.

"It's...a shadow," I whispered, eyes still glued to the screen. I couldn't see a single contour on its body, just the absolute blackness, like an empty space where nothing, not even light, existed. Those white figures had scared me, but this sent a chill to my very core.

"Why couldn't we see this in person?" Ford asked, brow furrowed. I glanced at him and he caught my eye. He had that same look he'd worn earlier in the kitchen, like he was trying to logically explain what we were seeing.

"We kind of could," Derek said, leaning closer to point at the screen. "It just came across as, uh well, as a shadow. I noticed the shoulders, see here?" he indicated the large, shadowy presence.

"But not as clearly," Emily explained. "Ghosts register on a lower frequency than what our eyes can see. Cameras, on the other hand, can capture them. When the camera captures it, it converts the wavelengths to spectrums that the human eye can pick up on more easily. It's why sometimes you don't realize there was a ghost somewhere until you look at a picture you took."

"Hey, I have a question," Hazel said, perched on the arm of the sofa. "Why did the ghost speak English? I thought you said it spoke some weird language?" she added, turning to me.

I shrugged, looking at Emily.

"We're definitely dealing with more than one ghost here," Emily said, not looking up from her computer. "No telling how many, but at least two from what I'm—"

Emily's eyes cut up quickly and I followed the direction of her gaze. Dana walked by, carrying a laundry basket and humming quietly to herself. She caught us looking at her and paused, smiling at us.

"Need anything, Roz?" she asked, pulling an earbud away.

"N-no. I'm good. Thanks!" I said, squeaking a bit.

"Okay. I'm going to take these upstairs and put them away," she said.

I nodded. "Great. Okay. Yeah."

We watched her leave and I ran a hand back through my hair.

"More than one ghost?" I asked when Dana's steps had disappeared upstairs.

Emily nodded. "No doubt. Probably quite a few more."

That was not what I wanted to hear. I had suspected it already, but I didn't like having it confirmed.

"Wait, wait, I'm confused," Ford interrupted. "Why would there be so many ghosts in one house? Isn't it like, just ghosts who died in the house or something?"

"Yeah," I said, glancing at Ford, then back at Emily. "He's right. I mean, I *think* he's right. I can't imagine so many people could have died here, the house is only, what, four years old? It's had *one* previous owner," I pointed out.

Emily bit her lip, shaking her head.

"Roz, I...I don't have an answer for you on that. I've never heard of multiple presences like this except for at ghost hotspots or places where a lot of deaths occurred. Like hospitals, or graveyards, or buildings where there were huge fires or...*something*, you know? I mean, Ford's right, it's usually about the people who died in that specific location. Or at least people whose bodies are buried there."

Hazel laughed nervously. "Could this house be on top of, I dunno...some Indian burial ground?"

I looked at her. "Seriously, Haze?"

"What? It happens in the movies..." she said, pulling at her sleeves as she glanced again at the picture.

I shook my head overdramatically at her. "It's not even *Indian*. *You're* Indian. That would be *Native Americans*."

"Yeah, but 'Native American burial ground' doesn't have the same ring to it," she countered.

Ford nodded at Hazel, then looked at me. "She's got you there."

I stared at them both, then turned back to Emily and Derek.

"*Anyway*. Is there a way we can figure out how many ghosts there are? And why they're all...here?"

Derek shifted to get a better look at the screen. "Hard to say right now. I mean," he clicked a few times to get to a new picture. "Here, you've got what looks like a man, right? That could be your first guy."

I nodded.

"But this," he said, clicking to a different shot, "looks more like a woman. I mean, it's hard to tell. I think she was moving. But it looks smaller, more feminine."

We clicked through more pictures, none of which made me feel any better. There were many different ghosts. It was hard to see them clearly, but I could make out distinctions: A child, a woman curled in the corner, a tall figure that I couldn't distinguish. It wore deep red, and hovered near the edge of our circle, looking like a blood-drenched statue. I shuddered, thinking it was entirely possible the figure *was* drenched in blood.

"Another question: Why'd they respond so fast?" Hazel asked. She looked at Derek. "You said they normally don't show up so quickly..."

Derek shook his head. "Never. We usually have to wait for a while before we get anything, but these ghosts showed up right away."

"Any idea why?" Ford asked.

Derek considered this. "Maybe since there are so many? Maybe this place is just so incredibly haunted, adding a séance to the mix is an automatic ghost-beacon. I mean, honestly, it was almost like they were already there, just waiting for us."

Ford and Hazel laughed at that, but I frowned, considering. I wondered if there had been something about that séance that was different.

"You know," Ford whispered, leaning over so only I could hear, "You *do* have a witch next door..."

I smacked him lightly, but I couldn't muster up a laugh. My throat was tight, my breathing shaky.

The garage door opened and I started, crashing into Ford. I heard my father dropping his keys in the bowl by the door and breathed a sigh of relief. This ghost business was going to make me hurt myself.

"Hey, Roz, I'm just stopping by, I have a—oh, hello, everyone," he said, spotting the others. He smiled. "What are you kids up to?"

"Just, hanging out..." I answered. Emily discreetly turned her computer screen away.

"Well, don't let me interrupt what you're doing, I was going straight into my office. I've got a call to make."

He disappeared down the hall and I let out a slow breath, wondering how long I'd be able to keep up with lying to him. It didn't come naturally to me.

We couldn't talk as openly with him in the house, even if he was on the phone in his office. Instead, we sat at the kitchen island and ate the Pizza Rolls I'd made.

"Definitely the coolest séance we've ever had," Derek said.

Emily loaded up her plate with her third helping of Pizza Rolls. "Oh, hands down."

"How did you guys get into this, anyway?" I asked. "All this...ghost stuff?"

Emily answered. "We had a school project. Eight grade. This eccentric teacher wanted us to explore non-scientific fields as though they were established, respected sciences. Derek and I and a couple other kids chose ghosts, and in the research, we got so into all this paranormal stuff that we decided to keep studying it even after the project was over. Our teammates didn't seem as fascinated as we were, though."

"There's a lot more science to it than we realized at the beginning," Derek said. "We wanted to see if we could get more actual proof about the existence of ghosts."

Ford sat back in his seat. "And you've been hunting ghosts ever since?"

"Yeah," Emily said. "Like I said before, Vegas is surprisingly haunted. And the city might be young, but the land has a lot of history. There are some great spots.

Not that I need them anymore," she said, glancing at me with a smile.

"Don't remind me," I muttered.

Emily laughed, and I ended up laughing, too.

Derek announced that he had to get to work and we got up, packing up the computers and any stray equipment left out.

"Hey, Roz, before I go," Ford said, his voice low.

"Yeah?"

He came up to me, looking to make sure the others were preoccupied. Then, he reached into his pocket and pulled out the folded slip of paper he'd almost shown me in the kitchen.

"That report on your house. Thought you should have it. Thought you might want to look at it yourself, first, before you show it to Mystery, Inc. over there," he said.

I accepted it, afraid to see what it contained.

"Thanks, Ford. For looking into this," I said, my voice tight.

He nodded. "Sure. And hey, don't get in any trouble without me."

"Yeah, you'd hate that," I snickered.

I helped Derek and Emily carry their equipment out to their cars. Emily drove a tiny little Fiat that was dark purple with black accents, same as her hair. It didn't look like it could hold half their equipment. She loaded up a few bags, and the rest they put into Derek's car, which was much simpler and older—black, faded, and generally sensible.

"Thanks for coming by and helping me out with this, guys," I said.

"Hey, thank *you*," Emily said. "We figure this out,

that grant is *ours*."

"Yeah, well, then for your sake and for my sanity, I hope we have some answers soon."

Ford walked home, and the other three drove off. I lingered on the porch for a moment, then turned and went back inside. I kept walking, though, heading for the backyard. I hadn't spent much time out there since we'd moved, and the weather wasn't too extreme today. I decided to stay out there. I slipped my shoes off and sat at the edge of the pool, legs dangling over the side into the water. It was quiet. Peaceful. All the grass and trees made the yard cooler than it would have been otherwise. Tall trees blocked the sun and cast shadows where I could hide from the more intense heat.

From here, the house didn't seem so imposing. I wished I could always see it like this—from a step back, bathed in sunlight on a warm summer's day. Windows gleaming. It really was a beautiful house. I hadn't had much chance to appreciate that since we'd moved here.

In the upstairs window, the one belonging to one of the guest rooms, I spotted a figure moving. My heart raced. It could be my father, but I doubted that very much.

Watching the window for more movement, I remembered my first day here, and the figure I'd glimpsed from the sidewalk. I could feel the paper Ford had given me in my pocket, but I wasn't quite ready to find out what it said. I turned my attention back to the pool's brilliant blue water and tried not to think about what dying felt like, and if I'd be bitter after, like the ghosts in my home.

Eleven

I couldn't believe it had only been a week since I'd moved into my new house.

I also couldn't believe that I was leading our sixth housekeeper around, explaining where things were and what she'd be doing.

Nadia was shy. Quiet. She tended to keep her eyes down and answer with a simple, "Yes" or "No" to most things.

I tried to be friendly, but her awkwardness triggered my awkwardness, and I ended up rambling.

"The kitchen's all stocked. Though you don't need to cook for a couple days because we have a ton of food left over from, um, restaurants. We eat out a lot. Because neither one of us can cook. Well, that's not true; my dad can cook. I just think that's the last thing he wants to do after he comes home from work."

Roz. Stop talking.

"But, uh, so yeah. Don't worry about cooking for now. Laundry, mostly. And...just...basic cleaning stuff. And, um. Yeah. That's it. That's, uh, that's the house. I mean, not the *whole* house. I didn't show you the guest rooms or my dad's room. Or the backyard, though I guess that's not technically part of the house."

Seriously, you have to stop.

I finally got control of my mouth and excused myself. I think Nadia was relieved to see me go and leave her to her job. Thank God I was going to meet with Emily and Hazel, or I'd have probably stood there chattering nervously for the rest of the day.

I grabbed my laptop and climbed in my car, cranking the air-conditioning as high as it would go. I was cold within a few minutes, but the stifling heat was impossible to tolerate when cooped up in a car. I kept forgetting to open my windows a little when I parked, and opening them when driving just made me feel like I was in an oven.

I drove a short distance to this pretty little shopping center with cobblestones and a fountain in the middle of the entrance. As I got out of the car, the clock perched high on the tower rang, signaling that it was a quarter to ten. It was a beautiful shopping center, with architecture reminiscent of old world marketplaces. I pulled out my phone and took a few pictures. Backgrounds were difficult for me, and I could use the inspiration later.

I walked around for a while until I found the café Emily had specified. I was glad I'd left early; by the time I found the right spot, I was just short of being late.

"Hey," Derek said as I walked in. He was wearing the black shirt of the café, with that little apron waiters wear for carrying around napkins and straws and order booklets.

"Hey, so this is where you work?" I asked.

"Yeah."

"It's awesome," I said, looking around.

Derek nodded. "I like it. Here, I reserved the best spot for us," he said, pointing me to a rectangular table under one of the many wide windows.

I sat down and pulled my laptop out. Emily had asked me to document my experiences from my own perspective for her grant proposal, and I hadn't quite had the chance to finish. I figured I'd work on it while we went over the séance notes.

Derek went back to work while I waited for the others to arrive. Ford wasn't sure he was going to make it, but Emily and Hazel would be there any minute.

I was typing up the last words of the time the ghosts had attacked me in my bed, cutting me in several places, when Emily walked in. She gave me a big hug when she saw me.

"I'm almost done with those reports you wanted," I told her.

"Great. That's going to help us establish a timeline and see if there are any patterns to what the ghosts are up to."

I shook my head. "I don't know, Em. There doesn't seem to be any kind of logic to what they do. They aren't even consistent with who shows up. I thought hauntings were usually just, you know, one or two ghosts?"

"I guess you're just that special," Emily said, dropping her bag in a chair. "Wanna order something?"

I followed her to the counter and scanned the menu. Emily ordered first, getting herself a large vanilla latte and a slice of cake. I got myself a tea.

"Hi, Derek!" Emily chirped when he came out from the kitchen. She hugged him, too, and he flushed a little. I made it a point to look away. No sense embarrassing the boy.

He had to return to his work, so Emily and I went back to our table and started working.

Hazel startled me by bouncing over to the table while Emily and I were going over my notes. She paused long enough in her whirlwind entry to tell us how excited she was to get back into ghost hunting. After that, she sped over to the register to order an iced coffee. As if she needed more energy.

Derek brought us our orders, and Emily waved him over to her side.

"Find anything new?" he asked, leaning on her chair to look over her shoulder.

"No, mostly just looking at things more closely. Ooh, look at all that cocoa powder," she said, derailed by her cake.

"Em," Derek said. "Focus."

"Right. Ghosts. I watched the video last night and I'm seeing some *weird* movement in the background."

"Okay. I'll be on break in a minute, show me then," Derek said, patting her on the head and turning toward the kitchen.

Hazel returned to the table and sat down, pulling out her phone and typing something. She gave a curious glance at all Emily's research and documentation, then at Emily's serious face staring fixedly at the computer screen.

"I think you have to call an exorcist," Emily told me, her brow knit as she clicked through the frames of our séance.

"I'm still adjusting to the fact that exorcists actually *exist,* Emily," I said, eyes glued to the scenes on her computer.

"Will an exorcist be able to help?" Hazel asked, looking up from her phone.

"More than I can. I mean I still want to be around and help, but we've got multiple presences here, one that looks downright...inhuman. This isn't something we can just reason with. I mean, I was thinking we could talk to the ghost, help him move on, but this...is way beyond anything I can do. And those things that attacked you in your bed? I don't even know what to make of that. I've never heard of *anything* like that outside alien abduction, which this obviously isn't."

I sagged a little at that. This was getting crazy.

"Hey, did you come up with anything that would explain the ghost that spelled out 'port'?" I asked, remembering the strange message.

Emily shook her head. "Either the ghost spelling that was named 'Portia' and she got interrupted, or the ghost was talking about ships. Maybe it was a sea-faring ghost."

"Out here in the middle of a desert, hundreds of miles from any ocean?" I asked.

"I have no idea. Retired, died here, longing to go back to return to the sea? I'm just making stuff up at this point."

"Well, okay, say that was true...wouldn't he just, go?" Hazel asked, still typing away on her phone.

"Who are you texting?" I asked.

Hazel looked up, blushing lightly. "Uh...Sean."

I raised my eyebrows. "Oh really? How's that going?"

"Irrelevant. We're talking ghosts now," she said.

"That's depressing, I don't want to talk about it anymore," I said, slumping in my seat.

Emily shifted slightly, taking a bite of cake. "Circling back to our original topic: The ghost probably won't just leave. Sometimes, they get stuck, and they need someone to free them. That's why I thought the séance would help. I thought we could figure out what the ghost needed and just help them along."

"Wait..."

They both turned to look at me.

"Maybe...maybe it wasn't 'port' at all. Maybe it was a different language."

"What?" they both asked.

I pushed my hair back from my face. "Well, the ghost? The one that talks sometimes? It doesn't speak English, right? Do we know what 'port' means in any other languages?"

"No, but we can find out," Emily said, turning to her computer and typing quickly. "Do you know what language it speaks?"

"Um, not really. It kinda sounds like...maybe French? Or...Russian?"

Hazel raised her eyebrows and grinned at me. "You do realize those languages sound nothing alike, right?"

"Hey, I'm in a near-panic whenever he talks to me. And he only says a few things."

"Do you remember any of it?" Emily asked.

I tried to think, but nothing was coming up. "No...I'd recognize it if I heard it again, but I can't remember what it is. Kwi-something. I can't remember."

We all went silent as our last shred of hope for figuring this out proved useless.

"How am I going to convince my dad to actually hire an exorcist?" I groaned, running my finger along the rim of my mug. "I mean, we kinda...discussed it...but I think he was just humoring me."

"He's not really a believer, huh?" Emily asked.

"No. I think he..." I trailed off.

"What?"

I looked down. "I'm afraid he thinks I might be losing my mind."

"Oh..." Hazel said, understanding.

"What? Why?" Emily asked, looking between the two of us.

"Because I told him I'm seeing ghosts," I said. I ran a hand back through my hair. "I told him...I told him what was happening. And it sounded so insane. Besides, my mother, before she abandoned us, she kinda...wasn't doing very well for a while. She hallucinated and stuff. Had to go see therapists, she was even in a psych ward for a little bit. It was really stressful. I'm just...I don't want my dad to think I'm turning into her, you know? But that's what he's going to think if I keep saying I'm seeing things no one else sees."

They were both quiet, and I regretted bringing it up. Of course no one knew what to say to that. What could they say?

"Well, hey, *we* know it's all real. And the housekeepers are seeing the ghosts, too, right?" Hazel asked softly.

I nodded. "Yeah, but none of them will admit to it." She kept saying *ghosts*, and that's what it seemed like, but something nagged at the back of my mind. The slender white beings. The massive black creature. These did not fit the lore around "ghosts".

"At least *we* know you're not insane," Emily said with a half-hearted grin.

I was quiet. *I* still wasn't sure about that, even if there were ghosts. Besides, if I lived with these ghosts much longer, I probably *would* go insane.

"Are you going to read the journal?" Hazel asked.

"I guess I should," I said. It wasn't really an answer, but she didn't bring it up again.

We fell silent again, then Hazel sat up straighter and looked between myself and Emily.

"Here's a question: Why did the ghost...or whatever...say 'gateway' at the end there?"

Emily considered this. "One of them was probably trying to get through to our world. Ghosts and demons and other ethereal beings are always looking for a way through, and séances are dangerous because they can open those pathways."

"Well, it was creepy," Hazel said, shuddering at the memory. I remembered the icy voice and shivered, too.

Ford walked in then, immediately catching my eye. He had this casual way of drawing attention to himself, which I guessed was a carefully crafted art. I rolled my eyes at his designer-ripped-and-faded jeans, but had to laugh at the very real grease stain on his left shin. Ford joined us, sitting down with his usual grin, and Derek took his break, sliding into a seat beside Emily.

"Did you guys figure out what that creepy shadowy thing was?" Ford asked, drumming his fingers on the table.

Emily and Derek shook their heads.

"We got nothing," Derek said.

"I think it's a demon," Emily commented around a bite of cake.

"Are you being serious right now?" I asked in a deadpan.

Emily shrugged. "Seems about as likely as anything else, doesn't it?"

"Ghosts. Demons," Hazel mused, nodding somberly.

"Witches," Ford added under his breath. I caught his eye and he grinned at me. I tried to look stern, but I couldn't keep from smiling.

Derek twirled a straw between his fingers. "Never encountered a demon before. Didn't really think they existed."

"But you believe in ghosts?" Ford asked.

"Well," Derek said. "Ghosts are kind of general. Spirits of people who were once alive and are now dead. Demons? That's a whole 'nother mess."

Ford nodded. "I hear that. Is there a different protocol for getting rid of demons, Em? I'm trying to make sense of all the rules here."

"Exorcists," she said. She was compiling her own notes now, typing without looking up.

"Trying to science it up?" I asked Ford with a smirk.

"There is logic to everything, I just want to know what it is," he said primly. I laughed.

"Ghosts are different. They're outside all that. Although they do have their own rules," Emily said.

Ford was quiet, but I could see he didn't agree.

I scanned the quiet café. There were a couple parents sipping coffee, their toddlers drawing or playing with toys. A few business people seemed to be having a lunch meeting. Others sat with their laptops, headphones on, absorbed in whatever they were doing. I wondered if anyone could hear us. All this talk of ghosts and demons being eavesdropped on would be kind of funny.

We fell silent for a beat as Emily jotted something down and Hazel stirred her drink.

"What if an exorcist *can't* help me?" I asked, my voice barely audible in the din of the cafe.

Emily looked up from her notes.

"Is there a step after that?" I pressed.

Hazel and Emily glanced at each other, but didn't say a word. Ford watched me with searching eyes.

Derek laughed darkly. "Next step? Burn the house down."

TWELVE

"Guess what," my dad said as I dropped my keys in the bowl on the counter.

"What?" I asked.

He grinned. "I took tomorrow off. Thought we could do something."

"Really?" I smiled. "That's awesome. When was the last time you even *had* a day off?"

He shrugged. "Technically, I was off most of Saturday for the party, but not counting that, um..." his brow furrowed, then he laughed. "I don't want to talk about it, okay?"

I laughed, nodding. "Fair enough. Well, I'm glad. You deserve a break. What do you want to do?"

"Whatever you want, kiddo. It's your day."

"Awesome. You're home early today, is that part of your day off?"

"Yup. Figured I'd take the afternoon for us, spend a little time at home."

My first instinct was to suggest something out of the house, but I knew my father was probably tired and just wanted to relax a little.

We took out the leftovers from the assortment of housekeepers and cooks who had passed through our house and made ourselves a very eclectic dinner.

"You know, Nadia's from a different agency," my dad commented lightly.

"Oh?" I asked, my voice a little too high to sound casual.

He nodded. "Yeah. The last one said they couldn't send anyone else over after having five girls quit."

It wasn't really funny, but I burst out laughing. I wasn't sure why, I just couldn't help myself. To my surprise, my dad started to laugh, too.

"How are the, um, ghosts?" he asked.

I shook my head. "I...don't know. It's been...the same. I'd rather not talk about it. Tell me something fun. Something from your work, or...anything else?"

He studied me for a moment, the smiled, nodding.

"Sure, kiddo. Um, your grandmother's back in town, so we're having lunch with her tomorrow," he said.

"That's a good thing. I like that thing." I was excited about the notion until I contemplated how my grandmother would react to all this ghost business. I didn't know if my dad had told her anything.

He laughed. "I thought you would."

We heaped our plates with an assortment of leftovers and sat at the island. He told me about this new intern they'd hired who spilled coffee all over one of the other partners. My dad had somehow managed to save the kid his job, though I'll never understand how. I guess that's one of his "lawyering" powers.

He asked about my new friends, and I told him what I could without bringing up ghosts. I talked about how Hazel had introduced us, how we were just enjoying hanging out. He was really happy to see me interacting with other people my age, and it made me sad to think that our time together was mostly about hosting séances and hunting ghosts.

"Hey," my dad said, grinning. "I know what we should do tomorrow. We should go to Red Rock."

"In the summer? Are you *trying* to die of heat stroke?"

He shook his head. "No, no, it's going to be nice tomorrow. Especially early. Plus, I haven't been there in forever. Do you even remember it?"

I couldn't honestly say I did, though I could recall the big, red rocks that gave the valley its name. Thinking of that place, I remembered my dream. I considered suggesting we go up to the mountains instead, but I held my tongue. I still didn't understand what was going on there, and I didn't feel like digging into it just yet.

"Not really. It's red and it has rocks, that's about all I've got," I said.

He laughed. "You want to go for a hike?"

"Sure. It'll be nice to get out of the house."

My dad laughed. "You've barely *been* in the house, you keep going to Hazel's."

"*You've* barely been in the house, you keep going to *work*," I teased back. "Which, by the way, is far less interesting than Hazel's house."

"Yeah, yeah, wait till I can tell you about this case. Then we'll see who had an interesting summer."

"Hey!" I said, mock-angry. "Don't taunt me with the case then refuse to share details! That's just mean!"

He laughed, then nodded to my plate. "Looks like you were hungry tonight."

I glanced down and realized I'd finished all my food. That was the first full meal I'd eaten in a while.

"Yeah, guess I was. In fact," I hooked the edge of a Tupperware with my fork and dragged it over to me. "I'm going to have seconds."

"Well, if you are, so am I. No judgment," he said, standing up to grab another container of food from the far side of the island.

We finished eating and cleaned up the kitchen together. I was acutely aware of the fact that I hadn't seen any ghosts, heard any strange sounds, or even felt an inexplicable chill. The thought was comforting, but disturbing, too. I never knew when the spirits would strike, and that made them all the more terrifying.

After dinner, we watched a movie. I kept expecting something, *anything*, supernatural to happen, but we were fine. We made it through the whole movie without incident.

"All right, kiddo, I've got to turn in," my dad mumbled sleepily, rubbing his eyes.

"Long day?" I asked.

He nodded around a yawn.

"No, it wasn't," I said, laughing. "You were home by like, two."

My dad gave his head a little shake. "Yes, but I was awake at four-thirty, so I'm running on fumes here."

I chuckled and got up, turning everything off. I kept up the calm act, but I was starting to feel the anxiety that always hit me when I contemplated going to bed. Even though they had shown themselves during the day, the ghosts really did seem to prefer the night.

My dad hugged me, kissing the top of my head. "Bright and early for our hike tomorrow, huh?" he asked before we bid each other goodnight.

In my room, I sat on the edge of my bed, restless. I could've woken my father up, but I didn't know what I'd ask of him once I did. So I sat, immobile, just waiting for something to happen.

But nothing did. The fact that no paranormal activity was taking place was almost scarier than it happening, because I kept wondering *why*. The silence was so loud. The stillness was so violent.

I went to bed, still buzzing with nervous energy that would no doubt keep me awake for hours. About twenty minutes after I turned off my lights, the room cooled, and I heard a woman humming, something like a lullaby, though not one I knew. I squeezed my eyes shut and wished to be anywhere else.

And just like that, I was.

I was in the clearing. The trees in a perfect circle around me, the wind whispering through them.I froze, startled. This felt more real than it ever had before. It didn't have the hazy quality of dreams. A sharp stab of pain shot out behind my eyes, and I squeezed them shut as a little moan escaped me.

It was dark this time, the stars and moon shining brightly above me. The moon was close to full, and it cast a cold light upon the scene, illuminating the forest around me.

A bitter wind blew and I shivered, but my pajamas were too light and thin to provide much protection.

Warmth radiated from behind me, along with a soft light. I turned to see it, but it grew, blinding me with its intensity. I shielded my eyes with my hands, squinting toward the light.

A towering, shadowy figure appeared, seeming to step forward from the light, obscuring it. I blinked, recognizing it. The angular body and jagged edges. The impossible darkness, swallowing up the light around it like a black hole.

"No. No, no, no," I whispered, backing away. I wanted to get away from that thing, whatever it was. I wanted to go home.

I woke with a start, curled in my bed, buried under covers. It was too hot under all the blankets, and I kicked them off, frantic and confused.

My body shook. The biting cold of the forest had felt so real, the stifling warmth of my bed seemed wrong now. The room wasn't cool anymore. I sat up and turned the light on, looking around.

This version of the dream had been different. It had been strange. I put my head in my hands and tried to make sense of it.

The shadow.

I didn't like that I'd seen it in this dream, and I didn't like how real the dream had felt.

Through my slightly-parted curtains, a sliver of brilliant moonlight filtered into the room, cutting a pale line across my bed.

Curious, I got up and went to my window, tugging the curtain aside.

It was the same moon from my dream. Almost full, illuminating the world below with its shining light.

I closed the curtains tightly and shook off the image of the towering shadowy figure. I told myself it was just a dream, trying desperately to ignore the fact that I was almost certain I hadn't been asleep when I'd had it.

"Almost there, come on," my dad urged me on.

I pulled myself along, enjoying the exertion. It was early—just past seven, now—and the morning was still relatively cool. The sun was already on the rise, warming the earth, but we had some time yet before the sweltering heat set in.

Naturally, we'd both wanted to do the most challenging trail we could find. Competitiveness was a classic Weissmandl trait, even if it was just being competitive against your own abilities.

My dad talked as we made our way through the milder portions of the trail, telling me about how he use to come up here with his friends. I thought of coming here with a friend, but Hazel, for all her health-nut nature-loving fanaticism, didn't much like physical activity *or* the outdoors, so I couldn't really imagine her hiking, at least not this far. Emily and Derek, despite coming out in the day, seemed in my mind more like wraiths. And even if they weren't creatures of the night, they both kept pretty busy.

I could see Ford here, though. He'd be awake now anyway, most likely managing his little business. Thinking about it, *he* probably had a bunch of stories about coming up here with his friends, no doubt getting themselves into trouble. I could see him being chased by a coyote or stuck to a cactus or something.

I snickered at that, turning my gaze up to the impossibly blue sky. I didn't know if it was the red of the mountains we stood within that drew that shade of azure from the sky, or the early hour of the day. Perhaps the Vegas sky was just incredibly blue, and I had been too busy with ghosts and goblins to notice.

No goblins. Not yet, anyway.

I decided not to dwell on the possibility of goblins.

We reached the top of the trail and looked out over the valley. I could see the Strip, shimmering in the early morning light. Around us on all sides, even the farthest side of the valley, I could see mountains towering up above the city, surrounding the millions lives playing out down there. Las Vegas was so much more than gambling and eccentric shows, and from this vantage point, it was more obvious. It all seemed weirdly small from here. It made sense, in a way, that ghosts would appear in cities. More life, more death. Out here, it was quieter. Well, save for all the dead people likely buried by mobsters back in the day.

Okay, enough of that, I thought.

We found a big, relatively flat rock and climbed to the top of it. There, we had our little picnic, watching the city. It wasn't a city waking up, as half of its inhabitants were already awake. In fact, a good chunk of them were just getting home from work, preparing to go to sleep. I wondered how well blackout curtains worked against the desert sun.

"This city has grown so much since I was a kid," my dad observed, looking out in the same direction I was.

"It's still growing," I commented. There was no shortage of work for construction crews in this town.

"Someday, you'll tell your kids about how small it was when you lived here," my dad said.

I laughed, wondering if I'd die from a ghost-induced heart attack before I got the chance to even consider having kids.

We sat up there for a while, until the sun had crept high enough into the sky to heat up the earth below. It seemed strange to have such natural beauty surrounding me when just a few miles away was a bustling city, but I sat back, enjoying the sun's rays like a basking lizard and ignoring the existence of everyone else on the planet, living or dead.

By the time we made it back to the car, it was hot out. Full-blown, triple-digit heat. We cranked the air in the car and I tossed my once-necessary sweatshirt to the back seat, not wanting it anywhere near me.

I was in a good mood after the hike. At home, I showered and changed, still upbeat. Getting out of the house, being in nature, that usually wasn't my thing. Today, though, it had felt nice. Maybe it was the time with my father, or the fresh air, or the complete absence of ghosts. Maybe that was just how it felt to have a normal, nice day and I'd so completely forgotten the feeling that it now seemed mind-blowingly wonderful.

My dad was taking a day off from work. Perhaps I could take a day off from ghosts.

We went out for lunch. My grandmother had chosen a restaurant on the Strip, which we usually avoided, but I had fun looking at the street performers and impersonators as we drove by the towering, shiny buildings.

We went to a tea room on the twenty-third floor of one of the elegant new casinos. It overlooked the Strip, and I took a seat by the window so I could appreciate the view. I snapped a few pictures of the opulent room we were in, and the other guests, but I put my phone away quickly. My grandmother didn't like people spending too much time on their phones, and I didn't feel like hearing a lecture.

The afternoon-tea style lunch was wonderful. I was relieved I was able to enjoy it. My only real concern was keeping kosher in front of my grandmother, who was stricter about these things than my father and I tended to be. But it was a normal, familiar concern, and I found myself reveling in it.

"So Rosalind, have you decided what colleges you'll be applying to?" my grandmother asked.

My stomach knotted. So much for relaxing. I hated these kinds of questions. I always felt like there was a right or wrong answer, and I didn't know what the right one was.

It certainly wasn't my answer, though: "Um...no. I-I haven't made any final decisions. I have a few in mind...but I haven't actually prepared my applications yet."

"Well, I think you should get a jump on that. You'll be entering your junior year, and many of the schools you'd want to apply to will already be accepting applications for your graduating class."

I nodded, agreeing passively as she talked about my future. Thinking about the next decade always made me anxious. I either had no idea what I wanted to do, or too many ideas, depending on the day. And lately, thinking about anything beyond "get rid of the ghosts" felt like an impossible task. She continued talking about colleges and how absolutely imperative it was to get into the right one.

"If you want, I know someone in the admissions department of—"

"Don't worry about it, Ma," my dad said, cutting her off and surprising us both. I looked at him as he calmly set his fork down and smiled at my grandmother.

"I just want her to have the best chance at getting into the school she wants," my grandmother said with an easy smile.

My dad nodded. "I know, Ma, but trust me—we've got it handled."

I tried not to smile, but I gave my father an appreciative glance when my grandmother wasn't looking.

After that, the matter was dropped. We discussed the new house and a few projects my grandmother was taking on at work, and my painting lessons with Joanne. At one point, my grandmother asked my father about interesting new cases, which he deflected smoothly. She didn't miss it, though, and I realized that he hadn't even told her about what was going on in his workdays.

After lunch, we parted ways, and my grandmother hugged me a little tighter than necessary. I wondered why, until she was walking away and I realized she hadn't once asked about all the strange incidents at the house, even though I knew my father had mentioned them to her. So, she was also worried about me.

We stayed on the Strip and went for a walk, stopping to watch the Bellagio's fountain and getting ice cream at this place that claimed to have the best ice cream in the world (it *was* pretty amazing).

"Maybe we should see a show tonight," my dad said, scanning a ticket site on his phone.

"Sure. I haven't seen any of them," I said around a mouthful of ice cream.

I left the decision to my father as I finished off my dessert. I felt good, and I didn't really care what we did, so long as this day continued far from the house and the ghosts and everything else I'd faced since moving here.

We grabbed dinner, then headed to the casino with our show. It was early evening, but the sun was still well above the horizon. The summer sun meant daylight would persist until about eight at night.

At the theater, my dad got us some snacks and we navigated to our seats. We were a little early, so we sat, talking about the various shows we should see in the future.

"I've got to run to the restroom before this starts," my dad said, glancing at his watch, then at the stage. "Do you have to go?"

"No, I'm good," I said. "I'll watch our stuff."

He got up and worked his way down the aisle while I skimmed my phone, searching for something interesting to occupy my time.

"Oh, my God. Miss. Miss? Are you all right?"

I looked up, confused. A woman three seats over was asking the question, but she wasn't talking to me. She was talking to the woman sitting one seat over from me.

I did a double take, not realizing her state of disarray at first. She wore faded, tattered clothes, and her stringy brown hair hung in her eyes. She looked incredibly sick. Her skin was ashen, and the circles under her eyes were deep.

I recoiled on instinct, before I even understood what repelled me from her.

Slowly, like the muscles in her neck weren't working quite right, she turned to look at me.

I couldn't meet her eyes. They terrified me, though I couldn't say why.

Not here, I pleaded silently. *Not here*.

"Miss? Can you hear me? You're hurt. I—Jack, do you see her? How did she even get in here? I didn't see her come in..."

I ignored the lady down the aisle who was still talking, my eyes fixed on the tattered woman beside me. She was a ghost; I could *feel* it. But she felt stronger than previous ghosts. There was something more intense about this one.

What could I do? I didn't want to get up and run screaming, not in public. Would she lash out? Was I in danger?

I scooted as far away from her as I could, but she didn't move, she just watched me, curiously. It was like she was as fascinated by me as I would be by her, were I not shaking in terror.

Slowly, she rose, walking toward me. I got up shakily and backed away.

Other people were noticing her now, noticing how she was striding toward me in a jerky, broken fashion, her intense eyes boring into me while I backed away like a cornered mouse. A couple guys in the row behind us got up, asking if she needed help. The woman ignored them, catching my arm in a sudden, swift movement as I turned to run. Her grip was surprisingly strong. I tugged against the very real feel of her dry, icy flesh, stunned by how solid she was.

Poltergeist, I realized as my stomach sank. Emily had warned me. I'd only heard of them so far, but I knew eventually I'd encounter one. I just wished it hadn't been here of all places.

One of the guys from the other row reached out and grabbed the ghost's arm.

"Hey, you can't just—"

A piercing shriek tore through the theater, momentarily silencing the hum of chatter as hundreds of people filed in. Everyone in the vicinity turned to look as she ripped her arm away from him, lashing out. She slashed her nails across his skin and he fell back, clutching the side of his face and wailing. Blood seeped out between his fingers.

"Hey! What's your problem?" his friend shouted.

I watched, stunned. She had hurt him. She was visible and tangible to everyone in this theater, not just me. And I could feel it in me, like a tug in my gut that was somehow tied to her.

Why is this ghost so powerful? I wondered.

By now, security had noticed the commotion. She still had one hand firmly wrapped around my wrist, and no matter how hard I struggled, I couldn't get away from her.

As security closed in, she broke and away, moving without much apparent hurry, but still evading capture easily, and literally disappearing into the crowd.

The guards set off in a search for her, with an usher coming to retrieve the guy who'd gotten hurt. I watched him guiltily, hoping the wounds weren't too bad.

"Did she hurt you?" one of the ushers asked.

I shook my head.

My dad arrived then, rushing to my side. He'd come back just in time to hear the tail end of the scene, but the surging crowd had kept him from getting to me.

"Roz! Roz, what happened?" he asked.

"Some crazy girl was here, started chasing her!" the woman from down the aisle supplied helpfully. I let her explain in great detail what had happened.

The start of the show was delayed a bit by all this, as they searched the theater for the deranged woman I knew they'd never find.

"Are you okay? Do you want to just go home?" my dad asked, his arm protectively around me.

I rubbed my sore wrist, contemplating my options.

"Roz? Honey? We can just go home if you want to, I think I might feel better if we got out of here," he said.

"Yeah, okay," I said.

And just like that, my day off was over.

THIRTEEN

The next day, things were back to normal, which was a problem for me. I didn't like living with ghosts. I wasn't sure how much longer my sanity would hold out.

After my encounter in the theater, I couldn't stop thinking about ghosts, and why they kept finding me. Did I have some kind of sixth sense? Was that why I always saw them? I hadn't really considered it before—in part because Emily hadn't brought it up, and in part because I had always assumed those things were life-long conditions. I'd never seen a ghost before moving to Las Vegas. Why would something like that take sixteen years to show up?

I decided I should stop basing my ghost-facts on movies and start looking at some actual research.

In my endless merry-go-round of questions and fears, I remembered Derek's comment about how quickly the ghosts had shown up at our séance. I didn't know why, but it bothered me. It itched at the back of my mind. I researched séances and hauntings, listening to another episode of *East/West* while I read. Most séances, as I was beginning to understand, didn't produce any results. Or if they did, the results were very minimal. Ours had had pretty big results.

Well, obviously, I thought. *My house is haunted.* Again, though, it felt wrong. I was missing something, and I knew it. As I dug through pages of information online, I stumbled upon a page that talked about "ghost sensitivity" and clicked the link, my interest piqued. What I read there seemed to indicate that some people are more prone to drawing ghosts to them. I bit my lip as my hands started to shake.

Goosebumps raced up my arm, sending chills along my spine. I yanked an earbud free, listening intently.

There it was again. A little sob.

I closed my eyes. *Not now, please. Not now.*

The room warmed a bit, and the house was silent again. I opened one eye, then the other. I looked around, confused. I didn't know how, but I could feel that nothing was going on anymore.

I sat there with my fists clenched, waiting for something to happen. When nothing did, I released the breath I'd been holding and looked back at my screen. I closed my computer and went downstairs to find my father.

"Hey, I was thinking of going to Hazel's house tonight," I said to my dad. He was preparing to head off to a meeting, based on his clothes and briefcase. I spoke casually, as if my friends and I hadn't planned this in advance.

"Ah, all right. Working on that project? With that girl, what's her name? Emily?"

"Yup, that's the one. And yeah, we want to do some editing tonight, maybe work on some new material."

I'd told my father we were doing a film project with Emily. Which was actually entirely true, as I kept reminding myself whenever the guilt welled up. I might have said it had to do with her college application, which was also true. It didn't do much for my guilt, but I kept trying.

My dad agreed, which I had known he would. He had no problem with me visiting his trusted and beloved sister to hang out with my cousin. And I liked having an easy way to get out of the house without raising too many questions.

We'd talked a little about the theater incident, but I'd downplayed it as much as I could and done my best to portray the crazed ghost as someone who'd had too much to drink and was just acting erratically. I was relieved, at least, that so many others had seen her. He had made no suggestions of imaginings or therapy, since it had happened so publicly.

On the other hand, it was really disturbing to think that these ghosts could turn up in other places, and even harm other people. I had preferred it when that sort of thing was contained to me.

I spent most of the previous night trying to see if anyone had died in that theater, but it was hard to pinpoint, especially since I wasn't much of an investigator. It seemed like plenty of people died on the

Strip. There were more than enough opportunities for unnatural presences to spring up.

I said goodbye to my dad and told him I'd be heading to Hazel's soon.

"Okay, I'll be at the office late tonight. Are there any more leftovers for dinner?" he asked.

"There's one big slice of lasagna and some of that Spanish rice, but after that, we're going to have to start ordering takeout again," I said.

He chuckled. "Well, that'll make a fine dinner whenever I get home."

I smiled, but my stomach twisted. "Are you gonna be okay without me?" I teased.

He didn't know it, but I actually was concerned. This haunting situation was getting worse. The ghosts were enough to scare off the housekeepers, and while he hadn't seemed to have any encounters yet, I was still worried.

Why hasn't *he had any encounters yet?* I wondered, not for the first time. I made a mental note to ask Emily when I saw her.

He smiled. "Of course. Go have fun. I'll be so tired when I get home, I'll probably just fall asleep on the couch again," he said.

"Well, try not to. You know you wake up with your back killing you whenever you do that," I pointed out.

"Yeah, yeah, way to remind me that I'm old."

I snickered and gave him a hug before heading out. I was still feeling guilty about leaving all the time. I couldn't help myself, though; it was getting to the point where I couldn't stand to be in my house anymore. This probably wasn't something I could keep up very long.

Spending the night at Hazel's wasn't a great long-term strategy for dealing with ghosts, but it was all I could think of for now, and it was the only way I was going to get any sleep.

I got into my car and sent Hazel a text, letting her know I was leaving my house. She sent back a text made up entirely of emojis.

I was looking forward to this. I wasn't just crashing at Hazel's, we were having a sleepover. A real, genuine, girls-hanging-out-having-fun sleepover. I mean, sure, we'd probably spend half the night talking about ghosts anyway, but I was still looking forward to it. I liked Emily, and Hazel was already my best friend. This was going to be fun.

It'll be normal, too, and I could use a touch of that before I completely forget what it feels like.

I arrived at Hazel's house to find an assortment of snacks already laid out by my aunt. Hazel and I sat with my aunt and uncle for a while, telling them about how I was liking Las Vegas so far. Haldi, Hazel's younger brother, was still out with some friends, so the house was quieter than usual.

The smell of incense and the tranquil atmosphere of their home soothed me. With four people in their family, the house always seemed more lively and active, which served to distract me from ghosts and hauntings. I thought of my father, who would be alone in ghost-infested territory tonight, and hoped he was safe.

"Do you like the new house?" Aunt Fiona asked. She poured some herbal tea of her own creation. She was always coming up with remedies, immune boosters, and all sorts of clever things to sell at the Apothecary. I could usually find her in her kitchen, grinding up ancient roots or whatever and mixing them like some kind of hippie version of a mad scientist.

"Uh...it's great," I said, sipping my tea and glancing at Hazel, who was actually biting her cheek to suppress a laugh.

I kicked my cousin lightly under the table. "What's really cool about it is my neighbor, Joanne Königin. Do you know her? The famous painter?" I asked, steering the conversation to something a little safer.

Aunt Fiona considered this. "Sounds familiar. She lives near you? How exciting."

"Yeah," I said. "She's giving me painting lessons. It's a lot of fun."

Uncle Naagesh smiled. "That's kind of her. I'd like to see some of her paintings sometime."

"I think she has a gallery downtown," I said.

"Ooh, Naagi, we should go!" Aunt Fiona said happily.

Emily arrived then, and I thanked my aunt and uncle for tea, and for letting me stay over. Again. We went up to Hazel's room so we could talk more openly.

The sleepover actually did end up being a lot of fun. Emily wanted to talk ghosts, of course, and while I had questions, I really didn't want to think about ghosts. Not here. I wanted to forget about the whole thing and have a peaceful night with my friends. Then again, ignoring the problem wouldn't get the ghosts out of my house.

"There was one in *public* this time?" Emily asked.

"Yeah. But, I mean, tons of people must've died on the Strip, right? And ghosts usually linger around where they died, so..."

Emily nodded vigorously, jotting down some notes.

"And where did you say this was?" she asked.

I told her the theater and she opened her laptop, typing quickly.

"I remember hearing about a performer dying in one of the shows not that long ago. I mean, *right* in the middle of the show. It was horrifying. Some kind of equipment accident."

I thought of the tattered woman's strange appearance. The ragged clothes, the sickly pallor. Perhaps she had died in an accident.

"Haze?" a voice called from the hall. I turned to see Haldi peeking in. He smiled when he saw us. "Hey, Roz. I thought when you moved to town you'd be moving into your own house, not ours."

"Your house has more Indian food," I said.

He snickered. "Right. What about you, Emily? Is Hazel going to let you live in her room, too?"

"I don't think she could put up with me for that long," Emily said.

"Well if she kicks you out, you're welcome to come hang out in my room," he said, waggling his eyebrows at her.

Hazel threw a pillow at him. "What did you come in here for, Hal?"

"Uh...I forgot," he said, and another pillow hit him in the head. Haldi laughed. "All right, all right, I'll go." He turned to us and smiled, still watching Emily. "Night, ladies."

With that, he slipped out of the room and shut the door, leaving us once more to our ghost work.

"I can't get much on how the performer who died looked, but it was a woman," Emily said, setting her laptop aside.

I nodded, considering this.

"I've been reviewing the séance footage," Emily said, shifting the topic to something she knew more about.

"Oh? Find anything?"

"Well, for one thing, you *do* have way too many ghosts in your house. We talked about this before, but seriously. I haven't had a chance to look into deaths on the premise, but I did some basic research and there's no way that many people died in or around your house."

"So what's that mean?" I asked.

Emily shrugged. "It could mean a lot of things. It could mean there's some kind of influx of energy in that area, it could mean the barrier between their world and ours is weaker there, or it could just mean there *are* that many around, and you have an uncanny gift for seeing them."

"Would that explain why your cameras and stuff saw them, though?" I asked.

"I don't know," Emily admitted. We had a box of pizza on the floor between us. She lifted another piece out and munched on it thoughtfully. "I mean, it is possible. I've heard of things like that before. If there's someone with a sixth sense, *you*, then sometimes, being in the presence of that person can make the ghosts visible to others, at least temporarily."

"Could it mean...could *I* be drawing them to me?"

Emily tilted her head to one side. "Well, I mean, I've heard of that, but it's more like an untested theory. Some people say those with psychic abilities or a sixth sense can attract ghosts, but not to the degree you are. And as far as I know, you're not psychic," she raised her eyebrows at me. "Are you?"

I shook my head, but then changed my answer. "Maybe? I have no idea. I only know about being psychic from books and TV."

Nodding, Emily sat forward. "Well, first of all, a lot of things fall under the blanket of 'psychic', especially once Hollywood gets involved," she said. "It could be subtle—it doesn't have to be predictions of big future events, especially if you don't have it trained or under control. I mean, symptoms of psychic awakening are weird...like...they can almost seem like anxiety or depression or being tense around some people. Then there's other random stuff like flashes of light, or having bad reactions to medicine."

I frowned. "That all sounds like some kind of disorder."

"Well, there's other stuff, too—visions, suddenly knowing things...ooh, one is being aware of events *as they're happening*. As in, something is happening and you know about it, even though it's miles away and you haven't heard news yet. Keep an eye out for that. I have more info on my blog."

I nodded. I had always wanted a superpower, and had thought being psychic might be cool. Now I was rethinking that stance.

"So that brings us back to the original question," I said. "Is it me drawing the ghosts out?"

Emily shrugged. "I won't say it didn't occur to me, but I didn't bring it up because it...it just doesn't fit. Usually, it's just one or two ghosts latching on to the person, not...a fleet of them. In your case, there are so *many* ghosts. If you had a sixth sense that was just drawing them to you, you'd only see ghosts who had inhabited the areas you're visiting. But...you're seeing way more ghosts than makes sense for your relatively new house. And not *everywhere* is going to have ghosts. I mean, Vegas itself is a pretty new city. It's just so weird to me that there are so *many*, but we'll figure it out."

Trying to wrap my mind around the science behind that made my head hurt, so I stopped. Ghosts, as far as I could tell, made no sense whatsoever, regardless of what Ford claimed.

"I don't want to talk about ghosts anymore!" Hazel declared. "I mean, no offense, Roz. I *really* want to help you out with this, but can't we just *relax* tonight? Some lunatic ghost jumped you on *the Strip*, for crying out loud. You deserve a break."

I laughed, and so did Emily.

"Okay, I surrender," Emily said, putting her hands up, her slice of pizza threatening to drip cheese on her head.

"Okay, Hazel, since you're an expert on this 'relaxing' thing, what should we talk about? I've forgotten how to have normal, non-paranormal human interactions," I said, making Emily snicker again.

Hazel flushed a little.

"Oh, I see how it is," I said, throwing my hands up. "Forget my ghost problems, Hazel has a *boy* she wants to talk about!"

"Hey! I finally got to go out on a date with him and we haven't even discussed it yet!" she shot back, giggling the whole time.

"Eww, you're still stuck on Sean?" Emily asked, finishing off her pizza. "Why?"

"What's wrong with Sean?" Hazel asked.

"He's so..." Emily snapped her fingers, "Sporty, hair-gel, doofus-y," she said. "He looks like he'd be all," she dropped her voice and winked at Hazel, making finger-guns. "*Hey, babe. Whassup?*"

"Oh, he does *not* sound like that," Hazel protested.

"They *all* sound like that in my head."

From there, the conversation branched off to our school, which I hadn't even seen yet. We discussed the various teachers, classmates, subjects, sports, and dramas around campus. It was fun, actually. I had almost completely withdrawn at my last school, and I was hoping to have a fresh start and be a little more involved this time around. Learning about the people of my new school, even if it was just a bunch of silly stuff, was a welcome reprieve from certain other people who weren't necessarily among the living anymore.

We talked well into the night before deciding to go to bed. Emily wanted to do more ghost hunting in the morning, and I would need all my strength for that.

Having the two of them to talk to was nice. I prepared for bed, my mind swimming not with hauntings and the anticipation of ghosts, but names of cheerleaders and mean teachers to look out for. It was a much more manageable kind of stress.

The three of us got comfortable and settled in for the night. Hazel's bed wasn't big enough for all of us, so we made up a sleeping space on the floor from pillows and sleeping bags.

Hazel turned off the lights, but immediately turned them back on.

I figured she'd just forgotten something, but when I looked at her, she had a stunned, frightened look on her face.

"What is it?" I asked.

She shook her head and laughed. "All this ghost stuff is really getting to me. I thought I saw something standing in the corner over there. Anyway," she switched the lights off once more.

This time, I saw it too.

The room was dark, but not completely black. There was enough light coming through the closed blinds to make out things like furniture, doorways, pictures on the walls...

...And the towering, impossibly dark figure that stood in the corner.

FOURTEEN

Hazel screamed and turned the light back on. Emily and I were sitting up now, alert and afraid.

But there was nothing there. With the lights on, it was abundantly clear that there was nothing in that corner of the room.

"You guys saw that, right?" Hazel squeaked.

"Yes," I said.

"Definitely," Emily added.

"Turn the lights off again, Haze. Just for a second," I said.

She flicked the lights off, and I kept my eyes fixed on the corner. Hazel yelped and turned the light back on fast, but I'd been paying attention. I'd seen what I needed to see.

The thing that had been standing in the corner—the corner that was now empty in the bright light of Hazel's bedroom—was tall. Too tall. And angular.

It was the creature I'd seen in Emily's séance photographs.

"It looks like..."

"The shadow," Emily interrupted. I glanced at her and saw my own anxiety mirrored back at me. She'd noticed, too.

"What do we do?" Hazel whimpered.

I got up, moving toward the door, all the while keeping my eye on the corner. When I twisted the knob, though, the door wouldn't open. Emily pushed me aside and tried it herself, shaking it furiously. The door wasn't locked, but she couldn't open it.

She pulled at the handle again and again as the lights in the room started to flicker. We all screamed.

"Open the door!" Hazel cried.

"I can't!"

"Quit messing around, Emily. Open the door!"

Through gritted teeth, Emily snarled, "It won't *open*, Hazel."

The lights flickered again and went out.

We all screamed, squeezing together in our panic.

The temperature of the room dropped, and we turned instinctively toward the corner where the creature stood.

It wasn't there.

All three of us were screaming. We pressed back against the door. Hazel kept trying to pull it open, but it still wouldn't work. She started pounding on the door while I cast around, trying to spot the figure in the darkness.

I found it, standing right in front of me. I could feel it reaching for me.

A cry escaped me. I pressed back against Emily and Hazel, and with all of us shouting, the door opened, slamming against the wall and throwing us to the floor of Hazel's bedroom.

I thought for a moment her parents or brother had heard us screaming and come to rescue us, but when I looked up, no one was there. Just the unnervingly dark, empty hallway. It was far darker than it should have been. I saw no light filtering in from the windows, and the nightlights my aunt kept in the hall were all out.

We started to charge out into the hallway, but when the creeping sensation emanating from the darkness hit us, we all stopped, uncertain.

I looked back. The creature was gone. That, at least, was a bonus. I didn't have much time to appreciate that, though; I was too busy looking around, wondering why the room looked so drab.

We stood huddled together, staring down the hall. I still wanted to run, but I couldn't move my legs.

"It's so dark," Hazel whispered.

"I can't believe your family didn't hear that. There's no way," I said, keeping my voice to a whisper, though I wasn't quite sure why.

Emily had her phone in her hand—probably about to call 9-1-1—and she woke it up, holding it out as a makeshift flashlight.

"Hello?" Hazel called. "Mom? Dad? Haldi?"

The house was silent. Houses are never completely silent. There's always noise. The hum of electronics, the whoosh of the air conditioner, the distant sounds of cars passing by or wind rustling outside.

I closed my eyes. I was developing what felt very much like a sinus headache. It was distracting, and it wasn't helping my nerves.

We weren't quite sure what to do. Going out into the hall didn't seem like an appealing notion, but staying rooted to the spot also seemed ineffective.

A presence behind us caught our attention. I can't even explain how we knew it was there. In the silence of the house, it was easy to tell if we were hearing anything, but that hadn't been it. There was no sound, no change in the light, no movement, there was simply the sudden and intense awareness that there was something behind us. It was the feeling you get when someone is watching you, but far, far more powerful.

We all glanced at one another, and slowly, nervously, we all turned to look over our shoulders.

A young woman stood behind us, barely visible in the darkness. She stared at us through a tangle of dark hair.

A jolt shot through me—it was the girl from the theater.

We all screamed, tripping over one another to get out of the room. She didn't pursue us; she just watched as we scurried down the hallway and to the stairs.

The ground floor was just as dark. There wasn't even the minimal light that would usually come from the microwave and oven clocks. I kept looking up the stairs, then around, trying to spot the girl, but she seemed to have remained upstairs.

"Mom! Dad!" Hazel screamed, so loudly her voice broke. I didn't blame her. It didn't make sense that they couldn't hear us.

"Haze, shh," Emily said. She was still using her phone to look around. The light on the back was on now. Somehow, she'd had enough sense in all that panic to switch on the flashlight. Even with the bright white beam cutting through the gloom, the darkness pressed in around us, almost aggressive. It swallowed the light, preventing it from penetrating the blackness shrouding us. I bumped into furniture and walls as I walked, feeling along blindly to guide myself.

We tried the light switches, but nothing worked. I wondered if the power was out; it would explain the unreal darkness we found ourselves in now.

Hazel came to me and I squeezed her hand, trying to offer what little comfort I could. I didn't feel like I had much strength to spare, but in all fairness, I was more experienced with this haunting business.

I used my free hand to rub at the bridge of my nose. It felt like my head was in a vice. I closed my eyes and tried to blink this away, but when I opened my eyes, we were still in the darkness.

Emily walked out ahead of us, swinging her flashlight around. With a sudden shriek, something grabbed her, knocking her to the floor and dragging her along. She screamed and we raced after her, trying to pull her back. Whatever had her was far too strong, though, and it ripped Emily right out of my grasp. She dropped her phone, its light pointing straight up at the ceiling, casting eerie shadows over the kitchen.

The thing that had Emily dragged her into the pantry, and the door slammed, rattling the glass panel. She pulled herself to her knees and pounded on the glass, trying the handle to no avail.

"Emily!" Hazel screamed.

"Grab the phone!" I said, racing to the door. I tried the handle, but it didn't even budge. Emily rattled it, too, but even with both of us working together, it wouldn't open.

Something slammed her up against the door, and she screamed. I could see blood smearing the glass as she pounded her fists against it. With a sudden jerk, Emily disappeared into the darkness of the pantry, and even in the direct light of the flashlight, I could only see blurred, shaky movements.

I cast around for something to break the glass with. Hazel's mother had a pestle and mortar sitting on the island, which she used to grind herbs. I snatched up the pestle and yelled at Emily to get back. I wasn't sure if she could hear me, or if she could even oblige, but I wasn't going to let her get killed in there.

I slammed the heavy stone club into the glass and it shattered, a huge, tremendous sound in the impossibly quiet house.

I knocked the jagged shards aside and grabbed Emily's hand as she reached for me. With Hazel's help, I pulled Emily free of the little pantry.

Whatever had attacked Emily was still there, breathing raggedly, but even though I kept waiting for it to strike, it never did.

The pressure in my head was becoming unbearable. It was so bad my vision was blurring. I stumbled, catching myself against the counter. I closed my eyes, squeezing them shut against the skull-splitting pain, wishing I understood what was happening.

"Roz!"

Hazel squeezed my arm. I opened my eyes, and the pressure in my skull vanishing. It left me with a dizzy, light-headed sensation.

We were standing in the kitchen. The dark, but not impossibly dark, kitchen. I looked around, confused, but everything seemed in order. I could see the glow of streetlights outside, and the green numbers shone from the appliances. One read 12:38, the other 12:39.

I blinked. The broken glass on the floor was gone. The pantry door was intact, undamaged. When I looked down at my hand, it was empty, though it still bore the little cuts from breaking the glass.

Emily climbed shakily to her feet, taking a few deep breaths. She ran her hands back through her hair. In the light from her phone, I could see cuts and bruises along her arms and face. Her nose bled in a slow trickle down her mouth and neck.

Hazel went into caretaker mode, turning on the lights and fetching the first aid kit. She sat Emily at the island and went about bandaging her up. There were certainly more than enough supplies, even if they were, as my dad called them, "hippie stuff".

I paced around the kitchen, hands balled into fists. I kept looking around, waiting for something to happen, but everything was normal. Perfectly normal. So normal it was making me sick.

This didn't make sense. I'd say we'd imagined it all, but...all three of us? Seeing the same things? And what about the broken glass? I looked at the cool stone club, sitting right where it belonged on the counter. I had cuts on my arm from smashing the pantry glass, but when I looked at the door, it was in perfect condition. The word "Pantry" sat cheerfully on the unmarred glass in soft, frosted letters.

Cuts coated Emily's flesh. Her long hair was a black and purple mess. Whatever had happened, it wasn't imagined. Maybe *I* was imagining it all. Or maybe it was a dream. An incredibly vivid, terrifying dream. Maybe I could wake up safely in Hazel's room. I squeezed my eyes shut, thinking, *Wake up.*

"Rosalind," Hazel said, and I looked up, realizing she must have been trying to get my attention for a while.

I swallowed hard. I couldn't find my voice for a moment. "Yeah?"

"What...what was that?" she asked in a quavering voice. "What just happened?"

I went to the other seat at the island and settled in beside Emily. I uncurled my fists and flexed my hand a bit, my fingers slow to move. I stared at them as I considered how to answer my cousin.

"I don't know, Haze. It was...weird. Nothing like that has ever happened before."

I looked back at the pantry door, unable to believe what I was seeing. I stepped over to the glass and ran my fingers along its cool surface. It was real, intact.

"Really?" Hazel pressed.

I was about to insist, but then I thought about it. I remembered having similar feelings in the past. The impossible darkness. The inexplicable silence. The oppressive fear. And my sudden headache. Maybe something similar *had* happened before...only I hadn't realized it.

I shook my head. "I don't know. Maybe. I..." I rubbed my temples, my headache returning. "I don't have any answers, Hazel," I admitted, slumping a bit. I was so tired.

"The glass is definitely freaky," Emily muttered, "but...what I really want to know is how, and *why*, the ghosts were *here*."

I nodded. I had considered that, too. I was supposed to be safe here. I was supposed to be away from all that. Out in public, I had accepted that I'd bump into ghosts. People died all over the place, after all.

"I think...I really do think they're following me, guys," I whispered.

Emily took a few deep breaths. "Well, whatever's going on, I can tell you this—it's a lot more than just ghosts."

"What do you mean?" Hazel asked.

"That..." Emily waved her hand. "Whatever all that was? That's not like any haunting I've ever heard of before. That's...something else entirely."

I remembered the blinding light and the tall, luminescent figures in my room. Ghosts had been too much for me already, and now they weren't even weird enough to explain what was happening.

With the adrenaline wearing off, we were all too exhausted to figure out what had happened, or why. We searched the house for a bit, but everything was as it should be. Feeling defeated, we set up blankets on the sofas downstairs and curled up there. None of us were ready to go back to Hazel's room just yet.

We decided to sleep in shifts, though once we were lying down, we weren't able to fall asleep. We sat awake, talking occasionally, but mostly just sitting in stunned silence, nervously glancing around the room.

I didn't mention to them that the girl we'd seen was the same one from the show. The one who'd tried to attack me. At least she'd stayed put this time, though I kept looking around for her.

I tried to distract myself with my phone, but that ended up making me feel worse; the voicemail notification was still visible on my screen, reminding me of the inexplicable call I'd received, and the message I hadn't been brave enough to listen to yet.

Anger swelled in me. I hadn't been brave enough to do a *lot* of things. Like reading my mother's journal, or make sense of all the research I'd done, or...I put my head down. I didn't know what else to do, and I was too afraid to do any of the things I *could* do. So I just sat there, feeling helpless and afraid, and hoping nothing like that would happen again, all the while knowing it would.

When the sun rose, the other two dozed off, but I still couldn't relax enough to rest. I had learned that nothing could protect me anymore. Not being out of the house, not being at Hazel's, not the daylight, nothing. There was something comforting about the sun's rays piercing the room, and I moved into the beams of light, trying to soak up some of their warmth.

But the fear had woven its way into me, burrowed deep, and I was starting to believe that I would never be able to get it out.

Fifteen

After that last encounter, we were having another meeting regarding the haunting. Emily wanted to do another séance, but I still wasn't convinced that was a good idea. So, fresh off our sleepless night in Hazel's house, we gathered in my living room. Now we absolutely had to face that the ghosts were following me. I'd already been suspecting it, and now it was confirmed.

"Emily," I whispered to her, pulling her away from the other three.

"Yes?" she asked, her voice quieter and more serious than I was used to.

"Do you really think...I mean, this whole séance thing might not be the best move, you know? After what happened?"

Emily shook her head. "We're getting to the bottom of this, Roz. I told you I'd get results, and I always keep my promises."

I swallowed hard. There was a fire in her eyes that gave me chills.

"You can't want that grant this much," I said softly.

She looked up at me, so small but so strong, her eyes still intense with whatever fervor was driving her. When she saw my face, her expression softened. She put a hand on my arm and gave a little squeeze.

"The grant...the mystery...the chance to interact with and maybe even help some serious ghosts? I know it's scary, but I can't walk away from this now, Roz. And honestly, neither can you. Maybe the others can, but you're stuck whether you like it or not, and I'm not done until I get some results. I'm not letting you deal with this all alone."

I smiled despite myself, then shook my head, the fear gripping me once more.

"What if we're just making things worse by messing with them?" My voice broke.

"What if we do nothing and someone gets hurt?" Emily countered. Her tone softened then. "Roz, we weren't doing *anything* to provoke the spirits when they attacked at Hazel's house. There's something aggressive out there and if we don't figure out what it is and what to do with it, someone *is* going to get hurt. Not because of you or me, but because the spirits, or whatever these particular entities are...they're angry."

She was right, and I knew it. There was no escaping this, at least not for me.

Unsurprisingly, Nadia had been, "unable to make it in" today, but the house was fine, so I'd told the agency to leave it be for a couple days. With all these séances going on, it was best if we didn't have anyone else around the house.

"What kind of séance should we try today?" Derek asked.

Emily shook her head. "Not sure. I brought a few different things, I still need to...see which one feels right. I did a lot of research after...Hazel's house. I have some ideas."

Emily's voice was strange. Distant, and fiercer than usual. If anything, this had made her more determined than ever, and that scared me almost more than the ghosts did.

Derek and Ford were still excited, but Hazel and Emily understood the reality of it a little better now that they'd experienced it firsthand. Emily still bore the injuries of her attack, and it sobered us. It also reminded me of the beings that had attacked me in my bed. I shuddered at the thought of those cold, metallic bindings digging into my flesh.

"You okay?" Ford asked, coming over to where I sat.

I twitched, looking up at him in alarm. He held his hands up and grinned.

"I come in peace. Sorry. You looked kinda freaked out."

I shook my head, then nodded, not even fully knowing what I was trying to convey.

"No, yeah. I mean, I'm definitely...it was scary, you know?"

"Well, no, I don't know," he admitted, still grinning, though there was something serious in his eyes. I knew he was trying to keep the mood light. "I haven't gotten to experience a firsthand haunting because *someone* never brings the party to me."

I rolled my eyes. "This is the furthest thing from a party."

"Breaking things? Inexplicable injuries? Not getting any sleep? Sounds like a party to me."

I smacked his arm and laughed, despite myself.

"Do you really think this can all be dealt with scientifically?" I asked.

He nodded. "Absolutely. The laws of physics are constant; just because we don't understand them all, or understand them fully, it doesn't mean they're not at work. It also doesn't mean it's not science."

I nodded. I wasn't sure why that comforted me, but it did.

"Besides," he added, "that...*shadow* thing? Looks more like an alien to me."

I raised my eyebrows at him. "Are you gonna start on that again?"

"What? It does!" he said, laughing.

I shook my head. "Nope. I can't deal with aliens, Ford. Ghosts, fine. Demons...I'd really rather not, but whatever. Aliens? No. Aliens will have to wait their turn."

He chuckled. "Hey, I'm just saying, aliens have a lot of potential to actually exist. Statistically speaking, there's no *way* we're the only life in the universe. I mean, our galaxy alone—"

"Are you going to science me some more?" I asked.

"Oh, fine. I'll just summarize: Aliens. They exist."

"Whatever you say, Shirley MacLaine."

Ford laughed. "Who?"

I opened my mouth to explain the reference, but Emily interrupted then.

"All right, we're ready," Emily said. I knew she was afraid, but the ferocity I saw in her impressed me. Hazel looked ready to cut and run, staying only out of Hazel's unique brand of unfailing loyalty. But Emily, despite being terrified, was still committed to this. Even if "this" was utterly absurd.

We gathered around the table and took our seats. Emily overturned a black pouch in the center of the table and a collection of carved stones spilled out.

"What are those?" I asked, indicating the stones with the interesting carvings in them.

"Runestones," Emily said. "They have inherent meanings tied directly to the spirit world. I figure, since we seem to be dealing with an assortment of different languages, something with a meaning beyond our spoken words might be better for communicating with the spirits. They have layers upon layers of meaning, so deciphering what the spirits tell us through them will take a little longer, but it might be easier for the spirits to work with."

"We might not get anything," Derek added. "But it's an option that's easier for spirits to use, and based on the last séance, this could be insightful."

Emily didn't touch the runestones. Instead, she had us grasp hands in the dimly lit room and close our eyes, breathing deeply and slowly.

"I'm curious, why do we have to hold hands?" Ford asked.

"Shh," Emily said, then added. "It helps with energy flow."

Ford gave me a significant look and mouthed the word, "*Energy*."

I rolled my eyes and chuckled.

We listened to her guide us through the opening of the séance, same as last time, and rather than feel silly or crazy, I felt sickly afraid. I still wasn't fully sure what was going on, but I knew I didn't like it. We were long past pretending I was having a nightmare, and there were too many people involved in my hallucinations for them to actually *be* hallucinations, so that theory was out the window.

I tried to concentrate and clear my mind, but it was harder than ever. I was starting to really worry—the ghosts had attacked Emily. I still had no idea why, but they had. They'd come after me, but never so forcefully. It seemed like things were getting worse, not better. I wondered if our meddling really was causing problems. I was afraid what else we'd uncover, especially calling them like this.

"Spirits, we call to you. Speak with us, tell us what you need," Emily said in the same soft, even tone she'd used before.

The candles glowed, the incense spiraled its smoke into the air, and the room was still. Our breathing fell into rhythm, the five of us all following the same pattern. It was actually calming me down, despite how afraid I was of another attack.

We sat in silence for a while before a breeze made the candlelight flicker.

"Welcome," Emily said softly. "Who has joined us?"

There was another soft breeze, more like a gentle sigh, but nothing more happened.

We were silent for a bit longer, then one of the candles winked out. I took a deep, steadying breath. *Stay calm.*

A few clicks alerted me to the runestones moving about on the table. Emily opened her eyes and studied them, brow furrowed. Derek picked up a notepad, marking their movements.

I wished I understood what the runestones meant. What they represented. Emily had explained them as a whole, but I still didn't know what the individual symbols meant.

Whatever spirit was with us now was very concerned with the stones, turning them over, spinning them around, arranging them meticulously. I watched, fascinated, heart hammering in my chest. One of the stones with a sort of X on it had moved to the edge, near me. Another, looking like a crooked cross, scooted closer to the first stone. Last, a piece almost like an F, but bent strangely, rolled over to the other two.

"What's—" I started to ask.

The stones moved wildly, scattered across the table. We all instinctively pulled back, but even breaking the circle didn't stop this presence. The candles went out, and I shivered in the dim light as another chill raced through the room.

"That's...odd," Derek commented, sounding shaken.

The table rose up, then crashed down. We recoiled. Hazel shrieked.

"Emily, what do we do?" I cried.

"I don't know," Emily called back. "This is new. S-spirit, please..."

The whole room shook, drowning out her voice. The trembling knocked things off shelves and threw us flat onto the floor. The table rose up once more, spinning rapidly and flinging the carved stones around the room.

Quiet at first, but growing so loud that it drowned out everything else, was a pulsating, electronic hum. I winced against the bright light that overtook the room as my hands clasped over my ears. I sank to the ground, my head throbbing so badly I thought my skull might have split open.

The room was so awash in light that everything looked white. I could barely see the outlines of the tall, slender figures moving toward me. I scrambled back, screaming, the volume of my own voice surprising me. The howling wind and the cries of the others were still audible, but they were far away, like it was all happening in another room. The electric hum overtook everything else.

The figures before me were pure white. I couldn't see faces or other features—just white outlines barely visible around the light shining off them. They almost reminded me of department store mannequins.

These are not ghosts, I thought in a panic.

Movement in the corner of my eye caught my attention. Derek was moving toward one of the cameras, trying to aim it at me. It seemed like the others weren't seeing these mannequins, but he must have caught sight of them.

One of the mannequin figures waved its hand at Derek, throwing him back and pinning him against the wall, high above the ground.

Someone shouted and the noise of the room became louder again. The mannequin figures seemed to fade, advancing on me like they were suddenly in a hurry. Hazel screamed while Emily shouted her commands to the ghosts, or whatever these were, her voice swallowed up in the rushing wind that filled the room with chaos. I caught sight of Ford, pressed back against the wall, as clueless about the situation as I was.

We are in so far over our heads.

The white beings closed in on me and I squeezed my eyes shut.

"Stop! Please!" I cried. There was nothing I could do. I felt helpless.

My head was throbbing again. The noise of the room, rushing wind and shouting voices, stabbed into my temples like searing hot knives. The electronic hum pounding into my brain grew so intense I could hear nothing else.

I closed my eyes and slammed my fists down on the ground, angry, afraid. "Stop!" I screamed again.

There was a tremendous crash as the table slammed into the ground. Derek, too, fell, dropping from the height of the twelve-foot ceilings with a sickening crash. The room went silent, save for the ringing in my ears. The sudden stillness in the room made my head spin. I was disoriented by the jolting return to normalcy.

"Derek!" Emily screamed.

I stared in horror, wondering for a terrified moment if he'd died. My stomach knotted; first Emily, now this. I was going to get someone killed. Derek groaned and I was immediately relieved. Hazel was already at his side, helping Emily check him over.

"He's hurt, he's bleeding," Emily said. Her voice was shaky, higher than usual.

"Come on, we have to get him to a hospital. Roz, grab my keys," Ford said, bolting up and helping Emily support Derek.

I was frozen, confused. I couldn't seem to get my body to move. My head was still spinning with pain and confusion. What had stopped it? Would it come back? What *was* that?

Ford glanced at me, then came over. He found his keys amidst the mess of scattered items and snatched them up before kneeling beside me.

"Roz? Hey, you still with me here?" he asked gently.

I shook my head and forced myself to focus. Then I nodded. "Yeah. Yeah. I'm okay."

I was beyond confused, but we had a more immediate problem to deal with. Ford helped me up and I climbed shakily to my feet, heading out to the van.

Ford and Emily supported a stunned and injured Derek between them. We helped him out to the van and I struggled to keep my hands from shaking as I unlocked the door.

Ford helped Derek into the back seat, and Emily piled in after him, her face pale and drawn.

Hazel climbed in with them, checking his wounds and comforting Emily more than Derek. I got in the front with Ford, my head still throbbing.

"Shouldn't we call an ambulance?" I asked as I slammed the door.

"There's a hospital real close, it's faster to drive ourselves, trust me," Ford answered.

"Are you speaking from personal experience?" I asked, brushing my hair from my face.

He grinned at me as we pulled away.

The hospital wasn't far. It only took a few minutes to get there. It helped that Ford seemed to know the route perfectly. He cruised right through the roundabout, maneuvering through the many lanes and bringing us up to the emergency entrance with a jolt.

We got Derek inside, and the nurses took him from us. There were a lot of questions, most of which I answered with, "I don't know." My head was hurting so bad I started to cry, and the nurses opted to check me over, too, just in case.

When they decided nothing was wrong with me, they gave me some painkillers and told me I could lay down for a while. Instead, I returned to the waiting room. I didn't want to be alone with my thoughts.

I rejoined the others and waited for the doctors to finish checking over Derek. After a while, I started pacing around the waiting room, somehow hyper and tired at the same time. Now that Derek was okay and things had calmed down, the guilt was starting to set in.

Derek had gotten hurt because of me—I didn't like that. I didn't want anyone suffering or getting into trouble over me.

And moreover, what had *happened* today? Our last séance seemed downright normal now. The things I'd seen today, the same things, I was sure, I'd seen in my room a few days before, didn't fit any ghost lore I'd read of. In fact, they didn't fit *any* stories or myths I'd seen.

Well, that's not entirely true...

I looked at Ford, almost expecting him to read my mind and interject with: "Aliens!"

"It's not aliens," I muttered under my breath.

"What?" Emily asked, glancing up at me.

"Nothing," I said, resuming my pacing.

I circled the waiting room so many times, I expected I'd started to wear a path in the tile. Hazel eventually gave up trying to get me to sit down and relax. Ford went to check on Derek after a while, probably just as much out of boredom as out of concern.

I continued trying to make sense of what I was seeing. The ghosts were confusing enough, but at least I understood them. Kind of. Okay, I didn't really, but they felt more familiar somehow.

These...things...didn't even really fit the style of aliens. They weren't abducting me and taking me to a ship, they were just...*appearing*.

"Alien ghosts?" I whispered, pausing in my pacing.

Now you're just being silly.

"Hey, you okay?" Ford asked as he walked back from the room where Derek was getting treated.

I blinked, looking at him in surprise. I'd almost forgotten where I was. "Yeah, just...is he okay?"

"He's fine. Head injury, minor concussion, broken arm, but the doctors said it's no problem. Nothing for you to worry about," he said tilting his head a little to the side.

Clearly, the look on my face said otherwise, because Ford added, "Seriously, he's completely okay, Roz."

"Yeah...this time...but it could have been so much worse! What if he'd broken his neck, or his back? What if he'd gotten really, really hurt? What if he'd *died*?"

"Roz, hey, that didn't happen, okay?" Ford said, putting a hand on my shoulder.

"But it *could* have," I snapped, knocking his hand aside and pacing again. "And it still might if we keep messing with this stuff."

He nodded, but he didn't say anything.

I ran my hand back through my hair. It occurred to me that Ford didn't know what I'd seen. He hadn't spotted the mannequins. I wondered if they'd showed up on the cameras. I half hoped they had, though part of me would be happy to never see them again.

"You ever read that report I gave you?" Ford asked.

"What? Oh, no, I forgot about that."

I was wearing the same sweater I had been the day of our initial séance, so I pulled the folded paper from my pocket and opened it.

Ford came and looked down at it with me.

There was a lot of information on the page, showing various specifications of the house. It was pretty new, built not four years earlier, and there had only been one family in it before my father and I moved there. I scanned the details until I found the section I was looking for: *Deaths On-Premise.*

I glanced at Ford.

He nodded back at the page.

I looked back and read: *"One death on-premise: Male, age 5."*

I swallowed hard.

"The little boy..." I whispered. "Do we know...how?"

Ford shook his head. "All I know is what I told you before. I didn't see much of that family, since their kids were younger than me. They kept to themselves. Real quiet, even when they were having issues with Joanne."

I folded the paper up again and shoved my hands in my pockets, frustrated.

"Wouldn't you have known a neighbor had died?" I asked, shuffling around nervously.

Ford shrugged. "I feel kinda bad that I didn't know, but...I didn't. None of us did, I don't think. We knew their son was having some health problems, but I didn't realize the kid *died*. I just thought he was sick, you know? And after that they barely came back to the house, they just hired movers and bam, they were gone."

"And when was all that?" I asked.

Ford pointed to the page. "Date's there. Little over a year ago."

I scanned the page once more, then resumed my pacing. "Again, though, this doesn't make sense. I'm seeing an adult man. A-and there was that tattered girl in Hazel's house. And that...monster," I added shuddering. I didn't mention the mannequins. I didn't want to think about them or what they implied.

"Well, everything I know about ghosts I learned over the past few days, so don't look at me," he said, grinning.

His usually contagious smile didn't catch this time. My stomach lurched. A little boy had died in my house. I thought of the crying I sometimes heard from down the hall and wondered if that could be him. I shuddered at the notion.

We had to sit for a long time in the waiting room. Even though it was clean and new, it was still a hospital, and those made me uneasy. I tried to keep myself entertained with my phone, but nothing was holding my attention. Hazel was on her phone, so was Emily. Ford was disassembling some mechanical component he'd had in his pocket, which struck me as odd, but rather fitting for him. I leaned my head back and closed my eyes. I was bored. I was tired. I didn't want to go home, but I didn't want to be in the hospital anymore, either.

I looked at my hand. It had a bandage from breaking the pantry door—the pantry door which had miraculously turned out to be fine—and a few bruises. I had wanted everything to stop. I had wished for it. And...it had.

My brow furrowed as I studied my injury. I had wanted things at the séance today to stop, as well. Again—it had worked.

If I can draw ghosts to me, I wondered, turning the thought over slowly in my mind. *Can I send them away, too?*

That was the first hopeful idea I'd had in a while. I was almost afraid to think it; if I couldn't, I'd go back to feeling helpless and trapped in this impossible situation. But it seemed like I had some kind of power in this whole mess. I just needed to figure out how to use it.

The hospital was cold, so I didn't notice a temperature drop. I picked up on the ghostly presence another way, a way I couldn't quite define. I was just *aware* of it. The little pull of a spirit jostled me, and I sat forward, scanning the room. I caught sight of a man around my father's age wandering the halls. He wore pajamas and a robe, and toted an IV along with him, though when he passed the nurse's station, none of them seemed to notice.

It disturbed me, seeing him there. It made sense that there were ghosts in the hospital, I just didn't like the idea of *seeing* them. My thoughts kept going back to the tattered woman in the theater. I kept my eyes down hoping he wouldn't notice me.

He did, though. When he passed in front of me, he came to a staggering stop. He turned slowly, his unfocused gaze finally settling on me.

Neither of us did anything. The others hadn't seemed to notice, and I couldn't find my voice. I was too afraid to speak, anyway. I didn't want to break the spell and draw some kind of reaction from the ghost.

Maybe I can send them away, the thought echoed in my mind, a fragile little hope that was all I had in this crazy situation. I had no idea how that might work, or how I was drawing ghosts to me in the first place, but I was almost certain that was what had happened at our séance today, and several times before. I took a deep, slow breath and concentrated on the ghost. On the idea of him leaving. I tried to clear my mind, like at the start of the séance, and push him away.

The ghost's eyes never left me, but he began to fade, disappearing entirely to reveal Derek coming down the hall toward us.

"Derek!" Emily said happily, springing up and racing across the waiting room.

I blinked, still caught up in what I'd just done. Derek was coming toward us, his head bandaged and his arm in a cast.

I shook off my possible new ability and stood up, trembling slightly. *Make a mental note of* that, I thought as I forced a smile onto my face.

"Are you okay?" I asked Derek as he joined us.

He nodded. "Yeah, I'm fine. Got my first broken bone—that's something, huh?"

I winced. "I'm so sorry, Derek."

"Hey, it's cool. Most exciting séance we've ever had," he said, looking at Emily. She laughed nervously.

"Man, I'm jealous. I never get any good injuries. I've never even broken anything," Ford said.

I turned to him. "I find that hard to believe."

"No, it's sad but true: As often as I cause trouble, I've never broken a bone. And I want a cast! So bad! I was even in a rollover once and nothing!"

I rolled my eyes and Emily laughed harder.

"Yes, you poor thing," I said to Ford.

"We'll all sign your cast, Derek," Hazel offered.

"Think we can get the ghost to sign it?" Derek asked with a smirk.

"He'll probably break your other arm," Emily pointed out.

"No! Hey, it's my turn!" Ford reminded her.

"We are all crazy," I said, trying to sound annoyed but ruining it with a laugh.

We waited with Derek until his mom came to get him. The hospital wouldn't release him without a parent's signature, and none of us were going to abandon him there.

I took a felt pen from my pocket and let everyone sign the cast. Then I asked Derek if he wanted anything drawn on it. He asked for a dragon, so I occupied myself with that until his mother arrived.

My guilt returned full-force when his mom showed up. We had interrupted her from work, and she had the look of someone who was already overwhelmed by her life. There was something so tired and worn in her eyes. Her drawn face reminded me of my father at the end of my parents' marriage. My gut knotted with shame as I wondered if I'd just added to an already heavy burden.

Derek's demeanor immediately changed with his mother. He became quieter, more withdrawn. He muttered some story about skateboarding that sounded reasonable enough. His mother accepted it without much questioning, which struck me as odd. My father would have had a million questions to follow that up, but Derek's mother seemed mostly concerned with getting out of the hospital.

"Thank you, all of you, for bringing him in," she said to us, sounding rushed and distracted. I nodded, but I couldn't meet her eyes. I should have dealt with this whole ghost thing on my own.

Derek's mother signed a few documents for the hospital. After that, they went home, and Ford drove the rest of us back to my house.

"I think next time we'll have to put up more defenses before we get started," Emily said as we picked up the mess and packed up her equipment.

"Next time?" I asked. "There will be no next time, Emily. We're done with this," I hissed.

She nodded, seeming to measure my words against her response. "I get what you're saying, Roz, but it's not going to stop just because we do."

I shook my head. “I don’t want anyone else getting hurt...”

“Let’s not worry about future séances right now,” Ford cut in gently. “I think we’ve all had enough stress for now. We’re lucky Derek’s in as good of shape as he is. We’ll just...figure it out later, okay?”

That was one point we could all agree on. Emily gathered her things from the house and loaded them into Derek’s car. She hugged me and said goodbye, promising to call soon.

Hazel gave me a tight hug, then drove behind Emily, who was taking Derek’s car to his house for him. Hazel would drive her back to retrieve her own car after. I’d offered to do it, arguing that it’d be less driving for me, but everyone insisted I should rest. I was likely too strung-out to safely drive, but I still felt bad. After they were gone, I stood out on the sidewalk with Ford, trying to recuperate from the afternoon’s events.

“So, anything exciting planned for tonight?” he asked.

I shook my head. “Just trying to avoid ghosts, I guess.” That was a bit of a lie—I had a plan forming, but I didn’t think he’d like my idea, and I didn’t want him trying to interfere.

“Sounds fun,” he said with a smirk. “If you ever need to get out of your haunted house, you can always stop by.”

“Thanks. I might take you up on that,” I said as nonchalantly as I could. “Though the ghosts might just follow me over,” I added.

“My mom wouldn’t have any of that. She'd send them away,” he said, and I laughed weakly.

Ford hung around on my porch until his mother pulled up to the house, home after picking up Ford's younger brother from his day camp. He'd mentioned his brother once, but I hadn't met him yet. As I watched, his mother got a toddler out of the back seat.

"Who's that little kid?" I asked.

"What? Oh, my sister."

"I had no idea you have a little sister."

"Yeah. That's Oops. She's three."

"...'Oops'?" I asked.

"Yeah, she has a real name, but I forgot it."

I gave him a look and he laughed.

"Okay, I didn't forget it. I just never call her that."

"Oops, huh?"

"Well, she was certainly a surprise," he snickered.

I rolled my eyes, but I was laughing.

"I should get home," he said. "My mom wants to cook tonight. She saw something on Pinterest...she means well. Anyway, that means I need to be on stay-by with a fire extinguisher."

"That bad, huh?" I laughed.

"You have no idea," Ford said, shaking his head dramatically.

I waved him off and he jogged across the cul-de-sac and back to his house.

Once he'd disappeared inside, I turned and made my way slowly toward the front door.

I sat on the couch and pulled up the *East/West* website, sifting through the various posts and pages. I found the show's archive and started downloading episodes. I didn't really know why. The show had scared me the first time I'd listened, but as I downloaded the old episodes, I put on my headphones and started listening to the first one.

Chad spent the first episode discussing mentions of paranormal activity in the news. He had a guest on the show and, according to him, the stories that made it into the mainstream media were just a tiny fraction of the paranormal occurrences that were actually happening in the world. He seemed to think they were keeping as much unexplained activity out of the public eye as they could in order to prevent panic.

"Why would they anticipate panic?" Chad asked.

"Because," his guest, a man named Dr. Oswald, answered, "Once the public realizes that these things are happening—regularly, and everywhere—and that we have no way of controlling or stopping these events, they will be very afraid."

"Do you think we should all be a little concerned about this?" Chad went on.

"Not necessarily. While I'm aware that the public would panic, I don't think that's the appropriate response. It's just how large groups of people deal with the unfamiliar."

"Is there any way to avoid mass panic, not only for paranormal events, but just any natural or man-made disasters?"

I scrolled through the pictures on Chad's site. Most were blurry or rather obviously faked. A few, though, stood out. I saved the ones I found interesting.

"None that I've found yet, which is why the government wants to keep these things under wraps."

"And you think these events are all linked in ways we can't see yet?"

There was a forum where others could discuss their alleged ghost/alien/Bigfoot/chupacabra encounters. I clicked on it a bit hesitantly.

"Oh, absolutely," the doctor answered. "There are entire government organizations dedicated to the preservation of these lies."

Chad chuckled, though not unkindly. "Like Men In Black?"

"Not quite. Hollywood tends to take these things and twist them into unbelievable drivel for their own purposes. Honestly, I suspect it might be to make these ideas sound so outrageous that we become desensitized and disregard anything resembling it. It'd be a great cover—make a mockery of a serious idea so the public can no longer take it seriously. That's why—"

"Roz?"

I almost fell off the sofa in my alarm. My father was standing beside me, smiling a little guiltily at me.

I pulled one of my earbuds away. "Sorry," I said. "You startled me."

"I was trying not to," he said. "What are you listening to?"

"Just some podcasts," I said, pausing the show and pulling my other earbud free.

"So," my dad asked. "What did you do today?"

I blinked at him. I'd always had a good relationship with my dad, so hiding things from him didn't come naturally to me. I didn't even *want* to hide things from him, but half the time, I just had no idea what to say. Most of what was happening didn't even make sense to me, so how could I possibly explain it to him?

"Um...just hung out. With Hazel. And Emily," I said.

My dad watched me, and I wondered if he was trying to decide if I was lying or not.

"Sounds fun," he finally said. "Anything else...strange...happen?"

I shook my head. "No. Pretty quiet day." The lie twisted in my stomach, like I'd swallowed a live snake.

He nodded, though I wasn't sure I'd convinced him.

"Well, I'm glad," he said. "It...feels like you've had kind of a rough transition with the move."

I chuckled, trying to keep things light. "I guess it could have been a little smoother, huh?"

My dad nodded, then cleared his throat. "I, um, did some research on exorcists today."

I blinked. "You did?"

"Yeah. If you still think we might need one..."

I was silent for a moment. I had told my friends he'd been humoring me on considering exorcists, and here he was talking about possibly getting one. I wasn't sure if I liked the idea or not, and I still didn't know if my father was just doing this to ease my mind. He didn't tend to believe very much in...well, anything.

He put his hand on my shoulder and squeezed. "You don't have to answer now. I just want you to know that if you feel like this is something we need to do, then, well, I'll take care of it."

I nodded. "Okay. Thanks, Dad."

I didn't mention ghosts or exorcists for the rest of the night, but I thought about them every second, and the possibility that I might have more power in this situation than I'd thought.

SIXTEEN

I sat on my bed, trying to clear my mind and breathe evenly, or whatever it was you were supposed to do when meditating. I wasn't quite sure if meditating was the right approach, but my Aunt Fiona insisted it was always the best thing to do, and Emily's séances kind of reminded me of meditation, so I'd decided to give it a shot.

After sitting for what felt like "long enough", which I had no real way of gauging, I opened my eyes and exhaled slowly. It all seemed a little over-dramatic, but it also seemed fitting.

This is stupid, I thought.

Don't be negative, I reprimanded myself.

Oh my God, don't argue with yourself.

I put my head in my hands. This wasn't working. Unless "working" constituted "confirming my suspicion that I was losing my mind." Then it was working *great.*

Sitting up straight, I slowed my breathing and tried again. Part of my problem was that I didn't know *what* I was trying to do. I had some ideas, but I hadn't decided on which to work with. So I picked one, and it was stupid, and I knew it was stupid, but I did it anyway.

I decided to try to summon a ghost.

Summoning a ghost seemed risky, but it was a good way to test this potential ability I might have. I considered all the ghosts I'd encountered. Most were horrifying, and the idea of calling them to me on purpose made me shiver.

Then I remembered the foreign ghost. He hadn't been so scary. He'd startled me a few times, but he'd never done anything malicious or violent. In fact, he hadn't done *anything*, really, except say that weird word. He didn't feel threatening or ominous, just...lost. In need of help. It made me sad, thinking of him. If I saw him, maybe I could help him. Or at least figure out what he was trying to say.

Focusing on the idea of the ghost, I closed my eyes and tried to push all other thoughts aside. I envisioned him as best as I could, concentrating on what I remembered. The way his presence filled the room, the rasp in his voice as he spoke, the soft fragrance that filled the air when he came around.

Nothing happened. This was frustrating. I flopped back on my bed and rubbed at my eyes. *Try again.*

I put one hand over my eyes and made another attempt at drawing the ghost to me. Nothing happened, but whenever I got discouraged, I remembered the séances, and how long it usually took for something to happen. *Calm down. Let go.*

A shiver ran down my spine as my stomach jolted and twisted. The change in the temperature of the room confirmed it. I sat up, finding him immediately.

"H-hello," I whispered.

He stared at me. I stared back. He was clearer than I'd ever seen him before—tall and thin, olive skin and light brown hair. I couldn't quite make out his features, but I felt the intensity of his eyes on me.

"Can you talk to me?" I asked.

He held my gaze, and I caught another whiff of that fragrance that always seemed to follow him. I'd smelled it before, but I couldn't place it.

Okay, time to test out the rest of this ability.

I fixed my gaze on him and concentrated on sending him away. The question of *where* I was sending him to popped up, but I pushed it out of my mind. There was no time to worry about that; I had to learn if this was real.

He started toward me, slowly, but not menacingly, almost as if he was afraid to startle me. My stomach still did a little flip anyway. His eyes were becoming clearer as he drew closer, but I concentrated, the same way I had in the hospital. Slowly, he faded, disappearing just as he reached the edge of my bed. As soon as he was gone, I fell back on my bed, shaking, heart hammering. I pulled a pillow to my chest and hugged it, uncertain why that had freaked me out so bad.

I obviously needed more practice, but I wasn't quite ready to try again, so I opened my computer. I was getting better at finding real information, even if piecing it all together still gave me a headache.

For background noise, I switched on Chad's show. It somehow made me feel less alone. The information provided wasn't usually all that useful, though. Then I did what had become a nightly ritual; I searched the internet for anything that could explain what was happening to me.

Interestingly, the problem wasn't a lack of information—it was *too much* information. There were more theories and explanations than I could process, and each one more ridiculous than the last. Aliens and ghosts all had lots of support from the good people of the internet. So did lizard people, hollow earth, and government conspiracies, to name a few.

"...In reality, these events are very logical and predictable. We just don't know how to follow the patterns. A lot of events seem paranormal and inexplicable, but are actually just the result of electromagnetism, alternating frequencies, and other perfectly measurable activity," a woman said. Her voice was low and confident, the kind of voice that sounded absolutely sure of everything.

"What if we could figure out a way to track those patterns?" Chad asked. "Do you have any methods you use for predicting paranormal events?"

I laid back on my bed, unable to look at anymore sites, and just listened to the interview.

The guest chuckled. "Unfortunately, no. While I know the patterns are traceable, I also understand that, from the third dimension, we simply can't comprehend them."

"Are you saying we'd have to be in another dimension to understand what's happening when we have things like ghosts or mystical creatures appearing in our world?"

I frowned. Something about that concept made me open my eyes and glance at my computer screen, like maybe it would suddenly have the answers.

"Somewhat," the guest answered. "It's not necessarily another dimension, so much as a higher or lower dimension. There's much more intermingling between the dimensions than we realize. Spirits and some of those 'mystical creatures' you mentioned tend to slip into our dimension from lower dimensions. We move between them relatively often, but as our society has no way to officially measure or track this yet, we don't recognize it. That's what my research has been about."

I was sitting up now, staring at my screen. It was just my music player. I clicked the track I was on for more info. It was called "EastWest-Ep-117_DrFallon _Dimensions".

I froze. I remembered Chad talking about this interview—I'd recognized Dr. Fallon's name and flipped through her book that night, but I'd forgotten by the next morning. Her book had seemed so over my head and out of place that I'd all but written it off. But hearing her on the show made me reconsider.

The book was still on my nightstand, under my mother's journal. I pulled both to me, setting the journal aside. I should probably open it one of these days, but I wasn't ready yet. I had been so careful to avoid having any contact with her, it seemed counterintuitive to read something she'd written now, even if it might help me.

Dr. Fallon's book was extremely scientific and mathematical. I didn't even think Ford would get most of it. Curious, I flipped to the back of the book. There was a color photo of the author on the back-jacket flap, with a small bio underneath. I blinked in surprise at the picture—Rowan Fallon was younger than I'd expected. Prettier, too. I had imagined someone older; frumpy and stern, but this woman looked around my dad's age. She had long, fiery red hair and piercing blue eyes. Something about her expression freaked me out. It was like she knew too much.

Her bio was short. It read:

> *Dr. Rowan Fallon earned her degree in Physics from Princeton University at age sixteen. She then studied at Yale, earning a PhD in Mathematics, and MIT, completing a Masters in Engineering. She has published seven books, taught at Stanford, and given lectures around the world for some of the most prestigious scientific conferences in existence. Dr. Fallon has spoken to world leaders about global affairs and how her research can change the course of human history. She lives in Cambridge, Massachusetts, and teaches at Harvard University.*

I frowned. Not much personal information in that bio. Mostly it was about her professional and scholarly achievements. But then, I supposed, it wasn't too unusual; clearly this was important to her. Maybe she was just private. A little self-important, too—"change the course of human history" sounded a bit lofty to me, but I guess we all have our dreams.

Turning back to the book itself, I went through the chapter titles again. *The Science of Alternate Dimensions* was one of them.

On the show, she'd specifically talked about ghosts, and the idea of having a scientific explanation made my heart race. Could this be what was going on? What Ford had been talking about?

I read the chapter carefully, sometimes reading a passage two or three times before understanding them. More than once, I would reread a line several times only to give up and move on. I wasn't an expert on geniuses, but I was relatively certain they weren't kidding when they said this Rowan woman was one.

The gist of the chapter was that multiple dimensions existed—possibly infinite dimensions—and while some of those dimensions could be incredibly similar to our own, others were drastically different. Rowan theorized that many of the inexplicable phenomena we experienced were the result of overlap or intermingling between the dimensions.

The chapter ended without saying much more on the subject, other than explaining some mathematical principles that would apparently prove the existence of other dimensions. I would have to take her word for it.

Closing the book, I ignored my mother's journal and turned instead to the internet. Maybe Rowan had more information about dimensions on her site or YouTube or something. When I typed her name in and hit "search", I found plenty about her online—articles by her, articles about her, videos of lectures and TEDTalks and interviews. To the right of the screen, a series of professional pictures showcased Rowan's striking face, telling me some little tidbits. She was born on a farm in Wichita, she was thirty-eight years old, and she *must* be a genius, because she had completed both PhDs and the Master's degree before she was twenty-five. At my age, she'd already completed one PhD and was teaching graduate courses in physics. For some reason her IQ was unknown, but it was estimated to be at least 190.

One headline caught my eye, towards the very top under the 'In the news' section. It read, "Rowan Fallon Refuses Comment on Leaving Department Head Job at Harvard to Move to Las Vegas". The article confused me. It was relatively recent, and the mention of Las Vegas made me curious. I clicked the link and watched the page load, frowning at the big picture of Rowan standing at a podium that filled my screen. She was actually pretty, but her features and expressions were so serious it was hard to appreciate her beauty at first glance. I was almost surprised she'd achieved the kind of celebrity status she had; usually, celebrities were personable, but she seemed intimidating. Harsh.

A quick skim of the article revealed that Rowan had resigned from her very prestigious post at Harvard, canceled an upcoming international book tour and several speaking engagements, withdrawn from an appearance on *The Late Show*, and moved to Las Vegas. And, stranger still, this had happened just a week after my father and I moved to town. Rowan had announced that she would be working at the University of Nevada, Las Vegas starting in the fall, though for the summer, it seemed like she was just doing some light research, and not taking on any classes or students. When asked what inspired the move, she'd declined comment and said it was for "personal reasons". She had even halted several projects, including an upcoming book and a research proposal she'd been putting together.

I frowned. Now *that* was all odd. Why would she essentially dump her career and everything she'd clearly worked so hard to create just to jet out to the desert? UNLV wasn't a bad school, but it certainly wasn't *Harvard.*

Sidetracked by this news, I spent a good twenty minutes looking for the most up-to-date information about Rowan and what had caused her move. Something about the move itched at the back of my mind, and I knew full well what it was: the timing. Rowan had moved just one week after we had. And it sounded like she had built her career around studying the very things that were happening to me.

I gnawed on my nails as I read yet another article that stated the utter bewilderment at the scientific community regarding Rowan's actions. No one could get an answer from her, she just kept citing "personal reasons" and refusing to comment further.

Frustrated with that, I clicked back to her research. It took a long time to sift through everything I'd found. Rowan wrote a lot about dimensions, and I didn't have time to read twenty-five years' worth of work.

As I read, I took notes on my phone. I was going to have to make sense of all this somehow, and the only way to do that was to check what I had been experiencing against what this expert in the field had discovered.

According to Rowan, she had found evidence of other dimensions. She had gone on about resonance and harmonic frequencies, all of which sounded more musical than scientific to me, but apparently it proved beyond the shadow of a doubt—at least to her—that other dimensions not only existed, but were accessible. Movement between the dimensions, she theorized, would take tremendous amounts of concentrated, directed energy. It was dangerous, she said, because it could easily go wrong and become harmful to large populations. This was why, despite believing she knew the formulas to make dimensional travel possible, no actual experiments had been done. I was honestly surprised she hadn't pushed for an experiment despite the danger; after reading her studies, journals, research papers, and articles for over two hours, it was obvious to me that Rowan wanted nothing more than to visit other dimensions. Or at least, to know *how*.

I sighed and sat back, drumming my fingers on my laptop. Was that what was happening? Was I experiencing some kind of...dimensional shift? The idea scared me more than ghosts had, but it seemed to make sense, too. According to Rowan, ghosts and everything like that were just energy signatures operating on another dimensional plane. I smirked to myself—thinking that sentence made me feel brainy.

I thought of the spirits haunting me; the girl in the theater, and the foreign ghost, and the whispers. The mannequins and the way they'd seemed so different from the ghosts, yet had appeared and disappeared in almost the same way.

I remembered Hazel's kitchen, and whatever attacked Emily. I remembered breaking glass that later was unbroken, holding an object in my hand that was later back on the counter, and the searing, raging headache that had overwhelmed me as we wandered through Hazel's too-dark house.

I glanced at my phone. My voicemail app still bore the little red "1" to remind me that I had not yet listened to that mysterious message.

My fingers brushed the journal, tracing the insignia on the cover. There were answers in there. My mother had known *something*, and more and more I was convinced that her madness, at least some of her madness, had not been true insanity. What if she'd been going through this, too? What if she'd seen the things I was seeing now? My mind drifted to her, and what it would be like to talk to her, to ask her for help.

No. She'd made her decisions and I'd made mine. There was no repairing the damage done; I'd get through this, and I'd get through it without her help.

I snatched up the journal and stuffed it into my nightstand drawer. I could solve this on my own.

SEVENTEEN

The next evening, I agonized over what I was going to wear. This wasn't something I usually worried about, but tonight was an exception: My dad had invited Veronica over for dinner.

It wasn't a date; he'd been very clear about that. He'd actually invited her and her brother Victor over, as well, to make it even less date-y. But Victor had canceled last minute, so now it was just Veronica. An awkward dinner with even less buffer between "old friends getting together" and "dinner where I meet my dad's new girlfriend". He'd deny it, but that's what it was. My dad liked her. She was a model. And if I was going to have any semblance of control tonight, I was going to have to really *feel* like I was in control. And that meant looking the part.

An insane thing to worry about, what with having just

sent Derek to the hospital yesterday, but such was life.

Hazel was there to help me pick out an outfit. She sat on my bed while I dug through my closet, proclaiming over and over that I had absolutely nothing to wear.

"Why are you stressing over this so much?" Hazel asked, going over some of my sketches. The batch she had was of the ghosts and other apparitions I'd been seeing. Drawing them soothed me somehow.

"Because, the woman is a model," I said, which wasn't actually an explanation, but I didn't know what else to say.

Hazel looked at me, raising her eyebrows. "So? It's not like you're competing with her."

"No, I know, but...I just...I want to put my best foot forward."

"You want to out-do her because you're competitive and controlling," she said, snickering and looking back at my sketches.

"Hey! I'm not controlling..." I argued, abandoning my search for a moment to turn and face her.

Hazel laughed. "Not all the time, but you can be. You like to have a handle on things, everyone knows that. It's why you—" she stopped, looking like she'd done something wrong.

It took me a moment to realize why: She'd been about to say something to the effect of, "That's why you're so upset over this whole thing with your mom." I returned to my search, trying to pretend that I hadn't noticed what she was saying.

"Oh hush, you're a super-perfectionist," I said lightly, trying to brush the whole thing aside. I didn't want Hazel to feel bad, and I didn't want to think about the implications of what she'd almost said. I was avoiding a lot of uncomfortable thoughts lately.

"I am," she said quietly. I glanced at her and saw how tired she looked. Was she having the same stress and sleep problems I had been ever since she'd been exposed first-hand to the ghosts?

I finally settled on a pair of slacks and a nice blouse. "This will work, right?" I asked.

Hazel went back to examining the sketches, but she had a far-away look, like she wasn't really paying attention to me. "It's fine, Roz. You'll look great. Are you done being ridiculously weird now?"

"No," I said. "I need to figure out what to do with my hair."

Hazel burst out laughing. "Okay, that's it, I'm getting out of here. I've never seen you freak out this much over how you're dressing. It's weirding me out."

I wanted to tease her, but I hadn't slept much in the past three days, so I couldn't think of anything witty to say.

"Sure, sure, run off. Leave me here to fend for myself."

She chuckled weakly. I recognized the weariness on her face. Hazel had the same hesitation about going home that I'd been suffering through since moving here. I hoped she'd be okay.

"All right, see you later," I said, waving her off.

"Have fun getting to know the *other woman*," Hazel said dramatically.

"I doubt it," I replied.

She left and I studied my reflection, trying to decide what was wrong with my look. All I knew was that I seemed off. I was not looking forward to this dinner—not one bit.

Before Veronica arrived, my phone buzzed. I pulled it out of my pocket, remembering the eerie call from before, and the voicemail I *still* hadn't checked. It was just Emily, though. I'd asked her to send me the pictures from the second séance. I'd told her to look for something white.

She'd sent them, along with a text: *Hey, this is all I've got. Not much to go off.*

I scrolled through the pictures, disappointed to find that she was right. The only pictures containing anything white were lens flares that made the entire image fade to almost nothing. There were no photographs of the mannequin things I'd seen. I frowned at my phone.

:/ OK thanks!

She sent a collection of dessert emojis as a response and I laughed.

Veronica arrived as I was making my way down the stairs. She greeted my dad with a hug and a kiss on the cheek. She was all tall and modely and annoyingly perfect.

"Rosalind," she said, smiling as I reached them. "It's so great to see you again."

I accepted her hug in the least-awkward way I could manage. "Yeah, you too."

We sat down, and a heavy tension settled over the table. The food smelled delicious, all laid out and ready to serve. My dad had ordered from some catering service. We were officially out of ready-made meals, and he wanted something more impressive than chicken and rice.

"So, Rosalind, how do you like Las Vegas so far?" Veronica asked.

"I like it. We used to come here often, so it's not too weird, but it's still been, uh...an adjustment." That was an understatement.

She nodded. "Do you like it better than Los Angeles?"

"Yeah, I guess so."

"It's better for work, that's for sure," my dad said. "I'm glad I don't have to fly out here every week for two or three days. That was exhausting."

"Sounds like it," Veronica said.

"Yeah, but now you fly from here to Chicago," I pointed out.

My dad shrugged. "True. But that's just this one case. Hopefully, I won't have to do any more of that for a while."

Veronica nodded. "So, what cases are you working on now?"

My dad chuckled and gave her a little half-grin. "I honestly can't say anything about it. It's a very high profile, dangerous case, actually. I'm not at liberty to discuss any of the details until a resolution is reached."

I looked over at my dad, curious again. He had mentioned it before, but I still didn't know much about it. Just that cases like this usually meant trouble.

"So, you have dangerous clients?" Veronica seemed impressed. I rolled my eyes. Who likes that sort of thing?

"Well, I do deal with some very high stakes. Fortune 500 companies, entire empires; when something that big is hanging in the balance, people can get crazy."

Veronica looked even more captivated. I started serving myself so I could look like I was doing something other than rolling my eyes at them.

I wanted to tune them out, but I was also tempted to listen in. I wanted clues on a few things, such as how serious this relationship...thing...might become. Also, what the heck was my dad working on? That was what really caught my attention.

"So, Veronica, you're a model?" I interjected, not looking up from my plate.

"I am, yeah," she said, smiling.

"How'd you get into that?" I asked, trying to keep things light, but also trying to get dirt on her so I could sit there and fester in silence some more. I knew it was stupid, but I couldn't stop myself. I was all out of energy—I was running on irritation and bitterness at this point.

She laughed lightly, but I could tell my attempted nonchalance didn't fool her. She knew what I was up to.

"Well," she said with a smile, "I was in college when I got into it. I got a part-time modeling job, and it seemed like a good way to pay the bills while I was completing my degree. After I finished school, I was making good money, getting to travel, and enjoying my modeling work, so I kept it up."

"Huh, that's cool," I said. I actually thought it was sad, giving up a life-long dream just because she could get by on her looks. That had to feel empty somehow.

She nodded and brushed her hair behind her ears. She didn't seem at all fazed by me or my thinly-veiled attitude, and that kind of bothered me, too.

I knew I was being ridiculous. I knew I was exaggerating the whole thing, but that didn't make me any less mad. Actually, it made me angrier. Here she was, enjoying her night, and I was stewing for no good reason. As if I wasn't frustrated enough after the week I'd had.

"Are you excited about starting a new school in the fall?" Veronica asked me.

"I guess so," I said. "I already know a bunch of my classmates, so it shouldn't be a big deal."

"Well that's good," Veronica said, sipping her wine.

I noticed a bit of bandage peeking out from her sleeve. There was a tiny spot of blood on it. I wondered how she'd gotten hurt. I couldn't see this girl doing extreme sports or, well, anything that might break a nail.

Speaking of which, her nails weren't manicured, either. I mean, they were clean and everything, but it was just her natural nail, clipped pretty short, with a bit of clear polish or buffed to shine or something. I also thought that was weird; I'd met my fair share of models when we lived in Beverly Hills. Every woman even associated with modeling had their nails finely manicured. Maybe Veronica played an instrument or something. I was pretty sure, at this point, that I was just *looking* for things to be wrong with her, but I couldn't stop myself.

She caught my eye from across the table, and smiled, but I had the feeling that she knew I'd been analyzing her. It made me uncomfortable. I looked away, pretending to be surveying the food.

The rest of the dinner went pretty well, aside from the fact that I got irritated every time Veronica spoke. I decided to blame the sleep deprivation.

After dinner, we had coffee and sat on the sofa, talking. Or rather, my dad and Veronica talked, and I stared into my mug, trying to ignore them.

My dad wanted to know everything she'd been up to, everywhere she'd gone, what she liked best about her job. He just kept asking her questions, and the weirdest part was how intently he listened to her answers. Every now and then, he'd pull me into it, relating her and I to one another with something like, "Oh, Rosalind read that book last summer," or "You took dance lessons, too, remember, Roz?" I would smile tightly and nod, and they would return to their conversation.

I was honestly a little relieved that talking to her had my dad so wrapped up, because it meant he didn't notice my lack of engagement. On the other hand, if he weren't so interested in her, she'd have probably gone home by now, and I could get back to...well, to be fair, I wasn't doing much but thinking about ghosts lately, but at least I'd be able to do that in some peace if Veronica weren't here.

My dad got up to fix another cup of coffee for himself and Veronica. He offered me more, but I shook my head, mumbling something about caffeine.

I zoned out a little, staring at this old clock my dad has owned since before I was born. The second hand ticked around and around, mesmerizing me.

My trance was broken when the second hand slowed, then stopped. An unwelcome but all-too familiar pressure built in my skull.

No. No. Go away.

"It's a little cold in here," Veronica said, shivering. I glanced at her, unsure what to say. She was trying to fill the silence, but I was listening, breathlessly waiting for what came next.

Veronica sat in front of the wide, floor-to-ceiling

windows that spread the entire back wall of the living room. She watched me, curious, and I wasn't surprised. I must have looked pretty freaked out.

"Rosalind?"

I didn't respond.

"Rosalind? Are you okay?"

Something was breathing on the glass behind Veronica. The window fogged in a little circle, which faded away, only to come back.

Go away, go away, I thought, but it didn't seem to be working.

Veronica turned around when I didn't answer her second inquiry, following my gaze.

I could see the shadow of a face forming behind the breath.

"Who is...?" Veronica said, rising from her seat a bit and turning to face the apparition. I wasn't sure how much she could see, but her eyes were alert, face serious, like she was sizing something up.

The face breathing on the window had taken a more solid form, though it was still a bit translucent. It was an old woman, and her eyes, black and empty, were fixed on me. I locked my gaze on hers and tried to keep my heart from racing. I needed to concentrate. I needed to make her go away.

She watched me for a moment, then started fading until she was gone. I couldn't tell if that was from my own effort, or if she'd just left.

For an instant, we were both silent. The room started to warm up, and a soft *tick* alerted me that the clock on the wall was working again.

I tore my eyes away from the last spot I'd seen the old

woman and looked at Veronica. She was tense, serious, but...oddly calm. I frowned.

"Did you see that?" she asked, turning to me, eyes narrowed.

I stared at her.

"I don't know, what did you see?" I asked.

"I thought I saw..." she said. She shook her head and ran her hand through her hair. Veronica gave a little laugh and sat back down. "Whoo, that was weird. I must be jittery from the coffee."

I didn't say anything. I couldn't. A moment later, my dad returned with the coffee, and Veronica put her smile back on as they continued chatting.

I was no longer foggy and unfocused. Veronica had my full attention, and in a whole new way.

Had she seen ghosts before? She'd seemed pretty surprised, but I'd seen them before and they still got me every time.

Maybe she'd just been shocked. Maybe she wasn't the delicate, prissy little thing I'd assumed. Even so, I thought the way she was handling it was unnerving. She was too...steady. It threw me off.

I was beyond tired when Veronica finally left, and I had concluded that I was more tired than I was afraid. I was getting some sleep tonight, I didn't care what else the ghosts did. Besides, there was a possibility I could shoo them away now, so if any showed up, I'd use them as practice. I changed into comfortable clothes and called Hazel immediately.

"Well?" Hazel asked when she answered.

"There was a ghost."

"*What?*" Hazel demanded.

I flopped onto my bed, closing my eyes. "Yeah...some old lady breathing on the window. It was weird. But you know what was really weird? *Veronica*."

"What do you mean?" Hazel asked.

"She saw it, too, and she..." I shook my head. "She wasn't nearly as freaked out as she should have been."

"I'll say again: What do you mean?"

I rolled over so I was on my back. "She just...she jumped up, like she was going to *do* something. I don't know, it was unnerving."

"Did the old lady do anything?"

I closed my eyes. "No. She just...looked at me." I opened my eyes then. I could still see her face so clearly. I pondered whether to mention my newfound ability to Hazel, but I decided against it. I still didn't fully understand it, and discussing it with the whole group felt more like the thing to do. Once I had something concrete to discuss.

"Sounds creepy," Hazel allowed. "But other than that, how was your dinner?"

"Eh. I don't like her, Haze."

"Of course you don't like her, Roz, you never gave her a chance."

"It doesn't matter. I'm right, she's no good, and she's just trying to get money out of my dad because she's a gold-digger. She's so completely...it's creepy! Me being bratty? Nothing. Ghosts in the yard? *Nothing*. The whole night, she was cool as a damn cucumber."

Hazel laughed some more. "Who even uses that phrase anymore?"

"I do," I said indignantly, mostly because I was still annoyed and there was nothing I could do about it.

"That sounds like something Grandma would say."

"It probably is," I said, cooling off a bit.

"So, you hate her, huh?"

I sighed, sitting up. "I don't *hate* her, but...I'm not particularly fond of her, either. The thought of her being around...bugs me. I don't want them to become some kind of 'item'. It'd be weird. He swears there's nothing there, but...I dunno. I hope not."

"I'm sorry, Roz," she said, sounding genuinely sad for me.

"Yeah, well, I'm okay. I guess. It'll be fine. I just need some sleep."

We said goodbye and I tossed the phone aside on my bed, flopping back. I was so tired. I just wanted to sleep, but all I could think of was my mom.

I don't even know how to describe my mom. She was selfish. Everything was always about her. It's not the kind of thing that I can say to my dad. He's still hurting over what happened. I know he thinks the same of her that I do, but he's not ready to speak ill of her. Or maybe he just doesn't want to talk to me about it. He probably doesn't want to put my mother down in front of me.

I tried for a long time to make her happy. My dad did, too, but you can't make someone happy when they completely refuse to accept it. She'd been diagnosed, seen a dozens of different doctors, been prescribed all kinds of different medications, but it didn't matter. She made up stories about all of her doctors—why they were quacks, why they could never help her, how they didn't care about her, just their paychecks. She refused to take her pills. She ran off sometimes, disappearing for days at time, coming home with no memory of where she'd been.

Even when she wasn't going off the deep end, she was difficult. Temperamental, demanding, insistent on getting her way, and with a strange talent for making it seem like she was always right. And always the victim.

I hate her for what she did to my dad. I would hear them fight. She had this uncanny ability to turn everything around so it was the other person's fault. She would twist and manipulate everything, and every fight would end with my dad feeling miserable and defeated. When I got older, she started doing the same thing to me. Honestly, a small part of me really had wanted her gone, I just didn't realize how much it would hurt to have her actually leave us.

My dad said I needed to forgive her. He said it was for me, to help me heal, but I didn't think I would ever be able to. He didn't push the matter and I didn't bring it up.

The hardest part of it, though, was that I could still find a million ways to blame myself. I knew none of this was my fault, I knew she was crazy and selfish and manipulative and cruel, but I still found myself missing her. No matter how awful someone is, you can still make good memories with them, and love them, and miss them. I was attached to my mother, I loved her, despite all her flaws. No matter what, she was my *mom*. So I still found myself thinking of how I could have done more to keep her around.

And the truth was, she *wasn't* all bad. My mother was exciting and creative. She had a habit of going far out of her way to do something to make you happy. I distinctly remembered once, after a doctor's visit that made me cry, she'd driven all around town to find me the particular ice cream I wanted, just so I would feel better.

When they were happier, she and my dad would often joke around. My dad has a kind of dry humor, but my mother could be downright silly. Sometimes, she would team up with me to prank my dad. Like once while he was away, she got an old, broken keyboard, put seeds in it and tended them so the keyboard grew all this grass, then switched it with the one in his office. He'd been utterly bewildered when he got home and we'd had a good laugh about it.

I snickered, remembering that, then wiped at my cheeks. I realized I was welling up, tears stinging my eyes and choking me, even around my amusement. My stomach churned. I curled up on my bed and took several deep breaths, forcing the tears down. I didn't want to cry over her, not anymore.

It wasn't that she was completely horrible, it was that she was so wonderful and so terrible all at once. I could see why my father had loved her. I loved her. I just hated what she became. I hated how she could hurt me so deeply. I hated not having answers.

I drew my blankets around myself and tried to sleep. Outside my window, a little light flicked on, as Joanne took to painting. I watched her, wondering what memories she was trying to escape tonight.

EIGHTEEN

I watched Joanne until I started drifting off, but I was pulled from my near-slumber by a jolt of energy that woke me up. It was like the ghost at the hospital—I didn't know how I knew he was there, I just knew. I was certain it was a ghost, now, too, even without knowing how.

At this point, I didn't know whether to be scared or just irritated. I had been so close to actually slipping off, and I had really been hoping to get some rest.

I sat up slowly, looking around the dark room.

Then I heard it: a familiar sound that made the hair on the back of my neck stand up.

It wasn't the foreign ghost, it didn't speak. Nor was it the tattered girl, who never made a sound. This was the sobbing, pitiful whimpers that came from down the hall.

My heart was hammering, my palms sweaty. A lump had appeared in my throat out of nowhere.

I am so sick of this.

I slammed my hands down on my bed and got up, marching out into the hall. These ghosts were working on my last nerve. I didn't bother with a weapon—this was a ghost, no earthly weapon would protect me. I'd see who it was and banish them. Hopefully.

I made my way to the guest bedroom, where the sobbing sound was loudest. I wasn't sure what I was going to do, but I had a couple options. I could try to send it away, like I had the others. Or I could see if it was calm enough have a conversation with. Emily had said something about talking to ghosts and helping them with their journey, so what could it hurt to try? Besides, I had gone so long without sleep that I wasn't even sure if this was an actual ghost encounter or genuine a hallucination.

My breath came in shaky, uneven gasps, but I forced myself forward. I turned on the light and stepped into the room.

It was neat and tidy, largely from no one using it. Everything was in its place, even the boxes that weren't unpacked yet were stacked in an orderly fashion. At first, I saw nothing, but the crying continued. Despite my earlier bravado, fear spiked in me again, constricting my insides until they hurt. Maybe it was the old woman from before, but I doubted it.

The weeping came from the other side of the bed. Slowly, feeling like my knees might give out at any moment, I made my way toward the sound.

There he was. A little boy, curled up in a ball. He wore dark blue pajamas, with stars and spaceships and little planets all over them. He had tan skin and dark hair, almost as dark as Hazel's. The child was crying too hard to notice me. Every now and then, he flickered, like a TV during a storm.

My pounding heart made it hard to breathe, but I forced myself to stand my ground.

One death on-premise: Male, Age 5.

So. This was the child who'd died in my house. I couldn't bring myself to will him away. It felt wrong. Instead, I looked around the room. Had this been his before? Had he died right here? How? Why? Was it the sickness, or something else? Something more sinister?

The tiny part of my brain that wasn't consumed by fear ached for him. Ghosts were often just as terrified by their predicament as the living. And sometimes they didn't even know they were dead.

Struggling to maintain my composure, I knelt down. "H-Hey..."

The boy twitched and looked over at me, still trembling and sniffling.

"Hey, are you okay?" I asked, making my voice as soft and steady as I could.

He stared at me for a moment, then wiped his eyes.

"I—I'm lost," he said. "I can't find my parents..."

Fear gave way to sadness as I watched him rub his teary eyes.

"Well, um, maybe I can help you." I had no idea if I could, and I didn't want to make a promise I couldn't keep, but he was just so pitiful.

"Really?" he asked, looking up at me.

"I'll try. I'm Rosalind, what's your name?"

"Diego," he said.

"It's nice to meet you, Diego. Do you have any idea where your parents might be?"

He shook his head, pulling at a loose thread on his pajama sleeve.

It was bizarre, watching him. He looked like a little boy, but a bit translucent. He was flickering less and less now, but he'd still fade out of focus now and then. It broke my heart to think he'd died so young. I wanted to know more, but I couldn't bear to ask him when he was so upset.

"Well, we can look for them together. I have some friends who will probably know what to do. We can call them in the morning. And for now, you can stay here, okay?"

"Okay. Your parents won't mind?"

"Nah. As long as you don't interrupt my dad during business calls."

He nodded.

"Do you know how you got here?"

"I don't know...I think this...I thought this was my house, but it's different now..."

I frowned. I didn't know how to explain that. He didn't realize he was a ghost, and the idea of telling a person they were dead was entirely too creepy for me to entertain.

"Well, we'll figure that out in the morning," I said. "Why don't you go to sleep for now?"

He climbed into the bed. He was more corporeal now. Had I not seen him translucent and flickering earlier, I'd have thought he was a regular little boy. But it wasn't just what I could see, it was what I could *feel*—his presence in the room grew stronger. I wasn't even sure how I could tell.

"Oh, hold on," I said, getting up. I went back to my room and snatched a stuffed duck from my shelf. I took it back to the guest room and handed it to Diego.

"To keep you company tonight."

He smiled and laid down with the duck.

"Do you need anything else?"

"Um, no...but I don't want that lady to come back," he said.

"What lady?" I asked.

He shifted, looking at the duck. "That scary lady. She was here today. She's mean."

I stopped in my tracks, confused.

He couldn't mean Veronica, could he?

"What did she look like?" I prodded.

Diego kept his eyes down. "She's tall. And blonde. And bad."

"Evil? Why? What did she do?"

He didn't say anything more, looking at me nervously.

"Well...uh...hopefully she won't be back," I said quietly, trying to fill the silence.

He nodded and fiddled with the duck some more. I studied him. Emily had mentioned that ghosts could be less rational than the living. She said they didn't see things the way we did, since they weren't bound to physical bodies. As such, according to Emily, sometimes they didn't make sense. I was starting to understand what she meant. Or maybe it was just that he was five.

I gnawed on my lip, wondering if I should say anything, or if I should leave the poor kid alone. I just couldn't shake the fear that it hadn't been an illness that claimed his life. Maybe it had been the ghosts. Or worse, those terrifying mannequin things.

"Hey, Diego?" I asked, trying to sound casual.

He looked up at me, his wide eyes dark and intense.

"Um. When you lived here before, with your family, did anything...scary ever happen?"

Diego's eyes took on a far-away look. For a long time, he was silent, and I wondered whether I should leave him alone or say something or just keep waiting.

"There were monsters," he finally said, so softly I could barely hear him.

My heart skipped a beat.

"What kind of monsters, Diego? Where were they?" I prodded. I needed to know if these were traditional there's-a-monster-in-my-closetmonsters, or if this child had seen what I was seeing.

"I don't know," he said, looking down at the duck. "Little ones. They came at night. They made me sick."

"Little ones? What did they look like?" I pressed. I hadn't heard of or seen anything like "little monsters". I tried to think what that could possibly be in reference to, but I was drawing a blank.

Diego shook his head and started crying again. I kicked myself. I'd pushed the poor kid too far and now he was upset again.

Way to be insensitive, Roz, I scolded myself.

"Hey, hey, don't worry. It's okay. You're safe now," I figured that must be true. Once you're dead, what more can really happen to you?

"No! There are scarier monsters now!" he screamed through his sobs. His anger startled me. The force of his voice shook the room. Around us, the lights flickered. His sweet little face had transformed, decaying and pale, and terrifying to look at.

I edged back, nervous. I didn't know what ghosts—even cute little kid ghosts—were capable of, and I was wondering if I'd yet again gotten myself in over my head. I wanted to ask about these new, "scarier" monsters, but that didn't seem like such a good idea.

Anxious as I was, I couldn't just leave the child. I sat with him while he cried, each sob and outburst causing me to shake. His anger began to subside, the trembling of the room easing away with it. His appearance, too, began to return to normal, though he was less solid now. I could see through him.

The lights were still unusually dim, though, and one bulb in a lamp seemed to have gone out completely. I couldn't figure out what that meant, or how to keep paranormal outbursts from destroying my house.

After a while, he cried himself to sleep, and I got up quietly, turning out the remaining light and slipping into the hall.

I wasn't sure if I was more or less confused about my predicament now. My encounter with Diego wasn't like my experiences with other ghosts, but in some ways, it had scared me far more than any of the previous episodes.

"Roz?"

I started. My dad was standing just outside his bedroom.

"Oh, hey, Dad."

"Did you feel the house shaking? I was in the shower and I could've sworn I felt a little jolt."

I blinked at him. "Um. I didn't notice anything."

He looked around. One of the pictures on the wall was crooked. He walked over and straightened it.

"I must not have felt it," I said as calmly as I could.

He nodded, then frowned. "Why were you in the guest bedroom?"

"Uh..." I was still jumpy. My mind raced with questions. What monsters had Diego meant? And what of Veronica, what had he seen? I wished I'd gotten more information before he'd become inconsolable.

"Roz?"

I looked back up at my father. "What?"

"Honey," his brow furrowed, "are you feeling all right?"

"Yeah, yeah, why?" I said, nodding and trying to look calm.

"Because I asked you a question and you didn't respond."

"Oh," he had a point. "Sorry. I'm just...tired..."

"Right, but, what were you doing in there?"

"Oh! That." The answer "talking to a ghost" would get me more questions and more stress for both of us. My mind raced. "Um, just...looking for some of my stuff. In the boxes," I said, adding another lie to the pile.

We said goodnight and I went back to the guest room. I had decided, risky as it was, that I was going to wake Diego up to ask him about Veronica. When I turned on the light, though, I saw the rumpled bed was empty, the duck lying among the sheets. Diego was gone.

I hovered in the doorway, wondering if I could draw him back. I could send the ghosts away—at least, sometimes I could—but I wasn't as practiced at drawing them to me. I was too tired to deal with all that, though. I decided I'd deal with it after a good night's sleep.

I went to my room, the whole time wondering what Veronica had done to be dubbed "the scary lady", and what kind of monsters were lurking in *my* closet.

Nineteen

My dad and I sat together, enjoying a breakfast of French toast and scrambled eggs. I made it a point to eat. I'd been acting weird lately, I was sure he was worrying. I was also trying to look alert. I'd slept for about ten hours, but I could've slept another ten. I was so tired, and my head was throbbing. My sleep wasn't complete. I'd woken up every hour or so, troubled by that dream of the clearing, and a new one, featuring my favorite terrifying, faceless white figures.

I didn't know what either of them meant, but I knew the dream of the clearing was getting more insistent, and more vivid. I'd had it at least five times last night alone, and it was always exactly the same: Me standing in a clearing, feeling this intense energy. There was nothing in the clearing. Not trees, not animals, even the breeze that rustled the leaves of the aspen trees surrounding me never touched my skin.

The wind in the trees made the leaves clatter, almost musical in the eerie silence.

"Rosalind."

I spun around, searching for the speaker, but no one was there. Instead, I saw a burning light, so brilliant it hurt my eyes. Each time, the light overtook me, and I woke with a jolt. It took a while to get back to sleep after that.

But I didn't want to think about that now. I was having a meal with my father. I was acting normal. I was fine.

"How's work?" I asked my dad as we ate. "I know you can't give me details, but is it going well?" I added quickly.

"It's...actually pretty difficult. This is a complicated case. I've even had a couple team members quit because they couldn't take the stress, and..." he shook his head. "Sorry, honey. I don't want to dump all this on you."

"It's okay, I don't mind listening," I said. I decided to change the subject, though, since I knew a thing or two about topics that weren't fun to discuss.

"So...are you going to grab lunch with Veronica or anything?" Not *my* first choice, but I thought it might make him feel better. Besides, I was curious. Diego's words were still on my mind. I doubted my dad would give me anything to work with, but it couldn't hurt to try.

"I don't know, we're both very busy. She's going out of town for a week to do some photo shoots at the beach."

"Oh. That sounds nice. No wonder she likes her job."

He chuckled. “How about you? How have you been?” he asked. “Having a good time with Hazel and your new friends?”

I nodded. “Yeah. Yeah. It’s fun. They’re really nice.” *And helpful when it comes to ghost infestations.*

“What have you guys been up to?”

I scrambled to think of something that sounded rational.

“Um...nothing, really. Just hanging out, watching movies, they’ve been showing me around town. That sort of thing.”

He nodded, finishing his breakfast. “I’m glad you’re getting out. It’s good for you.”

“Yeah. Definitely.” *I mean, I’m losing my mind, but whatever.*

“Have you been...” he paused, glancing at me. “I know you’re enjoying your friends, but you still seem stressed out.”

I bit my lip. I’d been hoping I’d be able to hide that from him. “I’m okay. I just destroyed my sleeping schedule and now I’m tired all the time.”

I don’t think he believed me, but he didn’t press the subject. I was grateful. He hadn’t brought up therapy again, likely because he was just as afraid to have that conversation as I was, and I wasn’t eager to give him any ammo on that subject.

He got up to take his plate to the kitchen and I pushed my food around with my fork. I grabbed my mug, but when I looked up, the tattered girl from the theater was sitting across the table from me, staring me down.

Her presence didn’t startle me like it should have, though, because I had already half-known she was there.

I could feel her; her presence was so strong I couldn't ignore it. We watched one another, my eyes locked onto hers as I fought off the instinct to run. The first time I'd seen her, she'd been aggressive. Now, though, like at Hazel's house, she was quiet. Contemplative. Her face was less frantic and more curious.

"Hello," I whispered.

She didn't answer. I held her gaze, my heart still racing. She might still attack, though honestly, it seemed unlikely. There was no malice in her dark eyes, only curiosity.

"What are you doing here?" I asked.

Again, there was no response.

"Do you need something?" I paused, waiting, but when she still didn't speak, I said, "I'll help you if I can."

She blinked slowly, tilting her head to the side.

"If I can help you..." I went on, "If I can do anything...please just tell me."

She stared at me, and slowly, her hand reached across the table to me. I froze, like I was dealing with an animal I didn't want to startle.

Her bony hand grasped my wrist, and the contact sent me reeling. An electric current ran from her hand into my body, not at all like at the theater. The connection surged in me, so intense I couldn't breathe or see, all I knew was pain.

I screamed and pushed back from the table, knocking my coffee mug aside and shattering it against the ground. I was on my feet and pressed back against the wall when my dad came rushing back into the dining room.

He was at my side in a flash, following my terrified gaze, but of course, the girl was gone. The chair across from me was empty.

“Roz? Roz? What is it?”

I was gasping for breath. Mila, today’s new housekeeper, hurried into the room. Apparently, my dad had realized I’d told the agency to stop sending people and had corrected my perceived error.

“Is everything all right?” she asked.

“Yeah, I think...I think so,” my dad told her, putting an arm around me.

“I’m sorry...” I whispered. “I’m sorry I scared you. I’m fine.”

She shook her head. “Don’t worry, don’t worry. I’ll clean this up.”

My dad led me into the kitchen while Mila set about cleaning up my mess. I was still shaking. My heart was pounding.

“Honey, what happened?” my dad asked when we were out of earshot of Mila.

“I...I don’t...” I shook my head. “Nothing.”

He looked at me sternly. “Rosalind. Don’t lie to me. What happened?”

I looked at my trembling hands. I’d have thought I’d be used to this sort of thing by now.

“I thought...I saw something. It startled me.”

“What did you see?”

I closed my eyes.

“Roz, honey, please talk to me.”

I put my head in my hands. “I thought I saw a woman. A girl. I don’t know. She looked...sick.” I left out the part about having seen her before, on more than one occasion.

My dad was quiet, gripping my arm. I peeked up at him, studying his serious face for some clue.

"I'm sorry," I whispered.

He sighed. "Why are you sorry, Roz? No one's angry...I'm just...here..." he sat down at the kitchen island and indicated that I should take the seat beside him.

I sat tentatively, wondering what this was about.

"I was thinking...that...maybe it would be a good idea if you were to...speak to a professional."

I blinked. I didn't want to talk about this—not now.

"I know it's been a while, and we thought after moving here you wouldn't need a therapist, but..."

So much for not bringing this up again.

"Dad, I don't want—"

"Please. Just...hear me out. I don't know what's going on, and I know you aren't making things up. I trust you, Rosalind, I always have and I always will, but this...I'm worried about you."

He looked at the bandages on my arms and neck. He couldn't meet my eyes. I read the fear etched into his face and tried to think what to say to calm him down. I opened my mouth, then closed it again, shaking my head.

I whispered, "I would really, *really* rather not go into therapy."

"I just think it might not be a bad idea, kiddo. I mean..." he looked at me pleadingly, squeezing my hands in his. "Something is happening to you and I don't know what else to do, honey."

A stab of irritation mixed in with the million other emotions I was feeling. I pulled back, looking up at him. "You're just afraid I'm going to start acting like Mom."

He cringed. "No...sweetie, it has nothing to do with that. I just feel like you've been under a lot of stress lately. We both have. It's not something to be embarrassed about—"

I shook my head. "No. No. I don't want to. Please, Dad." I could feel tears choking me. Going to therapy after my mother's abandonment had been one thing, but I didn't want to go back. Not like this. Not like her.

He gripped my shoulders gently, his expression pleading. "I understand that. I respect that. But...honey, put yourself in my shoes. I don't..." he closed his eyes, taking a moment. When he spoke again, his voice was low and strained. "I need to do what's best for you, even if you don't agree with me."

I looked down. I wanted to scream, but that probably wouldn't help with the "I'm not crazy" argument.

"I'm not the only one seeing them," I said, unable to meet his gaze.

He looked surprised. I closed my eyes and rubbed the bridge of my nose.

"The housekeepers keep leaving, Dad. Haven't you wondered why? It's the...the *ghosts*." I swallowed hard, feeling like I was choking. "And not just them. Hazel. Emily. My friends have seen them, Dad. It's not just me, I'm not..." I had to take a deep breath to steady my voice. "I'm not crazy," I said, barely more than a whisper.

My father looked stunned. He was quiet for a moment, then he took my hands in his and gave them a gentle squeeze.

"So...these ghosts..." he said slowly. "They're...really real?"

"Dad, I'm pretty sure even Veronica saw one," I said. "You can ask her."

"Why haven't I seen any?" he asked. He wasn't challenging me. He sounded genuinely confused.

I shook my head. "I have no idea."

He sighed. "Be that as it may, I don't know, I guess we really do call an exorcist now?" he rubbed the bridge of his nose. "Anyway, regardless of that, honey, I'm still worried. You're stressed. You're not sleeping, you're barely eating. You've been anxious and jumpy for almost two weeks, and...honey, that kind of stress...it does bad things to people. I don't want to...I don't want anything to happen to you."

My heart sank. He still wanted me to go to therapy. He was probably afraid, ghosts or no ghosts, that I was on the verge of a mental breakdown.

I bit my lip. Maybe I was. Sick as it made me, I *was* acting like my mother. I was reminding *myself* of her, and it horrified me. Just because the ghosts were real didn't mean I wasn't kind of losing my mind.

That was why his words hurt so badly. Because he was echoing my own fears. That made them real. That made them valid.

I was going crazy. Just like my mother had.

Was she haunted like me? She never told me, she just pulled away. Like I'd been doing.

My dad was still talking, trying to soften the blow. "We can still call an exorcist, okay? We can do that, too. But...I want you to see a doctor, at least a couple times, just to...to get you through..." he trailed off, looking at me helplessly.

I swallowed hard, forcing as much calm as I could muster into my voice.

"Okay, well, I have a painting lesson with Joanne. So..."

He nodded. "Go ahead, honey. Have fun. We'll...we'll talk more when you get home."

"Right. Okay. Bye."

I got up to leave, but he caught my arm and pulled me into a tight hug. I wish he hadn't, because I'd been able to hold it together until then. When he squeezed me, a sob escaped, and I started shaking.

He kissed the top of my head. "I love you, Roz. And I'll do whatever it takes to make sure you're safe, okay?"

I nodded against his chest, trying to compose myself. He released me, but his hand stayed on my shoulder as I wiped my eyes. I'd given up on being discreet about it.

"Have fun at your painting lesson, all right?"

I nodded again, unable to trust myself to speak, and left without a word. It probably hurt him—I know it hurt me—but I was all out of things to say. All I had was the fear that I would destroy him the same way my mother had.

TWENTY

"Rosalind, you're so punctual," Joanne said, opening the door to let me in. "How have you been?"

"Great, you?" I lied. I had taken a moment outside her house to pull myself together; I hoped I looked like I really was fine.

"Same old same old, not that I'm complaining."

I stepped inside and let the flood of artwork wash over me, immediately soothing my nerves.

"We're going to work with texture today, as that interested you last time," Joanne said as we made our way up to her studio.

This excited me. I listened as she went over the basic procedure. When she was finished explaining, I dove in, eager to see what I could do with it. I thought of the painting that dominated her stairway. Its beauty, its pain. I wanted to create something just as powerful and moving. I didn't know if I could, though. The very thought of it made me shiver.

I didn't use a reference picture this time. I just worked, letting my hands do what they wanted.

While we painted, we talked.

"How's the new house?" Joanne asked.

"Oh. It's...good."

Joanne looked at me and gave a little smile.

"You're not a very good liar, Rosalind."

I sighed. "I know. Sorry. I just..." I glanced at her. "I don't want you to think I'm crazy."

Joanne laughed. "Oh, sweetheart, I won't think that. Trust me, I have seen some strange things in my life."

I nodded, toying with my brush. "I...have kind of been...ghost hunting," I admitted.

"Ghost hunting?" she echoed. She didn't look at me like I needed to be locked up, though, so that was good.

Then it all came spilling out. The hauntings, the séances, the dreams about the forest. I told her about the mannequin-like figures and their cold metal examination table. The being in the corner of Hazel's room that seemed to swallow light like a black hole.

I told her about my sleepless nights and my constant fear, and how we couldn't hold on to a housekeeper. I'd have given in to the theory that I was insane long ago, but other people were having strange experiences, too.

Finally, I told her about my father. About him wanting to send me to therapy, and how worried he was about me. I told her how scared I was of what his fears might indicate, and what might happen if I went to a psychiatrist.

I did not tell her about my suspected role in all this; that perhaps I was causing it, that perhaps I was at the center of this whole mess.

Joanne listened quietly, watching me with an unreadable expression.

When I'd finished talking, I glanced up at her, wondering if I'd just cost myself painting lessons.

"Do you believe me?" I asked.

Joanne nodded. "I do, Rosalind. I do."

She came over and hugged me, enveloping me in her thin arms. I didn't want to cry, but it was hard not to. I was so tired. And so sacred.

"I'm sorry, my dear. But you know, this is how we find our strength. This is how we grow. Growing is always uncomfortable, sometimes downright painful, and when you come out of this, you'll be far wiser."

She leaned back and smiled down at me. "Remember what Winston Churchill said: 'If you're going through Hell, keep going.'"

I laughed, wiping away a few tears. "Smart man."

"He'd seen his fair share of ugliness, too. It makes us greater. You have greatness in you, I can tell," she said with a wink.

I pulled back then, feeling a little awkward. But Joanne was serene, and her calm put me at ease. I wondered *why* she believed me. What did she know? We resumed painting, and we were quiet for a while, but it was a pleasant kind of quiet. Peaceful. Calm.

My painting turned into a little boy with tan skin and dark hair sleeping in a big bed. I used the texture to create the blankets bunched around him. A little stuffed duck lay amongst the sheets.

As I painted, paranoia started to creep back into my mind. *Why* was Joanne so calm about what I'd said? Had she seen or heard something that made it seem commonplace? Had she had experiences of her own? Or was something scarier going on? I thought back to my first conversation with Ford. He had called her a witch, and once again, I found myself wondering if that wasn't too far from the truth.

"You...really...are being very understanding. I've said some weird things..." I said, glancing at her from the corner of my eye.

Joanne chuckled, returning my glance. "I've seen my fair share of evil, as well."

"Like...this? Ghosts?"

She set her paintbrush down, looking pensive.

"This is going to sound crazy," I said, realizing that line was becoming my catchphrase. "But...are you a witch?"

Joanne looked at me, confused. Then she started to laugh.

"A witch? No, dear, why would you think that?"

I blushed. "Not...like...I don't know. Everything I thought I knew is wrong, so I thought...maybe witches do exist?"

Joanne was still chuckling. "I understand your logic, but why *me*?"

"I don't know," I said, looking down. "I...um. Might have heard a rumor."

She nodded. "Ah, yes. The boy across the street?"

I smiled sheepishly at her. "Yeah."

Joanne chuckled. "No, dear, I'm not a witch. But you probably wouldn't be surprised to hear that I've dabbled in the paranormal in my time. I went to plenty of séances and haunted houses, particularly when I was younger. There are some things that simply cannot be explained with the science available to us, aren't there?"

"Yeah," I agreed. Something she'd said struck me as odd, but I couldn't place it, so I resumed painting and resolved to stop worrying about every little thing.

When I was done, I stepped back to survey my work.

"Oh, Rosalind, that's beautiful."

"Thanks," I said, studying the boy's peaceful face.

"This carries far more emotion than your last piece. You should paint from the heart more often."

I looked at the painting. She had a point. I wondered vaguely if she'd recognize the boy, but she didn't seem to.

"Yeah...maybe..."

I paused, unsure if I should ask what I was about to ask. I twisted my paintbrush in my hand as the words rattled around my brain. I thought of Rowan's books and theories, and how she was here, likely studying the wavelengths and harmonic whatevers that were causing all these ghost issues. If I wanted to solve this, I had to learn as much as I could.

"Joanne?" I blurted out, plunging on before I could think better of it. "Do you know what happened to the family that used to live in my house?"

Joanne turned slowly to me, her face becoming somber.

"The Marcelos. I knew them. They mostly kept to themselves, but I was in contact with them because..." she chuckled awkwardly. "Well, we were having a bit of a dispute. They planted a bunch of trees and, well, you've seen my garden. I'm rather particular about it, and their trees were hanging into my yard. Some of them even started to crack the wall. Anyway…"

She shook her head and went on. "Looking back at it now, with all that happened to them, it seems pretty silly. At the time, it bothered me, and I felt they were being very unhelpful about the whole thing. But then they lost their business, and their son got sick. I believe he developed a kind of cancer, poor thing. They moved to be closer to their family. Back in Texas, I think."

"Do you know anything else about them? What happened after all that?" I asked.

She shook her head. "No, I'm sorry. As you can imagine, they weren't exactly fond of me. I can't say that's one of my proudest moments, but to be fair, I didn't realize what a hardship they were going through."

I nodded. "Do you know…if their son died before they moved?"

Joanne looked a bit startled.

"Oh, no, I'm sure I would have heard about that. He got very ill, but last I knew he was still alive."

I studied her, wondering if she was trying to protect me, or if she really didn't know. I glanced instinctively at my painting. Joanne hadn't recognized the subject, or if she had, she'd said nothing.

"Why do you ask, dear?" she inquired gently.

I shook my head. "Just…wondering if maybe the troubles I'm having there might be part of why they moved."

"I see. I never heard anything about ghosts in that house, but like I said, I wasn't really their favorite person. I doubt they'd have confided in me."

"And...one more thing...did you know the name of the little boy?"

Joanne frowned. "Hmm, no. I don't recall. Sorry, dear. Why? Is he among your ghosts?"

I shook my head. I didn't want to talk to her about Diego. He hadn't come up in my story, and now felt like the wrong time to open a whole new topic of discussion. Besides, I didn't know what else to say. I had so many questions they didn't even make sense to me anymore.

I packed up and she set my painting of Diego aside to dry.

Joanne crossed the domed room to an easel off to one side. "Would you like to take your painting from last time?" she asked.

I looked at it and wrinkled my nose. There was something pathetic and empty about it compared to my painting of Diego.

"Um, sure. Thanks," I said. She probably didn't want it clogging up her studio.

Joanne walked with me to the front door and gave me a final hug before I left.

"Oh, one more thing," Joanne said as I stepped out into the day's heat.

"Yeah?"

"I'm going out of town for a few weeks. I'll be leaving in a couple days. This means we'll have to postpone our next lesson until I get back."

"Okay, no problem. What are you going out of town for?"

She rolled her eyes and shook her head, laughing. "My sister throws a big anniversary party every year. She makes a fuss, wants everyone to attend. I'm going to stay and visit with family; they live far away, so I only see them for holidays and, well, my sister's anniversary! Anyway, you'll see my assistant around, tending to a few things while I'm gone. So not to worry. She'll just be watering my plants and feeding my cat."

"Good to know," I said. I remembered what Ford had said about her cat and suppressed a laugh. "I didn't even know you had a cat."

Joanne chuckled. "She's so shy, you might never see her."

"All right, well, thanks again for the lesson!"

I headed home and stuck the puppy painting behind my bookcase, so I wouldn't have to look at it.

I checked my phone. I'd missed a call from Hazel, and had a text from Emily.

I think you might have some haunted artifacts in your house. Been reading about them all night. Could be an antique or heirloom. Could be several. Give me a call.

I called Hazel first. She wanted to check up on me. I told her about the ghost of the little boy and how eerie the whole encounter had been.

Next, I called Emily. She called Derek and put the three of us on video chat. I held my phone out, watching the two of them. They were so thrilled to hear that I had *two* new ghosts that they insisted we get everyone together again as soon as we could.

"Everyone?" I asked.

"Yeah, the whole gang," Derek said.

"Is that necessary?"

"It wouldn't feel right to do this without our usual group. We're all in this together now!" Emily said. She was back to being way too cheerful about the whole thing.

I agreed, a little grudgingly. I wanted to help Diego, but I didn't want my friends getting hurt. I could see Derek's cast in the chat window, though he hadn't brought it up once.

"Today?" Emily asked.

"Hazel's working," I said.

"Oh. Tonight?"

"I'm supposed to spend time with my dad..."

"Agh! Tomorrow?"

I laughed. "Sure, I think everyone's free. I know Hazel 's not working. I'll check with Ford."

We hung up after that and I sent Ford a text: *Hey are you free tomorrow? I have a new ghost and Emily wants us to help him.*

Fun. What time? He sent back.

No clue. I'll let you know.

Awesome. I'm in. A second message came through: *Now, what are YOU doing today?*

Um...nothing? My dad wants us to go out for dinner, but that's not till he gets home from work.

Soooo...you're free now?

I stared at my phone suspiciously, sending back, *Yeah?*

I was just thinking you might want to get out of there for a little while and do something. When I didn't respond right away, he added: *Instead of all the worrying.*

Worrying?

You worry a lot. You could use some fun

For some reason, I was a little annoyed by his concern. *I do NOT worry that much. And I have plenty of fun.*

Fair enough. But whenever I see you, everything's tense. And stressful.

He had me there. *I guess so.*

Right. And I don't want you to have negative associations with me.

Because my psyche is so important. I snorted as I typed.

IT IS. So what do you say?

I looked around my room. Getting out would be nice. *Sure, what do you have in mind?*

I'll pick you up. We can figure something out from there.

K

He pulled up to my house a few minutes later and actually got out and rang the doorbell. I grabbed my purse and a sweater and locked the door behind me.

"A sweater? You do realize we're in Vegas and it's like, nine billion degrees outside, right?"

"Yeah, well, it's cold in buildings. I guarantee you I'll need this."

We drove only a short distance, me wondering all the while where Vegas teens hung out. We pulled up to a little café with "OPEN 24 HOURS" written by hand in gigantic letters along the window, beneath the ransom-note style sign that declared it *The Madhouse*.

"What is this place?" I asked, glancing at Ford.

"The weirdest coffee shop I know," he answered. "But it's awesome. And they have really weird paintings and the best collector mugs. Also: Nutella. In basically everything. Being able to get Nutella-flavored coffee and pastries stuffed with Nutella at two in the morning is a high priority for me."

"I can imagine," I laughed.

I followed him inside, and we got some desserts and coffee; the kinds loaded with Nutella.

I was discovering that, in some ways, Ford was easier to talk to than Hazel. He got far more of my references, and liked a lot of the same books and shows that I did, so I spent less time explaining what I meant and more time trying to think up something witty to say, since he always seemed to have a comeback and I wasn't about to be shown up.

He asked about my "new ghost" as if it was a pet I'd gotten. I told him about both, Diego and the old lady. Like me, Ford found the old lady creepier. I steered the conversation away from ghosts after that.

Talking to Ford was simple, it was fun. It made me feel normal, like my life wasn't full of nightmares. Plus, he was new. It's nice, sometimes, to talk to someone who doesn't know you very well, because you get to tell your story, and you get to tell it your way.

Of course, talking to someone for hours will lead to more topics than you might be ready to address. I had expected it, but it was still difficult when it came up.

"Hey, why'd you call me Shirley MacLaine the other day?" he asked.

I laughed. "She's an actress from the golden age. She's in a couple of my favorite old movies. Anyway, she believes in aliens. She's pretty vocal about it."

He chuckled. "I see. So, you like old movies?"

"Love 'em. I mean, not exclusively. There are good movies made these days, too, but...there's something about those old movies. I think it's because..." I trailed off.

"What?" he asked.

I shook my head and busied myself with my coffee. "It's just...I think I love them because they...it was something my mom and I shared. It...makes me feel close to her. Which I usually hate, but...I dunno," I shrugged. "Those were some of our best memories together."

He nodded and we were quiet for a moment. Ford sipped his coffee and I studied the paintings on the wall, thinking of Joanne's house.

"So...not to pry," Ford said softly, "and you don't have to answer if you don't want to, but...where is your mom?"

I stirred my coffee idly as I considered how to answer the question. I decided to do so with as little detail as possible.

"She abandoned us," I said simply. "And...I would really rather not talk about it, because it was only about a year ago and..." *Dammit.* My throat tightened, changing my voice, betraying me. I wanted to sound indifferent, casual, relaxed, but it was coming through that I was none of those things. I was deeply emotional and tense.

"I'm sorry, we can talk about something else," he said, looking apologetic.

I shook my head. "Don't be sorry, it's a legitimate question. She just...didn't want to be around anymore, I guess."

"That must be really hard," he said, his brow furrowing slightly.

I nodded. "I think it's harder on my dad, honestly, but seeing him suffer is hard on me, too, so..." I shrugged. I didn't know what else to say and my voice was getting squeakier by the second.

Ford nodded and took a bite of his dessert.

"Um, tell me about your family."

He shrugged. "Pretty basic. Dad's a businessman, mom's a socialite. Does a lot of charity work, she's really involved with hospitals and stuff, especially since my grandfather died."

I nodded, happy to be hearing about his life so that I could stop thinking about mine for a moment.

"And I have a little brother and sister, you've seen them. Philip is twelve going on thirty. He's just," he shook his head and laughed. "He's so serious all the time. I drive him nuts, 'cause I'm always teasing him and poking fun at him. He doesn't know how to take a joke, you know?"

I laughed. "That must be rough, living with you."

"Oh hell yes," he said with a grin. "Good kid, just...needs to lighten up a bit. He's really committed to getting into Harvard Law," Ford said, laughing some more.

I snickered, too, amused by the thought of a twelve-year-old who had his life so planned out.

"And Oops—well, Olivia—she's just awesome. She cracks me up. I never worry about her, you know? She knows what she wants and she goes and gets it. Kid's gonna be great."

I smiled at that. I could tell he really loved her.

We stayed there a little longer, talking and joking and hanging out. When the sun started to set, we decided to get home.

"Hey," I said as I climbed into his van. "By the way, I have this book you should check out...it's kind of talking about what you're always trying to say about there being a scientific explanation to ghosts and whatnot."

Ford looked over. "Yeah?"

I nodded. "It's called *Between Worlds* by Rowan Fallon, and—"

"Oh my God! I forgot about that book! Yeah, I love Rowan, she's awesome!" Ford said.

I blinked. "You know her?"

"Oh yeah, she's one of my heroes. Super smart. Doing all kinds of awesome research. I haven't read *Between Worlds* yet, but I think I have it...man, I should remedy that." He glanced at me, raising an eyebrow. "Why are *you* reading her stuff?"

I shifted. "Well, she was interviewed on *East/West*—"

"She went on that show?" he asked.

I smacked him lightly. "Will you quit interrupting me? She was interviewed by that Chad guy and they were talking about ghosts and stuff...she thinks it's all caused by dimensions and...I don't know. It's all pretty heavy for me, but it's interesting, and..." I shrugged. "I'm open to any possibilities at this point."

Ford nodded thoughtfully. "Huh. Awesome. I'll have to read it tonight," he flashed me a grin and started his van.

"What, the whole thing?"

"Yeah."

I rolled my eyes, because I could tell he wasn't joking. Then I looked down. Now that I knew he was a fan, it was going to make the next part of this conversation more awkward.

"Um...there's something else about her that intrigues me," I said.

"Yeah? What's that?" Ford asked as he drove.

I glanced up at him, then looked out the window. "She lives here now," I said.

"What, in Vegas?"

"Yeah."

"Huh. I hadn't heard about that."

"It's pretty recent," I said. "In fact...it was just a week after I moved here."

"That's a weird coincidence."

I nodded. I suddenly didn't feel about telling him anymore; how suddenly and inexplicably she'd moved, and how no one knew why. Something about her—even the thought of her—still gave me chills.

We talked a little more about it, but I kept things light and steered us back to safer territory. When we pulled into our cul-de-sac, I sat in his van, looking up at my house.

"You okay?" he asked.

I shook my head. "I'm just...tired. And, honestly, I'm not really sure I can handle all this."

He grinned. "Ah, but you can, Roz. I mean, you've lasted this long in a haunted house, I bet you can do pretty much anything."

I rolled my eyes and laughed. "Your faith in me is so inspiring," I said.

"You're doing better than I would be, I think," he said.

I looked down at my hands, then glanced at him. "Wanna know something weird?"

"Always," Ford said.

"I think...I think I can kind of...send the ghosts away. At least, sometimes."

"What? Really?"

I nodded. "I figured out they were following me...and, well, I figured out that when I *really* want them to go away...sometimes it works. Like at the séance with Derek."

Ford considered this. "You made that thing stop?" he asked.

"I think so. I was angry, I wanted it all to stop, and...it did."

"Well that's handy," he said.

I shrugged. "Not always. But it's better than nothing, I guess."

"Hey, quick question," he said. "Did you ever listen to that voicemail?"

I looked down. "Uh. No."

Ford raised an eyebrow at me. "Well?"

I had my phone in my hand, but I made no move to use it.

"Do you not want to check it with me around?" Ford asked gently.

"It's not that," I said, keeping my eyes down. "It's...I don't want to check it at all."

He nodded. "Okay."

I sighed. It wasn't him. I hadn't stopped thinking about the voicemail since I'd gotten it. I just didn't have the guts to listen to it.

"Will you listen to it with me?" I asked.

"Sure, let's hear it."

I took a deep breath and woke my phone up, swiping my finger across the screen. My hands were shaking as I pulled up the message and hit PLAY.

I put the phone on speaker and set it on the seat between us.

At first, there was just crackling static. It grew and diminished in intensity, then there was a *click* and the line went silent. I glanced at Ford, thinking that was it, but before either one of us could speak, a very faint voice whispered over the line. It was twisted and garbled, words cutting in and out.

"...careful.... I just...you...need to know that this is...happening..."

There was a pause. Ford and I leaned closer to the phone, listening intently.

There was a shuffling, then the voice continued. It didn't sound like whispering, it sounded like it was far away.

"...she's dangerous. Stay away from her. You're not safe...stay away from—"

There was a loud *pop!* The line disconnected, and the voicemail ended.

TWENTY-ONE

Ford and I couldn't make sense of the voicemail, so we'd decided to talk to Emily and Derek about it. We were meeting up with them the next day, anyway, so hopefully I wouldn't have to wait long for answers.

I couldn't shake the sound of the voice, and the words it had spoken. I obsessed about it all night, and the next morning, it was still on my mind.

You need to know.

I needed to know *what*?

You're not safe.

Well, *that* was evident. Thanks for the super-helpful tip.

*Stay away from the...*from the *what*? The ghosts? The shadowy figure? Something else terrible I hadn't even discovered yet?

Stay away from her. This part freaked me out the most because it reminded me of Diego's panic over Veronica. I closed my eyes and rested my head in my hands. My head wasn't actually aching this time, I just didn't know what to make of all the questions swirling around in there.

My tea was taking a while to steep, and I was restless. I drummed my fingers on the countertop and tried to make sense of the few snippets I could make out from the crackly voicemail. Maybe if I listened to it again. I slipped my phone out of my pocket and thumbed to my voicemail. When I checked the list, though, it wasn't there. Frowning, I skimmed through the messages. Hazel, Dad, Grandma, a couple spam calls I'd never bothered to delete. Normal stuff, but no ghost messages.

Good thing Ford had listened to it with me. Otherwise, I might have doubted the whole thing. I rubbed my temples. *Now* I was developing a headache.

I froze. A headache. I had been assuming they were just stress reactions. Things like sleep deprivation, or anxiety, or not eating well. But I'd been getting headaches at very specific times: Right before ghosts—or something else inexplicable—showed up.

How had I missed this connection before? I kicked myself for not realizing the headaches always came before the encounters, but I didn't have time to be angry. Something was about to happen.

My first instinct was to look around, but I'd have better luck using my newly discovered ability to locate whatever was coming for me. I closed my eyes and tried to breathe evenly, focusing on the presence.

My eyes snapped open and I whirled around. The light drained from the room, and almost seemed to be pulled toward one point—one impossibly dark figure standing in the entry to the kitchen.

I was paralyzed. The shadow. I could feel its attention on me, and it wasn't standing menacingly anymore, it was racing toward me. I screamed and dodged, getting out of the way in time, but slamming against the counter. But I wasn't in the clear, and the figure moved fluidly, surprisingly fast for something so large, catching my wrist. A jolt of electricity ran through me, and I screamed, slumping against the cabinets, limbs tingling and stinging. The pain subsided, but I still couldn't move. The figure lifted me, and all I could think was that it was surprisingly strong for a shadow.

Focus!

But it didn't work. The shadowy creature was too solid, too real, and I couldn't push it away. Panic overtook me—I screamed and thrashed, weakly, because my muscles were still twitching from the shock. Around me, the world seemed to twist and shift, colors and lights fragmenting in my vision.

I closed my eyes as something metallic touched my wrist. It was cold and sharp, and I screamed again, trying to pull away. I could feel everything shifting around me like a whirlwind. It was like being in the middle of a tornado, and my cries were swallowed up by the roar.

Cold metal bit into my skin as I fought against the incredible strength of the shadow. It was so solid and strong, my punches and kicks had no effect.

The whirlwind increased in power and the shadow's grip weakened. I was being pulled in one direction, while it was being pulled in another. I squirmed against its loosening hold, fighting with everything I had until I twisted just right to rip my arm free.

With a yelp, I fell to the floor, opening my eyes to impossible darkness all around me. I sat perfectly still for a moment, gulping down air in ragged gasps. The thought of getting up and running occurred to me, but I couldn't make my body move. I lay there, sucking in air, unable to stand up. My eyes adjusted until I could see my kitchen, shrouded in darkness. The kind of darkness you get on a moonless night when the power is out.

Shaking, I recognized the feel of this darkness—it was the same as that night at Hazel's house, when something had attacked Emily.

As if responding to my memories, a scuffling sound hurried toward me. I squeezed my eyes shut once more and begged for home, for safety. Nothing happened.

Calm down, I ordered myself. *Focus.*

The sound approached slowly, but I was still high on panic from my last encounter with the shadow. Calming down seemed impossible, but I used a breathing exercise my Aunt Fiona had taught me, and slowly, my heartbeat returned to normal.

When I opened my eyes to check and make sure nothing had approached me, I found myself lying on the kitchen floor. I was a mess—sweaty and in utter disarray—but I was home. Not that home was particularly comforting these days.

My tea had spilled all over the counter and the floor, and my mug was shattered on the tile. I cleaned up the mess and went to get ready to leave. I still had to meet the others, after all, and I may as well leave early—I could just get tea there. Or drive around and clear my head.

As I straightened myself up, fixed my hair, and bandaged the shallow cut on my wrist, I wondered if maybe being locked up in a psych ward was exactly where I belonged.

I found Emily in the café where Derek worked, spread out on one of the larger tables with her laptop, a tablet, and stacks of papers, folders, and multi-colored pens. She had a pencil between her teeth, and she was muttering to herself around it as she typed.

Before she noticed me, I took a deep, steadying breath and relaxed my posture a little. I'd tell her about today's attack, but I didn't want to be tense when I did.

"How's it going?" I asked, pulling out one of the seats opposite her. I was careful not to disturb her meticulously arranged paperwork.

"Ngh..." she said, taking the pencil from her mouth. "Okay. But I wish we had more conclusive findings. I've got *so* much observation material—it's probably more than I would've ever needed, really—but nothing in terms of *solving* it all."

Emily ran her hands through her long hair, letting out a frustrated sigh, flinging strands of ombre black-to-purple hair all over.

"Any way I can help?" I asked.

"Did you figure out what the ghosts want?"

I shook my head, rubbing my bandaged wrist anxiously. "If anything, there are more of them now and I know less about them than ever."

Emily nodded. "I know. Ah, well. There's bound to be a break in the case eventually," she said, sipping her latte.

"When's your proposal due?"

"Um," Emily said, clicking something on her screen. "Not until December, so we've got time."

"But we're going to figure out the ghosts before then, right?" I pressed. A lump formed in my throat as I thought of all the days between now and December. I couldn't survive that long under these conditions.

"As long as I have a say, yes. In the meantime, I can always use more sketches from you for my project. You know, if you want."

I opened my bag. I'd been working on a few, since Emily knew I loved to draw.

"I drew that shadow thing," I said, pulling the folder out of my bag and handing it to her. I'd finished it in my car before coming in, since I'd been so early, though my hands had been shaking. This afternoon's encounter was so fresh in my mind I still had an adrenaline high.

Emily accepted it eagerly, scanning over it. She raised her eyebrows. "Wow, there's a lot more detail than I expected."

I looked down at the table. "I, uh, saw it again."

"What?" Emily said, louder than I'd expected. I twitched slightly and she giggled at her own surprise. A few people glanced over, but no one seemed to care very much.

I fidgeted. I'd known she'd demand all the details, and I wasn't sure I could talk about it without getting emotional. I gave her a quick summary of what had happened and kept my eyes on my wrist as I spoke.

Emily, for once, was speechless. She shook her head, letting out a low whistle.

"I think I need to read the journal, Em," I whispered.

She nodded, but wasn't as enthusiastic as I'd expected her to be.

"Yeah," she said softly. "I think you're right."

We were silent for a moment, which was interrupted by Emily perking up and waving Derek over.

"Hey, find something new?" he asked, standing over Emily and looking at my drawings with her.

"Well, I think so," I said. Then I remembered my time with Ford the day before. "But first..."

Emily's head snapped up. "What? What is it? There's *more*?"

I cleared my throat, strangely more nervous to discuss this than the attack earlier.

"I, uh," I said shakily. "I listened to that voicemail."

They wanted to hear it, but I explained how it had disappeared. That made it all the more intriguing. I told them what it said and Emily wrote it down quickly, eyes wide.

"What do you think it means?" she asked.

"I don't know, I was hoping you'd have some insights."

"Did you recognize the voice?" Derek asked.

His question made me pause. I considered it, brow furrowed. "A bit...but I've been hearing all kinds of ghosts lately. It sounded..." I shook my head. "I don't know. There was something frantic about it. And I couldn't hear it all that well—it was garbled and messed up by the machine and..." I trailed off, shaking my head.

Emily tapped the eraser of her pencil against her chin, silent in her contemplation.

"Ghosts are usually in a state of terror when they die. It carries over," Derek said. He sounded sad. Almost sympathetic.

"I guess dying would be scary," I said. I'd given it far more thought in the past year than I wanted to, and now death was literally haunting me.

"I better get back to work," Derek said, glancing at the register. "Roz, want anything?"

"Um, just a green tea. Thanks." I still felt a little awkward, ordering from a friend. Especially since his arm was in a cast and I couldn't imagine that made his job any easier.

"Ooh! Ooh! Bring me a cookie?" Emily added before he left. She was not awkward at all.

"Haven't you had enough sugar?" Derek asked, walking backward away from the table.

"Noooo. Cookie!" Emily said as he retreated into the kitchen.

I sketched absently on a napkin while I waited for my tea. Emily was absorbed in her work, looking between her notes and the screen.

"So, tell me about these new ghosts," Emily said as she typed.

"Well, there's not much more to say about the old lady, but Diego..." I drew the child for her and told her about his visit. About how strongly the room had reacted to his emotions, and how upset he'd been at the mention of "monsters".

Emily was interested in another part of the story, though.

"Wait, he was afraid of Veronica?" she asked, brow furrowed.

"I think so," I said. "He described her. Only one of our housekeepers has been blonde, and she wasn't tall. Besides, Veronica had *just* been there that night, so I'm guessing he saw her and that's what made him....I don't know, panic, react, show up?"

"And he was *afraid* of her? He called her *scary*?" Emily pressed.

"Yeah..."

Emily sat back in her seat, clicking her tongue as she thought. "Well, that's really weird."

I tilted my head to the side, trying to figure out which specific part of my really weird life she was referring to.

When she remained lost in thought, I asked, "What's weird?"

"That he was afraid of her. I mean, what earthly thing could scare a ghost? What mortal being would worry someone who's dead?"

I hadn't even considered that angle. "Well, I don't think he knows he's dead?" I supplied halfheartedly.

Emily nodded. "That's true. But even so, what could he have possibly seen or felt from a human that would scare him? Even if he is dead, I'd think something pretty significant would have had to happen for him to be so upset. Not just nervous, but really panicking, it sounds like."

I didn't like where this conversation was going. I shifted in my seat, the anxiety creeping back in.

"Did Veronica do anything while she was there?" Emily asked.

I shook my head. “Not that I saw. And I mean, she wasn’t exactly wandering the house alone. She was with my dad and I the whole time. And she didn’t do anything weird. Ate dinner, made conversation, drank some coffee, went home. It was...boring, really.”

Emily was tapping her pen again. Derek returned then with our drinks and Emily’s cookie. She clapped happily, momentarily forgetting our ghostly quandary.

“What are we discussing?” Derek asked, hovering at our table like he was taking an order. Emily’s face grew serious again. I chuckled at how quickly her emotions could shift.

“What would scare a ghost?” she asked him.

“According to a lot of publications, there are entities in the æther that could threaten a ghost.”

“I thought of that, but what about in the human world? Like, a person? Why would a living person scare a ghost?”

Derek’s gaze shifted. He wasn’t looking at anything in particular.

“Something personal,” he finally said. “Someone linked to their life. Or their death. The person or thing that killed them, most likely.”

Emily looked at me, and I wondered if I she could see me going pale as fast as I could feel the blood draining from my face.

“That—that doesn’t make sense,” I said, clinging to flimsy logic. “Why would Veronica have anything to do with Diego’s death?”

Emily gave a one-shouldered shrug. “No idea. It doesn’t make sense from what I can tell, but it’s the only lead we’ve got.”

"What's going on?" Derek asked.

"New ghost. Scared of my dad's...friend. She bugs me but," I shook my head. "A killer? I can't see that."

"I know he freaked out last time, but if you see him again, maybe you can ask him some questions, get *something* out of him," Emily said.

I stared into my cup of tea. "Okay," I said, voice flat, numb. None of this made any sense. I wondered for a moment if I should take my father up on the offer of therapy, though I had no idea what I'd ever tell a psychiatrist at this point. I was living in a house full of ghosts, some of which tried to kill us, others who were killed by blonde models?

Emily and Derek talked more about what my latest encounter might have meant. I sipped my tea and tried to look like I was listening.

I lost track of time, but soon enough Hazel was bounding across the café to our table, smiling and carrying a few books. She set the stack on the table between us and greeted each of us with a hug. Derek went back to the kitchen to get her drink, and she sat down between Emily and I at the head of the table.

"That's everything my parents had on the Eastern philosophies and the paranormal. Including some Hindu exorcism practices."

Emily's eyes lit up as she looked over the titles. I was slightly less enthusiastic, but I took a book from the stack and began flipping through it. I had been the one to ask for this research material, after all. I'd been looking into how other cultures interpreted spirits and the afterlife. I'd found some stuff online, but when I'd mentioned it to Hazel she assured me her father had a few old and relevant books in his collection—books I hadn't been able to find the contents of.

"Thanks so much, Haze!" Emily said. "This is going to be a huge help."

"Hopefully," I added dryly. Hazel looked a little wounded and I immediately regretted it. "Sorry," I said quickly. "Long day."

Hazel blinked. "Did something else happen?"

Before either of us could answer, Ford clapped me on the shoulder.

"Hey, Roz!" he said cheerfully.

"Hey, Ford," I said, sipping my tea. He sat beside me and looked with interest at the mess of papers and books spread before us.

"So. What's new?" he asked.

Emily looked at me, and I gestured to her.

"Please," I said. "Take it away."

I let Emily take the lead on updating Ford and Hazel. Derek came over and listened, too, but I didn't have the energy to contribute anything to another retelling of it all. I continued sketching, this time the face of the old woman I'd seen in the window the night Veronica had come over. Strangely enough, though the ghosts terrified me, drawing them didn't. Listening to Hazel's gasps and Derek's questions as Emily regaled them with the tale of my latest exploits was putting me on edge, though. Ford was silent through it all. His eyes never left my face, and I kept glancing up at him nervously, wondering what exactly he was staring at.

When she was done, they all turned to me. I shrank back in my seat a little bit. What did they expect me to say?

“Are you okay?” Hazel finally asked.

I thought about that question. I didn’t even know the answer. It was most likely “no” but that sounded too defeatist. “Yes” was an outright lie.

“Probably?” I tried.

That didn’t seem to instill a lot of confidence, but they resumed talking to one another, leaving me to my sketches once again.

“What’cha readin’, Em?” Ford asked.

Emily flipped through one of the books. “Well, since I can’t figure out certain elements of the haunting, we’re exploring some other cultures’ outlooks on the paranormal and how to cope with the presence of spirits.”

Ford nodded. “You know, I have some material you might want to read,” he offered.

Emily glanced up, then looked back at the book. “No thanks.”

Ford raised an eyebrow. “No thanks?” he echoed.

“Yeah,” Emily said.

“Why not?” Ford asked.

Emily continued flipping through the book, not looking up at Ford, with an expression I hadn’t seen on her before.

“Because you want this to be scientific,” Emily said. “And it’s not. It paranormal. It’s something outside what we can understand, and I don’t have time to waste on theories that will go nowhere.”

Ford shrugged. “That’s your theory.”

“Look, I get it, you’re analytical. You see the world in math and numbers, and that’s fine. But that just isn’t useful here.”

"Just because you don't know what the scientific explanation is doesn't mean it doesn't exist," Ford said coolly.

Emily's lips twitched in a sardonic smile. "Oh yeah? Kinda sounds like an 'I want to believe' situation. Then again you *do* seem to think this is aliens."

"I think aliens are as possible as ghosts. And I'm not discounting any of your views, I'm just saying there *has* to be a scientific explanation."

Emily laughed. "It's different, Ford. It's *supernatural*, it's outside all that."

Ford shook his head. "No. I just don't accept that. Something can be weird, scary, confusing, and inexplicable to us, but that doesn't mean it's *outside* nature. Nothing is *supernatural* because *everything* is part of nature, even the parts we have no understanding of. So yes, this has a scientific explanation; we just don't know what it is. Maybe we never will. Maybe it's a few hundred or thousand years ahead of us. But there *is* a quantifiable explanation to all that's going on, and researching that might help us."

"Just because you're uncomfortable with the paranormal—" Emily shot back.

"Uncomfortable?" Ford asked. "Who's uncomfortable?"

"I am," I muttered under my breath. No one heard me.

"Look," Emily said, snapping her book shut and setting it aside. "It's real cute that you think you can run some numbers and answer age-old unsolved mysteries, and it's real sweet that you have all this self-esteem and belief in yourself, but it's time for the grown-ups to work, and if we keep getting sidetracked on your theories, we're never going to solve Roz's ghost problem."

At mention of my name, I shrank back further. Why, oh why, couldn't I turn invisible?

Ford's eyes widened a bit. "Hey, that's a little unfair..."

"No, what's unfair is some cocky rich boy barging in on my investigation and trying to warp it to fit his beliefs."

"I'm not trying to steal your investigation, I'm trying to help my friend," Ford retorted, all lightness and humor gone from his face.

Emily glared across the table at him. "You keep diverting the conversation to theories that have no bearing on what we're doing here. That's not helping, that's slowing us down."

"How have I been hindering your research?" Ford demanded. "When have I ever stood in the way of your methods? I've offered new viewpoints, I haven't stopped you from one séance or reading or whatever. I just have my own ideas!"

"Ideas that are a slap in the face to everything I'm working on!" Emily snapped.

"I have participated in *everything*," Ford went on. "Without question, without ridicule. I'm in this, the same as you, and my ideas and theories are valid just like yours. You may be the ghost expert, but that doesn't mean I don't have anything to bring to the table."

"Actually, it kinda does. And I'm getting a little sick of your 'it's aliens, it's science' attitude, because frankly, it has no place here," Emily said.

"Em—" Hazel said, barely audible over the two of them.

"So you're just going to outright refuse to see another angle because it *might* go against what you think the answer *should* be?" Ford wasn't quite yelling, but he was close.

"That's not what I'm saying! You're twisting my words! Don't treat me like some kind of lunatic for knowing what I think!" Emily *was* yelling. "I didn't just wake up one day and invent a bunch of stupid ideas—these are based on *years* of research!"

"Same here!" Ford shouted back. "I'm not just trying to ruin your theories, I have real reasons for what I'm saying!"

"Guys!" Derek hissed, looking around the café. People had begun to stare.

Ford and Emily both sat back, fuming. I had slipped down even farther down in my seat, the napkin I'd been drawing on now crumpled in my tightly-clenched fist. Hazel's eyes flicked back and forth between the two, but Derek leaned on the table, palms flat, looking at Emily and Ford in turn with a level of command that surprised me.

"Are you two cool?" he asked after a few seconds.

They both nodded, though neither was looking at the other.

"Good," Derek said. "I'm going to get our drinks, and some Calm The Hell Down cookies, and take my break. Don't bite each other's heads off before I get back." With that, he headed back to the kitchen.

The four of us sat in tense silence. Hazel pulled out her phone and messed with it for a bit, and Emily went back to working on her computer. I glanced at Ford, who was staring down at the table with a look that was either irritated or embarrassed, or maybe a bit of both.

I sipped my tea. This was going to be a long day.

The journal was mocking me. Its existence tugged at the edge of my consciousness, always present, always calling out to me. The pull was getting worse. It was almost tangible now. Something I had to physically avoid. Keeping the journal in my nightstand was no longer an option. I put it in a box on the shelf in my closet. One that was too high for me to reach without standing on a step. Even in a box, on a shelf, behind a door, it nagged at me.

The draw of the journal was yet another reason for me to avoid my house. I was there for showing around the new housekeeper, and for spending time with my father in the evenings, but anytime I could get away, I did.

My father still wanted to call an exorcist, but I found myself putting it off. He kept asking, but the more we actually talked about it, the less I felt it was the right thing to do. He brought up therapy a few more times, and I promised to go. Somehow, that seemed easier to face than a rabbi burning herbs and reading scrolls in our house. Or a priest tossing holy water around. I wasn't even sure what my aversion was, it just didn't feel right. My father was reluctant, but he agreed. I had been calm, and we'd kept our housekeeper, Sarah, for several days.

For almost a whole week after I checked the voicemail, things were relatively quiet. It wasn't truly peaceful, but things weren't getting worse, so I considered this plateau a positive thing.

I had encounters, but they led nowhere. The tattered woman, the foreign ghost, glimpses of the white figures, and snippets of the whispers. Nothing of consequence. I didn't see Diego and, thankfully, I didn't see the shadow. When I told Emily about my suspected ability, she told me to try calling Diego to me, but I didn't. Part of me wanted to talk to him, but I also wanted to forget this whole thing. I sent the ghosts away when I needed to, but I didn't try to bring them to me.

I met with the others a few times, but I forced myself to sleep at my own house. I didn't want to draw the threat to Hazel's home, and while Emily probably would have loved to have me bring some ghosts to her, I thought it would be good for my father to see me sleeping through the night in our house like a sane person.

So I laid in my bed at night, closing my eyes against the whispers, gritting my teeth against the breezes of their passing, and burying myself under my covers like a little child. I could only push them away once in a while. My ability seemed less and less reliable lately.

Monsters under my bed. Monsters in my closet. Monsters everywhere.

I thought of Diego's words more often than I should have, pondering their meaning when I should have been sleeping.

I stayed by my father's side as much as I could when he was home. The ghosts never appeared around him. I had started paying closer attention, and it wasn't just a coincidence—it was consistent, and constant. One night, when he fell asleep on the sofa, I didn't wake him up. I let him sleep there, curling up beside him and reveling in the first night of uninterrupted sleep I'd had in weeks. I had no explanation for why my dad seemed ghost-proof, but I honestly didn't care anymore. I made a mental note to ask Emily after I'd enjoyed some peaceful rest.

The dream still came, as it always did, but I told myself it was just stress and put it out of my mind.

I took my lessons with Joanne. I hung out with my friends and helped Emily with her proposal. I spent time with my father. I tried not to roll my eyes when he talked about Veronica, and made nice when I saw her. Once, she dropped him off after lunch, and another time when she came by to pick up the scarf she'd forgotten at our house. Diego didn't make an appearance after that, and I wondered if he was just so afraid he had retreated completely. I decided not to bother him.

The relative peace wouldn't last; it couldn't. It never did with my mother, and it wouldn't with the ghosts, either. That was just a fact of life.

It didn't make it any easier when my delicate balance all came crashing down, though.

Twenty-Two

"Have you been sleeping at all lately?" Derek asked. His image was a little blurry on my screen, and it lagged here and there before clearing up a bit. I wondered if a storm was coming in.

"No. Have you?" I shot back incredulously. He didn't let my tone bug him. I adjusted the computer on my lap so I could sit more comfortably and still see my friends.

"You guys," Emily yawned. "Shhh. It's starting."

I snickered at the left side of my screen, where Emily's tired face looked out at me. Derek had informed me that, despite the fact that they did a lot of work a night, Emily was the kind of person who needed about ten hours of sleep and often got tired early. Since *East/West* didn't start till eleven, it was a stretch for her.

"Already falling asleep on us, Em?" Derek asked.

"Shut up, you," she said, propping her chin on her arm.

The theme music started up and I listened to the intro to the show. Emily and Derek had invited the rest of us to join in on their little tradition, but both Ford and Hazel had to be up early for work in the morning, so it was just the three of us.

They did this almost every week when new episodes aired, it seemed, and they thought it would give me a better idea of how to approach ghosts myself. We were having another séance soon, and Emily wanted me prepared to help Diego.

Besides, the ghosts had resumed their regular activity. Sarah had resigned from her post, and I was cold all the time. It was becoming disturbingly normal to me, which I didn't much like.

"Good evening, and welcome to *East/West*, the show that takes stories from all across the country. I'm Chad Letts, and tonight, we have a very special show for you..."

"I still think you should call in," Emily said, unwrapping a candy bar.

"Not happening," I said.

"I'm just sayin'," she mumbled around a bite of chocolate.

This episode focused on something called the "Mothman", which sounded completely horrible to me. Emily, despite being tired, was interested, and Derek seemed downright fascinated. I sat with a sketchpad, drawing out how the Mothman might look. I had a few different sketches going, based on the various descriptions given on the show.

Chad was interviewing an expert. There were several callers from around the country who reported having all sorts of Mothman experiences; everything from wildly outlandish encounters to barely-noteworthy sightings. I wanted to say they were all conspiracy theorists and paranoid lunatics, but it was hard to judge them when I was seeing strange apparitions in my own house.

"How many times has Mothman been seen since his initial sighting in 1966?" Chad asked the show's guest.

"It's very hard to say, really," the man speaking was some paranormal expert named Harlon Pax or something weird like that. He said, "It depends on what one considers a legitimate report. If you look at all reports, then Mothman sightings are well into the hundreds. If you restrict yourself to more thoroughly investigated claims, though, you'll still find close to one hundred reports of the Mothman."

I gnawed on my eraser as I considered one of my sketches. "Didn't they figure out it was some kind of huge crane that lost its migration route?" I asked.

"That's one theory," Derek said. "And it's possible that's what some people saw."

The way the two of them talked about all this paranormal stuff still fascinated me. They were so matter-of-fact, so logical about it. It threw me off a little, even now. Ghosts and Mothman and aliens were all still partially filed under "science-fiction" in my mind. Though I, too, was starting to think more openly about the possibilities.

"Of course," Harlon went on, "many reports are simply a response to the sensationalized nature of the Mothman. There was a time this creature was being reported almost non-stop, and fear mixed with fascination certainly generated more frenzy, and thus more alleged sightings. Some will be genuine mistakes, while others will be intentional deceptions. Some will be made by eager spectators trying to see something, while others come from paranoia and fear."

What bothered me, as I studied my drawings, was how the descriptions all seemed to match. They sounded different, people had their own ways of speaking and they focused on various aspects, but when I put pen to paper, the ideas all seemed strikingly similar. Maybe it was just my style. I was certainly no police profiler. It bothered me, though, despite my rationalization.

Emily fell asleep around twelve-thirty, which Derek said was rather impressive. Her computer was still on, though, so we could see her head resting on her arms, her shoulders rising and falling steadily.

"See anything weird today?" Derek asked.

"...Yeah. Remember that poltergeist from the theater I keep seeing?"

"Uh-huh."

"She was in my bathroom this afternoon. In the mirror behind me."

"Creepy. Did she do anything? Or was she just hanging out?"

I blew at a few stray hairs. "No. She never does, at least not since that first sighting. She just...looks at me. And it's a freaky look. I don't know how to describe it."

"Who do you think *she* is?" Derek asked. "I mean, you first saw her at that show, right? What's she doing hanging around your house now?"

"I really have no idea. I don't think she's..." I shook my head. "I don't know who she is, but then I don't know what that scary shadow monster is, either, and I gotta say, the shadow scares me more."

I drew the girl from the theater. I turned to a fresh page, not wanting to look at her eyes, even in illustrated format.

"I think all they have to do is be there to be scary," Derek mused, twirling a pen between his fingers.

"Yeah."

I continued drawing. My sketch was another of Diego. He soothed me somehow, and we listened to Chad wrap things up with the Mothman expert. Next up was a series of callers who had seen other strange beings, from chupacabra to humanoid lizards.

"Do you think these people are for real?" I asked Derek after a caller from Michigan came on the line, talking about a two-headed llama that he believed was the spawn of Satan.

"Some of them, yeah. Some of them..." he laughed.

"Chad's really nice, though," I said. "Always treats them like they're serious."

"I think all of them are, especially the crazy ones."

"Hey, don't knock insanity," I said dully, still drawing. "I'm likely headed down that road."

Derek chuckled and smiled, though it seemed sad. "I've had enough experience with mental illness to gauge. I think you're good."

"Well, so have I, and I would have to disagree with you there," I said. I tried to sound lighthearted, joking, but my laugh was strained.

He nodded, still snickering, and I bit back the urge to ask what he meant when he said he had experience with mental illness. I didn't miss the fact that he avoided asking me the same question.

"I don't know. Maybe we're all crazy. Maybe insanity is a normal part of human life," he said.

"If insanity is normal, can it be called insanity anymore?" I asked.

"Aren't we feeling deep tonight?"

"Ghosts plus sleep deprivation equals philosophical musings," I said.

"Makes perfect sense."

The llama caller was still on the line, saying, "...and I could hear it speaking to me. It said—"

"Derek!"

Derek's eyes went wide and he spun around. It was a male voice calling him, not his mother. He looked alarmed.

"What's wrong?" I asked.

"Derek!" The voice was louder now, more insistent. Almost angry, but not really about anything specific. It reminded me of my mother when she'd be having a bad day.

"Yeah, Dad?" he called.

I could hear his father speaking, but I couldn't make out the words.

"Sorry, I've gotta go," Derek said in a rushed whisper. His face was drawn and pale.

"Okay, bye," I said, confused.

His screen went dark before I had finished talking. I blinked at my laptop, now with half the screen dark and one the other half featuring the top of Emily's head while she slept.

I closed the chat program, figuring I should probably get to bed as well. The show was still playing, and I decided to leave it on for the moment. I was still drawing, Joanne at her easel now. I did another sketch beside it of her mother. My lines flowed easily to create the dark-haired woman who'd escaped Nazi Germany. What must that have been like? What had being her daughter been like? What kind of demons did someone carry with them after witnessing such horrors?

I set my sketchbook aside. I *should* sleep, but I didn't want to.

So I paced around my room. I lay on my bed watching shows on my phone. I listened to an audiobook. I did just about everything I could think of until I was yawning and fighting to keep my eyes open.

I laid sideways on my bed, flopping down lazily. I closed my eyes and tried to muster up the energy to reorient myself.

My hair moved. At first, I thought it was just the air conditioner. The room was cold, after all. Even more reason to move and get under the covers.

But then something slinked around my neck, squeezing me.

My hand shot to my throat, grasping at something very much like the bindings that had held me to the metal table before. I grabbed it and pulled, but it held fast, tightening with every second.

I thrashed. I tried to scream, but the rope was crushing my windpipe, and all that escaped was a strangled little moan.

Concentrate. Send it away. Focus.

But I couldn't. The panic was overwhelming me, amplified by the blinding darkness, and I couldn't clear my mind enough to do anything useful.

Still clawing at the rope, I tried to reach back and see what was attacking me. My hands brushed rough fabric. Massive arms pinned me against something firm, like a wall, though there was no wall in this part of the room.

I weakened, fading. My movements grew sluggish. Despite how dark it was, I could tell my vision was going black at the edges while little starbursts of light exploded in the center. Explosive pain shot through my skull.

You're going to send it away or you're going to die, Rosalind.

I closed my eyes and let the fear turn into anger. I let that bubble up inside me, building in my skull like pressure with no release valve. With my eyes closed, I couldn't see the swirling mess around me, but I could feel it like before, in the kitchen. Something about it made my head spin and feel light.

Go. Away.

But nothing happened. I thrashed, trying to scream but making no sound. I was helpless, and I was blacking out.

The lights flickered and there was a sharp breeze. As suddenly as it had started, it stopped, and I dropped to the floor, falling as though I'd been floating in mid-air. My ankle stung and my knees ached, but I didn't care much about that. I was coughing, gasping for air. The swollen skin of my face tingled uncomfortably. I ran my hand along my throat, still gasping for breath. My lungs burned, and I closed my eyes until the spinning stopped.

For a while, I just laid on my bedroom floor, shaking and hugging my knees. I cried a bit. I considered waking my dad, but that would only make him worry more. And what could he do?

As my breathing evened out, I thought back to other attacks from ghosts. The first was the one that gashed up my arms and legs when it pinned me down. Then there was Emily at Hazel's house, and Derek at the séance. Now this.

I sat up, trying to make sense of this information. I wanted to see how it all connected, if it connected at all. The room was still cold. I looked around, nervous. Every shadow made me twitch. Every sound sent me spinning around, looking for another attacker.

A floorboard creaked to my right and I whirled toward it, afraid I'd see the shadow creature, or the tattered girl, or some new terror.

But the figure I saw wasn't the monstrously huge shadow that I'd first seen in Emily's pictures. It was the figure of a man. It looked like the man I'd seen in my hall when my father was out of town.

"*Kwiaty.*"

I swallowed hard, but he didn't seem to be interested in attacking me. He just stood in the corner, watching me. I couldn't see him clearly. Then again, I never could. He preferred the shadows.

At least he wasn't like that other thing...which seemed to *be* a shadow.

"I don't know what that means," I croaked, my voice weak. I rubbed my hand along my throat again, hoping it wouldn't leave a bruise. The last thing I needed was for my dad to think I'd tried to hang myself or something.

"*Kwiaty,*" he repeated, more weakly, like he was fading away.

"What is kwia...what...what is that?" I asked more loudly. I wanted to help, I really did, but I had no idea how. Even Diego, who I could at least communicate with, was a mystery to me.

The man in the shadows stepped back again, and after a second, I couldn't see him anymore. Maybe he was gone, or maybe he'd just given up on me.

My room warmed and I sat up straighter, trying to make sense of everything that had happened. I was staring into space, looking at where he had been. He and his strange, foreign word that I couldn't make sense of. My eyes had adjusted to the dark, and something on the floor caught my eyes. I peered at it, then crept slowly closer. It looked like a scrap of paper, but when I picked it up, it had a smooth texture. A flower. I frowned. I examined it, wondering where it had come from. I didn't know what kind of flower it was, but I was certain it didn't grow in our yard or anywhere around here. I didn't have flowers in my room; we didn't even have flowers in our house.

I froze. Had the ghost brought me this? And if so, why? What was he trying to communicate with a flower? Getting up, I grabbed a small sketchbook and sat on my bed, flicking on a light. I sat staring at the page, my hands shaking. Slowly at first, then faster as I gained momentum, I mapped out each incident. The box of wedding pictures, the journal, the journal again, the whispering in the hall...

There were a lot. More than I realized until I sat down and put them all on paper in a list like this. I found myself remembering incidents, squeezing them into the proper chronological place on my list. Emily had asked me to do something like this before, but I'd been putting it off. Now, though, I *needed* to see how it all mapped out. Avoiding it clearly hadn't helped me—maybe this way, I could get some perspective.

By the time it was done, I had thirty incidents, including the one that had just happened.

I stared at the list in surprise. I had probably missed something, but still, it was a lot. I considered this, counting off days on my fingers. I'd lived in this house for just over three weeks. I shuddered at the list I'd made. Was it possible I'd had that many encounters in twenty-four days?

I shook my head. Something wasn't right here. Okay, *lots of things* weren't right here, but even for weird, inexplicable paranormal activity, this seemed a little out of hand. I'd read a lot about hauntings in the past weeks and this was excessive.

I wrote everything I could remember from every encounter and incident I'd had. I drew the ghosts. I drew the scene from that dream I kept having. I wrote about each day here and all the strange things I'd seen. The housekeepers, Joanne and Ford's stories around this house and the people who'd lived here before, all the times I'd felt anything off or weird or creepy.

Then I wrote down my questions and any notes I had to go with them. I had a lot. I dedicated a couple pages to them.

- *What makes the ghosts show up? Seems random.*

- *Dad has never seen ghosts—why?*
- *Housekeepers all see ghosts? Or just feel scared? Why?*
- *Veronica connected to Diego? How??*
- *Sometimes they attack?*
- *Darkness. Silence. What causes it? (Pantry door not broken??)*
- *CREEPY MANNEQUINS (humming, light, ropes?)*
- *Ghost attacks? Poltergeists?*
- *Who are these other ghosts?*
- *Shadow-thing. Attacks me.*
- *Headaches? Connected to ghosts?*
- *"Kweeatee"?*

Most of it was incoherent, but I didn't care. It was good to get it down on paper. It was good to give my fears a voice, and to lay my questions out. Somehow, seeing them made me feel more in control, even if it was all still chaotic. Even if I had no answers.

As I sat back and surveyed my work, a twinge of panic hit me. I knew what I had to do next, even if thinking of it made me sick.

Shaking, I crossed my room to the closet, dragging my desk chair with me. I climbed up and felt around for the box that contained my mother's journal, hidden on my topmost shelf. I found the box, but the journal wasn't there. I was almost relieved, but anxious, too, until I remembered that the journal had a habit of moving around. I climbed down and searched my room, but I couldn't find it anywhere. Had I lost it somehow? Had the ghosts moved it? After so long trying to get me to read it, were they now going to hide it from me?

But when I went to flop on my bed in defeat, the journal was there, sitting right on top of my notes, waiting for me. Despite being used to paranormal interference in my life, seeing it there sent chills down my spine.

Slowly, I sat down on my bed, unable to pull my gaze from the journal. Now that it was in front of me, I doubted my earlier conviction to read it.

But there was something useful there. It had appeared too many times, at significant moments, and my experiences too closely mirrored my mother's last I'd seen her. I held it in my lap, staring down at it. As I did, I realized for the first time that the insignia on the front had been *drawn* onto the cover. Carefully. Meticulously.

I sighed. Much as it made my stomach turn, I had to read it. I took a deep breath and opened the journal, tracing my fingers along the first page. It was day-planner style, with little binder rings in the middle. A pocket on the front was stuffed with papers, and there were newspaper clippings, printed sheets, and all kinds of other scraps mixed in with the pages.

The first entry was dated before I was born. My mother would have just been starting college when she'd written it.

Confused, I flipped through the pages. My head was starting to throb. I pressed my fingers to my temple as I turned the pages. Half-way through I paused on an entry from when I was about five.

Not bothering to read that one, either, I flipped to the end, wondering how much time this journal had covered.

I read the date without looking at the entry itself; it was the last day I'd seen her.

My eyes darted toward what she'd written in the hours before she decided to abandon me, but I quickly looked away, flipping back to the first page. I couldn't process the fact that this journal covered so much time. First entry—that was a good place to start.

The entry was simple. Her handwriting was different, though I could see similarities between my mother's adult writing and her teenage scrawl.

The purpose of this journal is to keep a record of the things happening to me. I haven't told anyone what's going on, but maybe I can start to make sense of it here.

The words hit me so hard I had to close my eyes for a moment. When I was ready, I opened them and continued reading:

I don't really know where to begin. Things started getting weird last year, and at first I thought they'd get better on their own, or at least just stay the same, but now things are worse and weirder than ever. Here's what's been happening:

- *Ghosts. Or what I thought were ghosts for the last few years. I'm starting to wonder, though, because a lot of them don't seem to fit the research I've done about ghosts. They don't all have a purpose or "unfinished business". Some of them don't even seem aware that they're here.*

- *Dreams. At least, they started as dreams. Now it's like my dreams are invading my day. They're popping up even when I'm awake. They've always been too real, it scares me.*
- *Headaches. They started as a dull kind of ache, but now*

I dropped the journal as pain like a burning ax shot through my head as a scream tore my throat.

Biting my lip to choke back the cries, I pressed my palms against my eyes until the burning subsided. I could feel the world spinning around me, but I couldn't focus on anything enough to make sense out of whether or not I was shifting.

Slowly, the pain edged away and I lowered my hands, looking back at the journal. Reading her words had made me sick. Literally. I decided to read little by little, and give myself periodic breaks.

I went downstairs and made a cup of tea, taking an aspirin while I was waiting for it to steep. I stayed in the kitchen longer than was really necessary, and I wasn't sure if I was avoiding my mother's words or the skull-splitting headache this time.

In my room once again, I sat on my bed, clutching my mug of tea. Hand shaking, I picked up the journal again. I'd caught sight of a bold, underlined phrase in the journal. When I'd dropped it, it had opened to one of the middle pages. The sentence I was staring at read:

*In my dream, the red-haired woman introduced herself as **"The Red Knight"**, and* *she said she could help me "quiet the voices" (her words, not mine).*

"The Red Knight" was underlined, gone over several times with the pen to make it bold. And the symbol from the cover was sketched messily on that page, as well. I wondered why. I'd been having strange dreams, too, but I hadn't encountered anyone who spoke to me in them.

Yet.

Searching for additional references of this "Red Knight" turned up a few more cryptic entries, but nothing I could work with. I decided to give up on it for the moment. The only thing I could be sure of regarding the Red Knight was that they were interested in my mother, and contacted her often.

Instead, I hunted for key phrases that might lead to understanding. "Ghost" came up a lot, but that wasn't exactly what I wanted to read about. I wanted to know *why*, and *how*, far more than what kind of encounters she faced. Even seeing her handwriting was making my throat tight, but I pressed on, searching for answers.

My hands skimmed through pages and across words, eyes flicking along, looking for anything that might help, despite barely knowing what to look for. It was overwhelming, and only made the pressure in my skull intensify.

Just as I was about to give up for the night, a word caught my eye, making my heart skip a beat.

Portal.

I sat up a little straighter as I pulled the book closer, holding it carefully as I read the entry.

I've finally found another portal. This time by the sea. Seems like they turn up in nature a lot, though the last one was in a bus depot.

I'm getting better at closing them, but this one was a challenge. I blacked out after sealing it, and Sana couldn't carry me back to the car, so she just sat with me until I woke up. I think I was out for almost an hour.

The process for this one was a little different. I've added it to my notes on that (page 71), but suffice to say I felt like I was being ripped apart from the inside. I don't like that this is getting harder. I'm worried I won't be able to close them in the future, not if it keeps feeling like this.

The words made me shiver. I checked the date and saw that it was from about a year and a half ago. I remembered my mother disappearing that day. It was, in fact, one of the first times I'd felt panic at her absence. The first time I'd wondered if perhaps she wouldn't be coming home this time.

I tried to read more, but my head ached again, and I closed the journal, clumsily dog-earing that page for future reference. I had a lot of questions, like who was Sana, and why had she been there? I had never heard of her, but she must have been important to my mother if she'd been around for something like this.

I rubbed my eyes and temples, desperate for relief. An ache blossomed in my chest at the idea of how little I'd really known my mother. The séance with the cards flashed through my mind: P-O-R-T.

Portal.

After a moment of rest, I turned to page 71 and read through this “process” for closing portals. It all seemed impossible to me, but I took notes in my own journal. According to her, the portals were how ghosts and various entities leaked into our dimension from others. And if she could close them, maybe I could, too.

The more I dug though—slowed by headaches, but still making decent time—the more I saw that there was a kind of haphazard order to it. At first, I couldn’t understand her process. Mostly, I think, because she couldn’t either.

As it turned out, the whole thing seemed pretty simple. Not easy, but simple. It would require a few things, and meditation seemed to be a key component, which I was terrible at. I tapped my finger against the page of my journal, contemplating whether or not I could pull this off. I was supposed to have the ability, but that was in theory. In practice, I’d displayed very little control over it—my results were hit or miss, and usually left me so drained I could barely stand.

When I couldn’t read any more of her words, I set the journal aside and returned to my own. I wrote and drew, spilling my thoughts and theories and fears onto the page until the pain in my head moved into my hand, and my heart beat evenly for the first time in longer than I could remember. Finally, I could see light at the end of this tunnel.

Twenty-Three

I had another dream about the clearing that night. The same dream, which left me with the same nervous energy. I woke with a jolt, pulled from sleep, but by what, I didn't know. I looked around, startled, but saw nothing out of place.

Waking up like that left me disoriented. I had fallen asleep atop my covers, draped over the scraps of paper on which I'd jotted down various notes, drawings, or ideas. I'd crumpled a few of them with my body, folding one of the pages of my sketchbook. The dim light on my nightstand was still on, and there was something odd about waking up with the sun still down, artificial light softly illuminating the room.

I rubbed my face as I sat up, stretching my back and trying to work out the kinks I'd gotten from sleeping wrong.

My phone was beside me, battery low, as I'd forgotten to charge it. I checked it, squinting my eyes against the too-bright light. It was almost five in the morning. I yawned and gathered my papers together, trying to create some semblance of order.

After I sorted the loose pages, I took the sketchbook onto my lap and tried to fold the bent page back along the seam, smoothing it out.

There was something drawn on the page. I stared at it, still half-asleep and confused by what I was seeing. At first, it seemed to be just a jumble of lines and squiggles. I turned it slowly, trying to see it from another angle.

When the sketchbook was upside-down, the lines all clicked into place, and I understood what I was looking at. It was a roughly drawn map.

I stared at it, bewildered. What was it a map of, and who had drawn it? I didn't think I had, and I didn't recognize the landscape, so it was unlikely I'd done so, even in my pre-sleep daze.

I thought of the ghosts. It was probably one of them, though which one, and why, nagged at my mind.

But all those concerns fell away when I saw the messy scrawl in the lower right-hand corner of the page. I smoothed my fingers over the words, reading them several times.

Mount Charleston – Echo.

Echo. It sounded familiar, but I couldn't place it.

That didn't matter, though. I knew what I was looking at. The entire map converged around a small circle in the center, and somehow, I recognized the indiscriminate little patch of gray amidst a vast expanse of illustrated woodland.

I didn't need any more explanation than that; this was the location of my dream.

I stared up at the building before me. It was more intimidating in person than it had been online.

"What are your plans for today?" I remembered my father's question from breakfast this morning.

And I remembered my lie. "Nothing much. I might go for a drive, look for some drawing inspiration or cafes or something."

Well, the "go for a drive" bit hadn't been an outright lie—I had driven to get here, after all. But this wasn't a random destination, or somewhere I'd chanced upon.

I took a deep breath and stepped into the physics building of the university. This was where Professor Rowan Fallon would be working in the fall. Rumor was she had an office here that she sometimes visited. Rumor also had it she'd be in today.

My grandmother had a good friend on the school board, and I may or may not have used that connection, and a white lie about Ford's interest in Rowan's classes, to get this information.

The girl at the information desk smiled at me as I walked in, but didn't say anything. I did my best to look confident, like I knew what I was doing. I passed classrooms and labs until I found Rowan's office. The door was ajar, and I could just see her inside.

I froze. I didn't know why I'd come here. What was I thinking? What did I hope to accomplish? She studied physics, sure, but why would she be able to help me? And why would she even *want* to?

"Yes?" she said, leaning a bit to see me through the crack in the door.

I stiffened. I hadn't been quite prepared to speak to her yet.

"Uh, um, h-hi," I said, moving closer to the door. Time to commit or bail. And I had to know if she could help me.

"If you're a student, my office hours are—"

"Actually," I said, pushing the door open and stepping part-way into the office. "I'm...not a student here. Just...someone with a few questions. About your research."

Her eyes narrowed slightly. "Are you with some paper? No, too young. School paper, maybe. I'm not giving interviews."

"It's not that, either. I just..." I glanced down, unable to maintain eye contact with her. And here I had thought *Veronica* was intimidating.

"Well?"

I glanced up at her. She wasn't angry or cross, but it was clear she thought I was wasting her time, and she didn't like that.

"What if...I knew of a portal that had opened?" I asked, holding her gaze despite how it made my knees wobble.

Rowan raised an eyebrow at me. For a moment, I was sure she'd send me away, but she sighed and gestured to one of the chairs in front of her desk. I sat down, grateful to have the support. This was more stressful than I'd anticipated.

"Have you read my book, then?" she asked.

"I...yes?"

"Is that a question?"

I winced. "Um. No. I-I read it. Most of it."

"And you think, based on what you've read there, that you have a portal?"

I nodded shakily.

"Well," she said, sitting back in her chair. "You realize, theoretically, there are portals all over, right?"

"I-I've heard that, b-but," *God, when did I develop a stutter?* "Um...thing is...I think I might have a-a...particularly *big* portal..."

She raised her eyebrow again. My hands started shaking. I gripped my purse tighter and tried to remember everything I'd wanted to say. It all seemed to have fallen right out of my brain.

"How, um, how would I go about...closing it?" I asked. I could barely breathe.

Rowan studied me, and I shrank back a bit, feeling like a specimen under a microscope.

"Why would you want to close it? It could be studied, understood. Where is it?"

I tensed. I didn't like where this was going. "I...I'm not sure."

"You said you wanted to close it, that implies you know where it is."

Lie. "It's....it's in Red Rock canyon..."

She stared me down, and I had a feeling she knew I'd made that up.

After a charged moment, she nodded. "Very well. You don't have to tell me. What signs of this are you experiencing?"

I shifted in my seat. "Um. Temperature drops. W-weird changes in lighting. Like, it'll go really dark all of a sudden. Sounds. Uh...seeing...strange things..." I withered under her stare, wondering what she thought of my ramblings. I almost told her about the shadowy creature that tried to kill me, but when I looked at her face, it made me hesitate. She didn't look confused, or concerned, or annoyed, even. She looked...vindicated. I stopped talking, my stomach churning more than before.

"That certainly does sound like it could be linked to a portal...assuming you aren't suffering from some psychiatric disorder. Are you sure you're in the right building?"

I blinked. I didn't quite know how to answer that.

"Let's go with the assumption that you're correct. If you *are* experiencing a dimensional rift, there is some speculation about what can close them down. As I said, however, the presence of portals is actually far more common than you might think. I've visited a few in my research. They're naturally occurring."

"Yes, but—"

"However, for a portal to cause enough disruption that you would come down here and willingly subject yourself to what I'm assuming is a social-anxiety induced panic attack in search of a solution...then I'm inclined to believe you have a real problem. A bit of advice: *don't* Google 'how to close a portal'—you'll mostly get a bunch of new-age mumbo jumbo. Here, use this," she turned to her computer and typed something. Behind her, a printer rumbled to life and spit out a few pages. She stapled the pages together and handed them over.

"Um, thank you," I said.

"It's my most recent scientific journal submission. It goes into the principles behind portal minimization. It's rather densely scientific, but if you were able to follow my book, you should be fine with this."

I decided not to tell her I'd struggled with her book. Maybe Ford could help me. Or maybe I could just muddle through—I had the internet, I could probably figure it out.

"Thank you," was all I said. I stood to go, then stopped. "What...causes portals to open?"

Rowan shrugged. "Various kinds of energy fields, like electric or magnetic. High concentrations of energy interacting with their environment in just the right way. I discuss the possibility of a global grid in some of my past writings. Why?"

I looked into her piercing eyes. It was like she wanted a particular answer, but wanted me to come up with it on my own. My legs turned to jelly again.

"Um. Just curious."

She nodded, then sat forward, pulling a business card from the holder on her desk.

"Do me a favor; let me know how this goes. I'd love to learn more about your personal experiences, and any real-world applications of my work," she scrawled something on the back of the card and handed it over to me.

I stepped back toward the desk and took the card.

"Thank you," I mumbled, barely audible, and ducked out of the office.

I made it down the stairs and out of the building, but had to find a secluded little bench on the campus to sit and calm myself down before I could drive home. Talking with her had been almost as terrifying as facing the shadowy beast that always attacked me.

I clutched the pages she'd given me, unsure if they would provide answers, or lead me down an even more dangerous path.

TWENTY-FOUR

"We need to go up to the mountains," I said, putting the sketchbook down on the table, open to the page with the hastily-drawn map.

Derek tugged at the edge of the sketchbook, pulling it around so he could see it. "Where is this?" he asked.

"The spot I keep having dreams about," I answered.

The four of them looked up at me in surprise. After leaving Rowan's office, I had called them all and arranged an immediate emergency meeting. Now, we were sitting around the weird café Ford had taken me to before, huddled over my sketches. Everyone was clearly afraid I'd become completely unhinged, but they were all tip-toeing around the topic. I was so strung out at that point I didn't even care.

When none of them had a response, I whispered, "I need to see it myself."

Hazel nodded. “All right, we can head up there tomorr—”

“I need to go *now*. This séance is going to have to wait. I need to be there *today*.”

They looked at me, a bit confused. It was afternoon, and heading to the mountains now might mean being up there at night, where darkness fell much earlier and inexperienced hikers could easily get lost.

“Look,” I said, setting out the pages I’d worked on the previous night. “I mapped everything out. I charted ghost appearances, and the intensity of various events. I wrote down *everything* I could remember, and I...” I glanced at Hazel. She was studying me closely. “I read my mother’s journal.”

Hazel’s eyes widened.

“You did? What did it say? What did you learn?” Emily demanded.

I cleared my throat. “Do you remember that séance where we got the letters ‘P-O-R-T’? It wasn’t spelling a name, or a word in another language; it was spelling ‘portal’.”

“Whoa...portal? To what?” Derek asked.

“To...” this time I glanced at Ford. “To other dimensions.”

Everyone was silent.

“Here, look,” I said, indicating my work from the night before.

They leaned forward, examining the diagram I’d made.

“What does this mean, Roz?” Hazel finally asked.

I pointed to how many ghosts I had encountered. "See that? See how the number of ghosts present keeps increasing?" I asked.

Emily nodded. "Yeah, we'd noticed that..."

"Yes, but look here," I said, indicating the instances of the recurring dreams.

There was a silence as the realization dawned on all of them, as it had on me.

"Every time you have the dream, more ghosts show up," Ford said.

I nodded. "Consistently. Have the dream? See more ghosts. Then the ghosts I see remains the same, until I have the dream again. Then, suddenly, more ghosts."

"How many are you up to now?" Hazel asked.

"It could be anywhere from eleven to seventeen. There are a few events I can't be certain of; could be a separate spirit, could be the same ones I've already seen."

"This is a lot of information, Roz," Emily said, flipping through the pages of my sketchbook. "How did you ever make sense of it all?"

"I stayed up all night," I said. They all looked at me and I shrugged. "What? Like that's different from usual anymore? Anyway, I thought if I put this together with all your observations and data, Emily, we can probably figure out a lot."

Emily nodded. "Yes. Definitely. We've got energy readings and spirit signatures. I knew there was a steady increase in the number of spirits, but I had no idea why. I didn't realize it was related to the dream."

"I didn't, either," I said. "Honestly, the dream seemed kind of irrelevant compared to all the crazy stuff that was happening. So I wasn't really thinking about it, but..."

They all watched me, but I was having a hard time getting the next words out.

"What else, Roz?" Hazel finally asked, her voice gentle.

I bit my lip, then sighed. "I...think...I think *I* am the thing that opened the portal. A-and I think I can close it."

Ford tilted his head to one side. "Is *this* why you need to go to the mountain today, Roz?" he asked.

"Yes," I said. I turned to the page with the map. "That," I said. "*That* is where my dream is happening. *That* is where the portal is. *That* is where I need to go."

Emily nodded slowly. "Energy vortexes, like portals, can be a huge draw for supernatural entities."

Derek nodded. "Yeah, but...why would *this* location—miles away from her house—have anything to do with Roz and her house? This doesn't fit with anything we've ever dealt with or even heard of."

Emily frowned. "I know, but...this is all we have to go on."

We were silent. Hazel made a face.

"What?" I asked her.

She shook her head. "I don't know, Roz. It's just...you need to think about who exactly is drawing you there."

I blinked at her, wondering what she meant.

Hazel fidgeted in her seat and pulled the map over to herself. "This map, for example. Where did you get it?"

It was my turn to shift uncomfortably. "I...well, when I woke up, it was there."

Hazel looked at me, shocked.

"So, a ghost drew it?" Emily asked.

"I don't know. Maybe...I did, but I don't remember? Is that even possible?"

"Possession?" Derek offered. I didn't like the thought of that.

"My point is," Hazel cut in, "we have no idea where this information is coming from. We don't know why you've been getting the dream, we don't know who drew the map, and we don't know what this specific spot has to do with the ghosts. What we *do* know, though, is that it's related somehow, and that even dreaming about this place has increased the whole....ghost activity thing in your life."

I was quiet. She had a point. Blindly following directions wasn't going to help me. It could very easily get me killed. Rowan popped into my head and I bit the inside of my cheek out of nervous reflex. Most of the ghosts seemed largely directionless with their assaults, but a few were downright hostile. And that shadow...it was actively trying to kill me. Maybe this was a dumb idea.

Hazel's eyes lit up as she studied the map. "Unless..." she mumbled.

"Yes?" I prodded when she fell silent.

She glanced up at me, as though she were uncertain. "What if this is...*someone*...who's trying to help you?" she gave me a pointed look and my mouth went dry.

Emily pounced on the idea, saving me from having to think of a response. "Oh!" she said. "That could be it! I mean, if one of the ghosts wants help, or closure, then this could be how they're trying to help you get to where you need to be!"

Derek frowned. "If we don't know for sure what we're doing, and we try to do *anything*, we could end up making even more of a mess."

Emily deflated a little at that. "Yeah, I guess so," she admitted.

"That doesn't mean we can't *go*," Ford said. "We just don't *try* anything. Right?"

Derek's brow furrowed. He glanced at Emily.

"Well, at least we won't make anything worse," she said.

I looked at Derek's cast. I looked at Emily, a few faint scratches still visible. I absently touched the bruises along my neck, the ones I'd hastily covered with makeup and a decorative scarf before leaving my room.

I didn't know the correct course of action. But I didn't like just sitting around waiting for something to happen. I wasn't comfortable with that, and if there was a chance we could learn something that could put an end to all this, I had to know. I had been helpless and without direction this whole time; now that I had something to go on, something to do, I was eager. Between the notes from my mother and the printout from Rowan...there was a possibility I could end this. I had to try.

"Maybe you're right, maybe we shouldn't go," I said, measuring my words carefully. "This sounds like it might be more trouble than it's worth."

I'd have probably gotten away with the lie if it was only Derek, Emily, and Ford. The three of them all nodded in consideration.

But not Hazel. Her dark eyes narrowed at my words, mouth twisting into a frown. "Oh, don't you *dare*," she said.

"What?" I asked.

"You're going to go alone, aren't you?"

I blinked. Knowing someone your entire life could be really inconvenient at times. "No, of course not," I lied.

"Don't give me that, Roz. I know that look. That's your crazy-determined, willing-to-do-anything look and you *know* it's dangerous, but you're still going to go! And worse, you're going to go *by yourself!*"

Emily's eyes widened. "Roz, you can't go alone."

"Why not?" I asked. "If these ghosts are after me, they'll get me eventually. Doesn't mean they have to get the four of you, too. If I go alone, I can check it out and not put any additional people in danger."

Ford shook his head. "We can't just let you go up there by yourself," he said.

"None of you can 'let' me do anything," I snapped.

"At the risk of taking us all back to first grade..." Ford said, "I'll tell on you."

"*What*?" I demanded.

"Your dad. We can't stop you, but he probably can."

I glared at Ford. "Don't threaten me, Abramovich," I snarled.

He put his hands up in a gesture of peace. "I'm not threatening you, Rosalind. I'm just...worried about you," he said. He looked a little surprised at my reaction. "You don't have to get all last-name on me," he added, trying a little smile.

I wasn't in the mood for his jokes. I snatched away my papers and tucked everything back into my sketchbook.

"Roz...in all fairness, I'm with Ford here," Hazel said.

"So if I do something you guys don't like, you're going to have me locked up in a psych ward?"

Hazel's jaw dropped a bit. So did everyone else's.

"No, Roz, that's not—" Ford started to say.

"That's what's going to happen, you know. He thinks I'm losing it," my burgeoning fury gave way to grief at that, and I glanced at Hazel, no longer shouting. "You should know that," I added softly to her.

Hazel looked down, and her expression of shame instantly made me regret my words. Everyone else fell silent.

Emily got up and came over to me, grasping my hands gently. "Look, why don't we just do what we'd originally planned: Go up there and look around. *Only* look around, no messing with anything," she added, looking back at the others.

My hands were shaking a little. Other people were around, some of whom were looking curiously at us.

"Yeah, okay," I whispered. My anger was dissipating, replaced by a weariness that tugged at the corners of my mouth and stung my eyes.

"Let's go now," Derek said. "Before it starts to get dark."

We got up and headed outside, toward Ford's van. It was the only vehicle we could all comfortably fit in.

"Hey," Ford said, hanging back to catch me. I was a little behind the rest of the group, walking slowly.

I didn't say anything, but I looked up at him.

"I'm sorry. I didn't..." he shook his head. "I didn't mean to sound, like, threatening or anything weird like that," he said. He was looking down, glancing up at me like a wounded puppy.

I sighed. I was still annoyed, so I didn't know what to say that wouldn't be mean. I tried to stay neutral by saying, "I know. Just...I don't respond well to that sort of thing."

He nodded, looking solemn. "I get that. It came out all wrong. I didn't..." he ran a hand back through his hair and sighed. "I'm just sorry. I was trying to be a good friend and look out for you and I think it came across weird," he said, wincing.

I laughed weakly. "It's fine. Just...don't look out for me. I take it all wrong."

"Yeah, she really does," Hazel said, catching my arm and linking it with hers as she circled back to me.

"It's your own fault," I said, smiling apologetically. "You should know better by now."

Hazel shook her head, giving me a little hug. "You know I can't stop."

We piled into the van and I pulled out the map, trying to orient it to any roads I knew.

"We should paint your van green and call it the Mystery Machine," Emily said, clicking her seatbelt into place.

"No way," Ford said. "That would be a disgrace."

We all laughed at that.

"What? I have my standards," he said, crossing his arms.

I typed up a text to my dad as Ford started up the van and steered us onto the road.

Heading up to the mountains for a hike with the gang :)

He responded a moment later with, *Great. Have fun. Be back before sundown, OK?*

I stared at his response, the guilt gnawing away at me. My reply was a simple "*OK*"—a promise I had no intention of keeping. I was lying to my dad. Again. I didn't like it, but what was I going to say? "Sorry, Dad. I opened a portal in the mountains and had to try to close it or else people might start dying"?

The others chattered a lot on the drive up, but I couldn't seem to focus on their conversation. I was too busy going over my notes and trying to perfect the method for closing the portal. If I could pull it off, this would all be over.

"Roz?"

"Hmm?" I glanced at Ford, pulled from darker thoughts. I looked at the other three in the back. They were absorbed in some video Emily had recorded and was showing off on her phone. I turned back to Ford.

"Do you have any clue what to do with a portal if we find one?" he asked.

I studied his anxious face, then turned my attention back to the mountains ahead.

"No...I just...I feel the need to be there. So strongly. Have you ever felt like you really needed to be somewhere? Or do something?"

He shook his head.

I sighed. "How about...do you ever just...*know* something? Not because you read it or heard it or figured it out...you just, you *know* it?"

That sparked some recognition in his eyes. "Yeah. I have. It's how I fix things most of the time."

I nodded. "Yes, that, exactly. It's...it's like that. I just *know* I can have an impact on this whole situation. I've been feeling it for a while, but now I...I can't put it off anymore. I need to be there. I need to *see*. I need to try."

He nodded, seeming to accept that. There was still an air of tension in the car. Hazel fidgeted, nervous, twisting her hair around her finger as she drummed her other hand against her knee. She was asking a bunch of questions, to which Emily responded with things like "mmmhmm" or "dunno". She was busy, writing quickly on a notepad, no doubt compiling notes for her grant proposal and making lists of what to do when we got there. Derek sat quietly, looking out the window. He was surprisingly still, face drawn, frowning slightly, his too-old eyes clouded with emotion I couldn't read.

Beside me, Ford was also quiet. I studied him out of the corner of my eye. He was usually much livelier. Seeing him still and contemplative bothered me.

And what about me? I had no idea where I was in all this. I thought I'd be scared, or worried, or at least questioning, but I was eerily calm. It was an odd calm, though. Abnormal. Unsettling.

The calm before the storm. My mother grew up in the Midwest, with tornadoes ravaging towns; she used to say that all the time. I understood now.

We drove on, largely in silence, save for Hazel's nervous chattering. The desert gave way to forest rather abruptly. One minute it was rocks and dirt, the next, we were surrounded by trees and greenery. I spotted a cluster of deer watching us from a hillside. The temperature dropped, I could feel it even though the van was sealed. Again, the change in scenery stunned me. Living in Las Vegas was proving to be much more intriguing and complex than I'd imagined.

I snorted. That was a bit obvious.

"Where are we headed again?" Ford asked.

"Echo," I said.

"That's by grandma's cabin," Hazel noted. She reached into the front and took the map, guiding us along the twisting mountain roads better than I could have. I was glad, honestly. I wasn't in the mood to talk.

We drove past some houses, leaving the paved road and turning onto a path of rocks. There was an area that looked like it might be a parking lot, but there were no cars there.

Ford parked across from a little cluster of buildings behind a chain link fence. They looked like housing for generators or water pumps or something.

I climbed out of Ford's van and shivered. It was cooler here, even with the sun shining. The others looked at me, and I nodded, heading toward the forest. There was a path, almost like a road, that I followed at first. After a few paces, I turned, weaving my way between some boulders and heading to a big, wide-open clearing.

"Is this it?" Hazel asked, studying the sign that announced we were standing on a historic site.

"Not yet," I said.

I moved out of the clearing and deeper into the woods, the others trailing behind me. Under the cover of the tall trees, it was colder, and darker, giving the illusion of it being later in the day.

I could feel the pull stronger than ever. My head was pounding, but I couldn't turn away from it. I had to press on.

And then, with stunning suddenness, I was there.

The pressure in my head released all at once. I was standing in the middle of a little grove. The ground here was clear, and around us was a circle of aspen trees.

The wind whispered through the leaves, sounding almost like the ocean.

I closed my eyes and shivered. This must be the portal; the energy here was exactly like when ghosts showed up, but intensified to an incredible degree. I swayed a little at the overwhelming sensations; it felt so like my dreams it was unreal.

"This is it?" Derek asked.

"Yes..." I whispered.

"There's nothing here," Hazel said.

"Yes, there is." I heard my voice like it was someone else's. I was disconnected.

Emily and Derek took out their phones and started taking pictures. I wasn't sure why, but I didn't interfere. I didn't care. I looked at the hastily drawn map in my sketchbook, then up at my surroundings.

"Whoa...look at this," Emily said. I turned to see her holding out her phone, a picture she'd taken displayed on the screen. I was in the picture, my back to Emily, staring into the distance. But instead of the ordinary landscape before me, the picture showed a warped, twisting circle of light before me. It was subtle, but still clear.

"Is that the portal?" Hazel asked.

I turned back to the clearing, trying to see the light with my own eyes. I did my best to clear my mind and "let go", but it was harder than I'd thought, even up here, and I couldn't make it visible to myself.

I stepped out into the center of the clearing, where I always found myself in the dreams. I could feel the energy here, so strong I could almost touch it. Goosebumps spread up my arms.

It was just like in the dreams. It scared me, how accurate they had been. I turned slowly, studying the trees. The earth. Even the color of the sky was the same as in my dreams. I shivered, wondering what that meant.

My headache was returning, but different, fuzzy. It didn't have the sharpness it usually had, but instead rolled in, like the tide, slowly rising in my skull.

"Roz? Are you feeling anything?"

I didn't even know who'd asked the question. I was so lost to the rest of the world.

"Roz?"

I turned at the sound of my name, slow, like I was moving through water. It was Emily. She had come a little closer, though she seemed hesitant to step into the clearing.

She can feel it, too.

I paused at the thought, unsure if it had come from me or not. It was an odd sensation.

"Our equipment is going crazy. Are you getting anything?" Emily pressed, looking up from the device she held. Derek had another little measurement tool in his hands, one earbud in his ear, listening to whatever the sensor was detecting.

I nodded at Emily's inquiry, squinting at the clearing. "Yeah," I said. "There's something here..."

I was going to say more, but I forgot the words before they even formed in my mind. I could see things moving, but it was unlike anything I'd seen before. This was not one or two apparitions, like in my house. It was more like an entire world overlaid atop mine.

I stepped back, instinctively, but this vision was settling all around me. There was no escaping it. I sank to the ground, shrinking away from the solidifying forms. Beside me, the warped circle of light was becoming visible, just as it had been in Emily's picture.

"Ah! Hey!" someone cried. I looked up to see Hazel, eyes trained on one of the figures.

She could see them, too, which only scared me more.

I closed my eyes, hoping that when I opened them, the beings around me would be gone. The pressure in my head was building steadily, and I could feel the scream rising within me. Somehow, I hadn't imagined finding the portal would be like this.

I concentrated with everything I had on pushing the beings away. I focused my mind, using the techniques I'd read about to close the portal. Maybe I could seal it, maybe I could end this. I squeezed my eyes shut, pressing my fingers into my temples until the ache started to dull.

Slowly, I opened my eyes.

It hadn't quite worked. I could still see some figures, though there were fewer of them, and they were more translucent. I frowned. Sitting cross-legged in the center of the clearing—right where the portal was—I closed my eyes and fished the quartz crystal from my pocket. I hadn't told the others, but I'd read about it and found one in a bag of crystals my Aunt Fiona had given me a few years back. Apparently, they were supposed to be useful for focusing energy and working with portals.

I took several deep breaths, ignoring the chatter of my friends and the soft rattling of the aspen leaves. I slowed my breathing, calming my mind. It was hard, but years of coping with anxiety meant that I had developed a few ways to settle my racing mind. It wasn't quite the mental clarity of meditation, but it seemed better than nothing.

I tried to visualize the portal, and see it closing. I squeezed the crystal as I focused, using the feel of the sharp edge biting into my palm as an anchor, focusing my mind on the task at hand.

I wasn't sure how long I sat there, concentrating on closing the portal, but slowly, I started to feel the pressure of the shadowy entities release, softening until they were almost gone. Tentatively, I opened my eyes.

My wish was granted. The ghosts, or whatever they were, had gone, and we were in an ordinary forest again, just like we should be.

Save for one brilliant, shimmering figure standing before me.

Twenty-Five

"Rosalind," a voice said. It was weak and distant, but clear. I looked up at the figure before me, squinting at it.

"Y-yes?" I asked. It wasn't the shadowy beast. It was smaller, human-sized, with softer edges.

"I'm sorry."

I blinked. "You're...sorry?"

This voice was different from the others I'd heard. Familiar, though I couldn't place it. It was still too wispy and weak to fully recognize.

The figure solidified, and as it started to take shape, my stomach dropped.

"Honey, listen to me. You—"

That was when I recognized the voice. "No!" I screamed.

The voice cut out when I started yelling. I recoiled. The shimmering, glowing figure before me coalesced into something more real, more concrete.

My mother.

"Stop it! No! NO!" I shrieked. I pushed away, scrabbling back toward the edge of the clearing.

"Roz, what is this?" Emily cried.

"Go away!" I screamed, ignoring the questions of the others. I tried to concentrate, to push her back, but it was useless.

"*Rosalind...*" she whispered.

"*No*! I don't want to talk to you! Get away from me!" I shrieked. I shook with fury. My voice didn't sound right.

She looked so sad. She reached out to me. "*Please...*" she begged, more real than ethereal now.

"No! No! You can't just come back now!" I snarled at the ghost of my dead mother.

"*Roz...*"

"You can't just start haunting me and scaring me and expect me to be happy to see you!" I raged on, climbing to my feet. "You *left*. You *abandoned me*. I wanted to talk to you for *years* and you wouldn't! I did everything to help you and you just...you ignored me and you hurt me and you *left me*!"

My throat was raw. Tears were streaming down my face. I had forgotten everything—the headache, the ghosts, the clearing, the portal, my friends, all of it. The only thing I could see was her, giving me that damn piteous look, trying to convince me not to be mad at her anymore.

I hated that it was working. I hated her for turning my own emotions against me, and for making me feel guilty for being angry with her.

I had a right to be angry.

"Get away from me!" I said.

She moved closer, speaking, I think, though I couldn't hear her words over my own shouting.

"No!" I pulled back again.

Still, she advanced. "*Rosalind, listen, there's—*"

"Get *away!*"

I slammed my fists against the trunk of a tree, glaring as much hate as I could at her. The ground shook, and the ghost of my mother retreated, dissipating until she was no more. The portal shimmered again, shining brighter in the flare of my anger.

We sat in a strained silence for a moment. Everyone was looking at me.

"What the hell was—" Derek started to ask.

A blinding light erupted from the center of the portal, and a terrible sound filled the quiet forest. It was like metal groaning under an immense weight, but impossibly loud. I clapped my hands over my ears, squeezing my eyes shut and screaming against the sudden torrent of wind. It was so cold I could feel frost collecting on my exposed skin. It spread across my nose, my fingers, my neck, and arms. I shuddered against the chill and tried to turn away.

The earth shook, throwing me to my knees, and the others screamed. I was screaming, too. The whirlwind tore the words right out of our mouths.

There was a blast. A huge force, like an explosion, but frozen, not burning. It threw us back, tumbling across the ground, scattered around the clearing. The blast hit me twice—outside of me, knocking me down as a physical force, and within me, making my heart ache and my head throb. The portal burned clearer than ever, and every fracture in it rippled through me as the air split open. When it finally cracked, I almost fainted, my vision fading to black.

The stars cleared from my eyes, and I could see brilliant white light push to the edges of the trees, rising up into the sky, lighting up the forest like a star going supernova.

The wind died down and someone screamed. My head snapped around and I opened my eyes to see two very large feet standing in the center of the clearing.

I looked up, up, up at the too-tall figure before me.

The shadow.

It was like looking into a black hole—all light swallowed up into nothingness by its massive form. Even standing in the midst of this brilliant glow, it was pure darkness; a shadow come to life. The massive size of it reminded me of a bear. A towering, humanoid figure carved from obsidian.

I couldn't move, I couldn't scream, I just stared up at it in horror.

No. No. Leave. Go away.

I didn't know what to do. What *could* I do? I concentrated, using my newfound ability, but it was futile. The being was huge, and as it came closer, it solidified. Whatever powers I had before to send it away were nothing against it now.

I could feel it, somehow. It reminded me of when a butterfly perched on your finger. It was this faint awareness of something *there*.

Without knowing how, I understood that this thing was now corporeal. It was real. It was *here*.

And that meant it could hurt me. Hurt my friends.

The creature stepped toward me. It drew what looked an awful lot like a gun from its belt. I couldn't see its face, but I could feel its gaze on me.

Gun? I wondered amidst my terror. *Why does it need a gun?*

Above us, I saw rolling clouds. Thunder crashed and lightning cut the heavens, illuminating the darkening sky in fleeting bursts. The glow cast from the portal was eerie, a cold light that twisted in the air behind the shadow.

"Rosalind!" someone screamed. The voice snapped me out of my daze and I scrambled away, managing to climb to my feet as the being crossed the clearing in one long stride.

I had backed up to the edge of the clearing, my shoulders pressed into the trunk of a thin tree. Pathetically, I grabbed a fallen branch and held it up against the shadow.

He leveled his gun at me. I saw something within it glow and pulsate.

I'm going to die.

He fired, but his weapon's charge didn't reach me. I saw a blinding light strike the leaves above my head. I ducked and screamed. The trees sizzled and blackened, a burned hole left in their wake.

Hazel was shouting. I saw Ford throw a rock at the creature. It clanged loudly against its head. The monster turned to him and fired. Ford ducked, barely avoiding a direct hit.

A kind of bubble spread out around us, sealing the clearing and blocking the others from reaching us. It was dark, but I could just make out the forest beyond it, and my friends, frantically beating against the strange shield.

I stared up at the creature before me, barely visible in the darkness, and wondered what kind of shadow-ghost-thing carried a ray gun and set up force-fields. That definitely did seem more like an "alien" thing than a "ghost" thing. Provided we lived through this, Ford would never let me hear the end of it.

Its dark gaze fell back on me and once again it fired. I screamed and stumbled back, crashing against the shield. It hummed, sending my hair standing on end with its buzzing energy.

There was something weird, though. I mean, besides the million weird things happening. But there was one that was *really* confusing thought: *Why is he missing?*

Part of me was stuck on that, but some other part of me, some braver or crazier part of me, let out a strangled cry and charged the monster, driving my makeshift weapon into the creature's abdomen.

It struck with a clang, like I was hitting metal. I struck again, and again, my arms rattling with the effort. I swung over and over while it was preoccupied with whatever was keeping it from killing me. The creature was distracted, seeming to fight something I couldn't see.

I didn't care. I continued my assault until the branch I was holding splintered and broke, becoming a stub in my hand. I threw it aside and snatched up a rock. I threw it at the creature as it tried again to fire at me. I was so scared I could barely grip the rocks, but my father had always taught me that if I was being attacked, I should fight with everything I had. That was how I intended to go out. This thing might kill me, but I wouldn't make it easy.

I found a larger rock, hefting it up with both hands. I threw it as hard as I could, hitting the creature square in its face. This time, it wasn't just a metallic clang—it was a *crack.* The faceplate of the mask it wore broke off, revealing a shockingly humanoid face.

I was about to hit it—him?—again, but stopped, stooped over holding a rock in bewilderment. I was looking at what could easily be an abnormally tall man. I recoiled.

"What are you?" I demanded.

He tried to aim his gun at me again, but once more, it was pushed away. This time, I could see a hand pulling the gun back. Just like the tall man, this being began to take on a solid form.

It was my mother.

I shrank back from both of them, clutching my rock, ready to attack, though I wasn't sure how much good it would do.

"Enough, Miranda!" the man roared.

"I won't let you," my mother snarled, though she was still translucent.

"You know I have to," he said, sounding almost apologetic. "Look how much damage she's done already."

In response, my mother tried to pull the gun away. He tried to shoot me and I dropped to the ground, screaming, barely dodging the shot. I could see my friends outside the strange forcefield, watching in horror.

"She's too dangerous!" the shadow-man shouted, tossing my mother aside.

While they fought, I spotted another branch in the clearing. Smaller, but long enough that I could use it. I snatched it up and tried to knock the gun away from him.

He was distracted enough that it worked. The weapon skittered away and a huge, gloved hand closed around my throat, lifting me off the ground like I was a misbehaving kitten. I clawed at the hand, futilely trying to pull his fingers back. He was so shadowlike that I could barely see what I was grabbing at. My vision swirled as it became harder and harder to breathe; everything was going black around the edges.

Lightning struck outside the dome, illuminating it just enough for me to see few lines of difference on what I had figured was his armor: an insignia on his breastplate.

The same one that was on my mother's journal.

A jolt ran through his arm and he dropped me, roaring in anger. I fell, stumbling and gasping. I hadn't regained my composure before that same giant hand struck me across my face, throwing me back. My head spun and I tasted blood. He reached out to strike me a second time, and surely this one would kill me, but again my mother thwarted him. She couldn't do much, though, just slow him enough that it dazed, rather than destroyed, me. Sooner or later, he'd win out.

The strange, armored man lunged for his gun and snatched it up. He snarled and fired at me again. This time, he held down the trigger, drawing a line of light that followed me, shaking and wavering where my mother interfered. It incinerated trees within the shield, turning sand to glass. Everyone was screaming. Above us, thunder clapped and lightning flashed.

I scooted back and tried again to push him away, to banish him with whatever capability I had for sending ghosts packing.

To my surprise, it kind of worked this time. There was a tremendous shattering, and the shield seemed to fracture, falling in shards that disappeared before they reached me. I raced out of the clearing and into the trees.

The monster of a man threw something and I dove away instinctively. It was a good instinct, because it turned out to be some kind of grenade. It rolled into the forest, and I veered away from it. The little grenade exploded with a ridiculously powerful blast, and countless little bits of metal cut me, slicing me, burying themselves in my flesh. I gasped, dizzy from the pain.

Behind me, new light blossomed. Orange and flickering.

The man pointed his gun at me again, but something struck him, something new, knocking it from his hand. He cried out, clutching his hand as blood spilled from it. He looked like he was missing a couple fingers. Confused, I turned to see what had hit him. Instead, I saw a fire spreading through the trees.

"Oh, no," I whispered, all thoughts of the mystery ninja-star vanishing from my mind.

It ripped through the forest with incredible speed. Before I could even process it, the inferno had raged over to our clearing, blindingly bright and painfully hot.

"Rosalind, run!"

I didn't question my mother's command. I clambered to my feet, stumbling and falling in my panic.

I turned back to the creature, the man, who'd attacked me to see my mother make one last strike. She was solid now, real, and she struck him with surprising force while he groped on the ground for his weapon. He crashed into some trees and she swept over to him. I watched her rip something from his suit and throw it violently away. Placing her hand on his chest, she concentrated. He glowed and yelled in rage before disappearing.

My mother looked back at me, watching me sorrowfully as she, too, vanished.

"Roz!"

Someone grabbed hold of me, pulling me along. I stumbled, looking around for the others.

Regaining my footing, I ran on my own, turning to see the woods behind us completely consumed by an unnatural flame. The roar of the fire was deafening, and we ran all-out, chased away by the blaze. Lightning still struck, thunder booming so loudly it felt like we were in the bellies of the clouds.

We scrambled into Ford's van just as it started to rain, heavy, as though buckets of water were being dropped from the sky. Ford sped away, the flames raging behind us, somewhat subdued now by the downpour.

Still, though, I could see the fire consuming trees and spreading along the mountainside.

"We have to call someone!" I cried. "There are houses up here, it could hurt someone!"

"I don't have reception," Emily said, checking her phone. She hit it against her palm a few times.

We passed the fire station, where trucks with sirens blaring were already heading out into the torrent. They must have seen the blaze and mobilized without needing a call.

Ford pulled to the side of the road and we watched the big yellow trucks race by. It wasn't far to the fire, luckily, but my insides still clenched in terror at the thought of the flames consuming any homes.

When the firefighters had passed, Ford steered us back onto the road and kept driving, going as fast as he could on the slick roads.

My heart ached. Why had I needed to come here today? What had made me think I could fix things? I hadn't closed the portal, I had annihilated it, and at what cost? I'd put the lives of everyone living on the mountain, all the firefighters, and my friends in danger.

I dropped my head into my hands and tried to ignore the throbbing pain all over my body.

"Does that hurt too much?" Hazel asked, holding my arm in one hand and a pair of sterilized plyers in the other. We had decided against the hospital—they would ask too many questions we had no hope of answering. So we went back to my house, and Hazel patched us up as best she could.

"No," I lied. I kept my face turned away. I could stand having the shrapnel pulled from my skin. I couldn't stand to watch it happen.

Lucky for me, Hazel was good with this sort of thing. She'd done plenty of first aid for her brother, after all. Haldi had spent the last few years trying to master movie stunts, and his lack of skill was apparent.

"Does anyone know what actually happened up there?" Ford asked.

"Well...we did technically manage to close the portal," I finally said. *Destroying* it would have been a more accurate term, but I didn't feel like getting technical. Besides, was this really a win? We'd torn it open, and I wasn't sure how much...stuff...had gotten through before it was shattered.

I glanced at the news, playing on mute in the background. It was flooded with reports and speculations. They kept interviewing experts on-air, asking how this was possible. There was a fire, a huge magnetic storm, and reports were confirming what several people on the edges of town had felt: An earthquake.

"What did that...guy...thing...say to you?" Derek asked.

"Um...he said..." I winced against the pain as Hazel pulled another bit of metal from my skin. "My mother...he knew her. I think. It sounded like they knew each other, at least. And he said...'You know I have to.'" I left out the other thing he'd said, though it echoed in my head like a threat.

She's too dangerous. Look how much damage she's done.

Part of me was in complete denial. How was *I* dangerous? Another part of me, though, knew he was right. I glanced at the muted television. At my injured friends. I was plenty dangerous, whatever my intentions.

"...Roz?" Ford asked. The hesitation in his voice was palpable.

"Yeah?" I said, distracted by pain.

"Why...why didn't you tell us your mother was dead?"

I looked at him, then looked down at my injured hands. "I don't know," I admitted. I laughed, but it was weak, hollow. "I know this sounds stupid, but I just...wanted to leave all of that behind me, I guess. She didn't just die, you know? She...she killed herself. And I was angry. I was...I couldn't..." I stopped talking, the words catching in my throat.

It sounded absurd, saying the words out loud. I gnawed on the inside of my cheek, wishing I could pull them back. I didn't want to be this bitter, petty, selfish person who was angry about her mother, but I was. I didn't want to explain the thousands of conflicting emotions that cluttered my mind and blocked-up my heart, but I feared I would have to.

Hazel gave my shoulder a little squeeze. Derek nodded, a kind of quiet understanding taking over his face. No one else said anything. It was silent again.

We watched the news coverage of the fire for a while. Despite the speedy response, there were a total of five injuries and two deaths. A young couple caught in the blaze while out for an evening hike. At that, I thought I might throw up. Two people were dead because of me. Two families devastated thanks to my actions.

Hazel sat beside me and gripped my hand, saying in a small voice, “You’ll be okay.”

I shook my head. When I spoke, my voice trembled, on the verge of tears. “I don’t know about that, Haze.”

Hazel nodded, then bit her lip. “You know...”

I glanced up at her, already knowing what she was going to say. “I could ask my mother?” I offered.

She looked down, and I sighed. Hazel had been circling this idea ever since we’d accepted the existence of ghosts, but I’d been avoiding even addressing it until now.

“I guess. I mean...I don’t know how to get in touch with her, but...” I flipped through the journal. “Obviously it *was* her trying to get me to read this.”

Hazel looked back at the news. “Should we tell someone what happened?”

“Haven’t you ever watched a movie?” Ford said. “If we say anything, we’ll either be called crazy, or the government will come take us away. Or both.”

“Wow,” Emily deadpanned. “I didn’t realize you were a conspiracy theorist, too.”

“Says the paranormal investigator,” Ford countered with a grin, diffusing what could have easily become another fight. Emily chuckled, sounding tired.

I ignored them, flipping through the journal instead, eyes scanning over sketches and lists and newspaper clippings. It was aimless, and futile, but it made me feel like I had some semblance of control. But I had none. The symbol on his breastplate. On this book. What did it mean? Why had my mother known so much about that...shadow man? Why did he know her name? What was their connection? What had she tried to tell me before we were interrupted?

It occurred to me that I should try to summon her, but I was still so shaky with my ghost-related abilities. Besides, if I expended any more energy, I might actually fall into a coma.

"Anything that'll help us now?" Emily asked, glancing at me.

"Probably not," I admitted. "I mean...it sounds like my mom was going through the same thing I am now, and she had some ways of coping but...she died. She—she *killed* herself."

"That doesn't mean it'll happen to you," Emily said firmly. "Sixth senses can be hereditary, so you might see what she did, but...you're not her. And you're not alone."

I smiled at her. "Thanks, Em. But...is it even a sixth sense? That shadow...he turned out to be..." I held my hands out helplessly. "That wasn't a ghost."

She sighed. "I know. That was...something else entirely."

"What do we do about that?" I asked.

"I wouldn't even know where to begin," Emily said, staring blankly at her notes. Seeing her at a loss, without a plan, without a handle on things, made my stomach churn.

"What if..." Derek started, glancing at me, then looking away.

"What?" I asked.

"What if she's...not dead?" he offered.

Everyone fell silent.

"Not...dead...?" I asked, a little dumbfounded.

Derek fidgeted, realizing everyone was staring at him.

"Wait, do you mean...like...stuck in another dimension?" Ford asked, catching on before I did.

Derek nodded. "If she had this ability, too...and if she was trying to escape, or...I don't know, draw the threat away from you? Or maybe something went wrong...?"

I stared at him, then at the news. I couldn't feel the presence of *any* ghosts right then, and wondered if that meant I'd somehow cut myself off from my mother.

Even so, I should have felt victorious; the portal was gone. I'd done what I'd intended to do. But clutching the slightly singed journal in my hands, I also knew this wasn't over. More entities would find their way back to us. More creatures would come to my world. There were other portals, and other monsters lurking in the darkness.

There was still so much I didn't know—why did I have these abilities? Who was 'The Red Knight', and what did they want? Why did one of the ghosts in my house fear Veronica? Who was the woman, Sana, mentioned in my mother's journal? What did that symbol I kept seeing mean? How was this all connected? A million questions raced through my mind, making my head spin.

And that shadow man in armor that seemed to be made of nighttime? I didn't know who or what he was, or why exactly he'd come for me, but there had to be others like him, and where he had failed, they would return to finish the job.

"More will come," I said, not realizing at first that I'd spoken aloud.

My words seemed to reignite the fire in Emily, because she sat up a little straighter and squared her shoulders.

"We'll be ready this time," she said, nodding to the journal.

I looked around the room at them, heart hammering. "You guys don't have to do this," I whispered. "It's only going to get worse."

Hazel gripped my hand. "I'm not letting you do this alone. Besides," she glanced at the news. "Doesn't look like we can really avoid this, even if we want to."

I looked to Derek and Ford.

"Can't quit now," Derek said simply.

"Exactly. Not when aliens are officially on the table," Ford added with a grin.

I looked around the room at my friends, realizing there was no way to dissuade them.

"Well then," I said, trying to force determination into my trembling voice. I looked down at the journal in my lap. "Let's get to work."

SNEAK PEEK:

DARK SENTINELS – THE ASSASSIN

I held the flashlight as steady as I could while Emily typed away on her computer. Beside me, Derek was taking pictures and making notes.

"There," I said, looking toward a darkened corner.

Derek followed my direction, nodding as he caught sight of the ghost on his screen.

It was less apparent to me when technology helped, since I could see the ghosts regardless. Usually, ghosts are only visible sometimes, but in the last week, I'd found myself able to see all ghosts, all the time, whether or not they wanted to be seen.

They didn't seem all that thrilled about my new ability, either, but what could I do?

The ghost in the corner snarled and withdrew further. This one was strange—human, but oddly feral. An animalistic poltergeist who liked to bite.

The house we were in was old, but not old enough to warrant generations upon generations of ghosts. Las Vegas doesn't have old buildings the way the east coast does, or Europe—a fact Emily often complained about.

Now, though, it seemed age of the building was irrelevant: No one had ever died on the property. It had had two owners since it was built, and as far as we could tell, they'd all lived happy, peaceful lives. The second owner still lived here, as she had for almost thirty years, and she'd never had any kind of paranormal disturbances until a week earlier.

They'd gotten so bad in that time, she'd temporarily moved out. Her church's priest had come to try and exorcise the house. That hadn't worked. Emily was her last hope.

Or rather, *I* was.

"Okay, Roz—do your thing."

I hesitated. "My thing" was apparently banishing ghosts, but I still wasn't completely sure how I did it, and I didn't feel particularly confident that I'd be able to call up that talent when I needed to. I didn't have the best track record, though in fairness, I had been getting a *lot* of practice lately.

The ghost let out a guttural growl and I swallowed hard, trying to concentrate.

He lurched toward me, ungainly and awkward in his movements. I backed away, bumping into a wall. It grabbed a chair and threw it at me, and I ducked, letting out a little scream.

"Concentrate, Roz!" Emily shouted.

I squeezed my eyes shut and focused on the ghost. I could still feel him—it was almost like seeing him, but worse—as he moved closer.

I saw the wavering light of his energy, and imagined it dissipating. Vanishing. Slipping away into wherever it was that ghosts belonged. It wasn't this world, but I didn't really know where it was. Something to do with dimensions, I was sure, but I just couldn't care about that now.

The ghost stopped, hesitating, weakening. I opened my eyes a crack to peek at him. Emily and Derek stood on either side of us, watching.

Go back, I willed him.

His image flickered, dimming.

Then, he roared, launching at me. I screamed and swung at him instinctively as he charged me. My concentration broken, the action had no effect. He knocked me back into the wall, and I smacked my head hard, my vision spinning.

"Roz!" someone shouted. Strong hands grabbed me, trying to pull me away.

The room was still out of focus, but I was able to pick out the ghost's energy. It was moving closer, stronger and more corporeal now. I raised my hand to the ghost and concentrated, ignoring everyone and everything else in the room. I put all my power, all my energy into that moment, that ghost. I pushed as hard as I could with my mind, with the new, unfamiliar part of my consciousness that somehow dispelled ghosts.

The room seemed to bend and twist around me, and for a moment, I could see through everything. It was almost like an x-ray, but so much more. Everything around me was shadowy, half-there, semi-transparent. And mixed in with all the things I expected to see—the walls and furniture of the house, my friends, the equipment—were other things. Other structures and objects I couldn't make sense of. It was all too fuzzy and disjointed for me to piece together.

My stomach churned with a sudden wave of nausea and my head throbbed so hard I lost my footing, sinking to my knees.

Around me, the room darkened.

I mentally pushed at the ghost again, and I could feel it slipping away, pushed back behind whatever barrier that divided the living and the dead.

I shuddered, slumping to press my forehead against the cool tile floor. Emily was the one who'd grabbed me, and she stumbled under my weight.

"Did it work?" Emily asked.

Derek was checking his EMF detector. He looked up and nodded, crossing the room to us.

"You okay, Roz?" Derek asked, crouching down beside me.

I nodded. "Yeah. Sure. I think," I said, my vision still spinning.

They helped me to my feet and led me to a chair where I rested, taking slow, measured breaths. They picked up their equipment, chattering excitedly about this latest ghost expulsion.

"That one was harder, wasn't it?" Emily asked.

I nodded, testing whether I could stand on my own. "Yeah...it really didn't want to go."

"This seems to be a pattern; every ghost is worse than the last," Derek commented. He looked at me. "Any theories?"

I shrugged. "You're the ghost experts. I'm just..." I let it hang. I didn't know what I was.

"Maybe we should be more careful next time," Derek said, glancing at Emily. She looked at me, then at the cast Derek still wore. While we hadn't encountered anything quite as violent as the ghost that dropped Derek from twelve feet in the air, we'd faced a few challenges in our almost-never ending string of ghost removals, and it was getting harder for me, not easier.

Emily frowned, but nodded.

"Yeah. We had another one scheduled for this afternoon, but maybe we should do it tomorrow," Emily said, glancing at me. I must not have looked all that great, because Derek nodded in agreement.

"Which one?" I asked.

"What?" Emily replied.

"The other...expelley-exorcism-whatever thing we had scheduled for today. What's the case?"

Emily blew at her bangs absently. "Uh, another poltergeist."

Two poltergeists. Must be my lucky day.

"Who's it haunting?" I pressed.

Emily glanced up at me. "Just...this woman."

Her tone bothered me. "And?"

Emily sighed. "And her two kids."

I leaned back against the wall. "Well, we shouldn't put that off," I said.

"Roz," Derek said. "I don't really think that's a good idea."

"Why not? I don't think it's a good idea to leave them in a house with a poltergeist. Those things can be dangerous."

"Yeah, but," he looked at Emily for help.

"It's just," Emily started. "You've been pushing yourself *really* hard this past week, and..."

"This is my fault, Emily," I said.

Emily and Derek exchanged a look, but I went on before they could argue. We'd had this conversation too many times already.

"It's my fault and it's my mess to clean up. If I hadn't..." I shook my head. "I still don't know exactly what's going on here, but I know I caused it, so I'd better make it right. Plus, no one knows better than me how awful it is to live with ghosts in your house."

"You know I don't agree with you that this is all your fault," Emily said. "But...I don't know. I won't cancel just yet, but I'm gonna check in with you before we go, and if you're not up for it, I'm calling it off until you're at full capacity."

"Fair enough," I said.

They drove me home after that and I contemplated whether I had enough energy to go all the way upstairs and sleep on my bed. The sofa was so much closer.

Just as I was getting a blanket to curl up with, the doorbell rang.

Frustrated, I threw my blanket onto the sofa and went to the see who it was. I must have been exceptionally tired, because there was no explaining why I just opened the door without even checking to see who was there.

"Oh, hello," I said to the short woman standing on our porch. I was surprised to see her there, as if the ringing doorbell hadn't signaled to me that someone would be waiting.

She smiled. "Hello. My name is Elixabete Otxoa, I was sent by the agency." She spoke with an accent I couldn't place, though it had a musical quality to it.

"Hi," I said, still a little startled. She had deep olive skin, with twinkling dark eyes and an impish smile. "Um," I stuttered. "You...the agency sent you?" I asked, brow furrowing. My father had mentioned hiring another housekeeper, but I hadn't expected anyone today.

"Yes, said you needed a housekeeper? Said you were having a bit of trouble finding a good fit?"

I blushed a little, wondering how in the world I could explain that in a way that wouldn't sound like we were troublemakers.

"Um, right, yeah, for some reason...that has been kind of an issue," I said. So much for eloquence.

Elixabete's smile broadened. "Well, I'm the one they send in for special cases," she said, adding a wink.

Oh, that makes me feel so much better.

"Right. Um. Can I see your paperwork?" I asked. I didn't get any weird ghostly-sense from her, but I had become suspicious of everyone. Besides, normal people could be dangerous all on their own.

She nodded and handed me an envelope. I opened it and skimmed the documents there. Everything was in order. Trying to look like I also had my life together, I smiled and stepped back, letting her inside.

"Glad to have you here, um, Elixabete? Is that right?" I asked, checking the paperwork again.

"That's it!" she said brightly, looking around the house.

I gave her a quick tour, explaining where everything was. Elixabete put a hand on my shoulder as I was showing her around upstairs.

"Rosalind, if I may say so," she said gently. "You seem tired. Why don't you go back to whatever you were doing before I arrived and I'll get started with what you've shown me so far. If I have any questions, I'll find you," she said with a reassuring smile.

"O-okay," I said, returning her smile.

I shook myself a bit, trying to clear my head. I didn't know what I'd tell my dad if this housekeeper left, too, but I couldn't worry about that now. I had to get some rest, so I could go back to fixing all the problems I'd caused by going up to the mountain and...doing whatever it was I did. I'd closed the portal, but something else had happened, too. And it was causing even more of a mess.

I collapsed onto my bed and drifted off for a while.

The soft buzz of my phone woke me. I grabbed it, still half-asleep, and pulled it to me.

It was a text from Ford. I checked the clock and saw that I'd slept for almost three hours. I was surprised—sleeping didn't usually come easy anymore. I rubbed my eyes and opened the text.

Hey, how'd it go today?

I reoriented myself so I could type, *Eh*

That bad, huh?

Not really. I just hate it, I sent back.

Ford responded in his usual style: *Right. Having a super power. SO lame.*

I don't have a super power, I replied.

Ford's indignation was palpable. *Well I know I can't send ghosts away. WITH MY MIND.*

I rolled my eyes, *You poor deprived soul.*

lol.

I thought perhaps he was done, but then I received, *You still going to take care of the poltergeist this afternoon?*

Apparently he'd been in touch with Derek or Emily. I sighed and texted back: *Yes.*

Cool. Can I come?

Sure. I stared at my phone, suddenly suspicious, and sent a second text. *Why?*

I want to test a theory.

I rolled my eyes. *What theory?*

He sent an angel emoji.

Ford. I hoped the severity of my tone could be conveyed via text.

You'll all-caps at me.

I scowled. *What is it?*

...Aliens.

IT'S NOT ALIENS!

SEE!?

I laughed, despite myself. *Whatever. It's at 3. I'll have Emily send you the address*

Excellent

I got up then and decided to check on Elixabete.

She was happily cooking in the kitchen. When she spotted me, she gave another broad smile.

"Hello, Rosalind! Can I fix you anything? Tea? Coffee? A snack?"

I shook my head. "No, thank you, I just want to make sure you're doing all right."

"Everything's just fine," she said.

I nodded. More awake now, I noticed that Elixabete wore a collection of bracelets and necklaces adorned with crystals and intricately-carved symbols. They reminded me of the kind of thing Aunt Fiona's hippie friends wore.

"Well, I've got a load of laundry going, and dinner will be ready in about half an hour. I also noticed that there are still some unpacked boxes in the guest rooms, so if you'd like me to take care of that, I can."

I blinked. "Oh. Okay. Uh, I'll ask my dad."

She nodded and returned to her cooking, humming softly to herself.

I studied her movements. She seemed very relaxed. Very at ease. That didn't mean anything, though. She'd only been here three hours. I had tried expelling the ghosts around my house, but it didn't seem to work long-term. I hadn't seen the foreign ghost for a few days, or Diego since that first night, but the creepy old woman, the girl from the theatre, and a few new ones were keeping up with regular appearances, despite my best efforts to banish them. Even knowing that I was at the epicenter of this, I didn't fully understand what was happening; I only knew one thing—no one was safe here.

Well, save for my father, who seemed to repel ghosts naturally.

Either way, I hoped Elixabete would at least get enough cooking done to last us a few days before she left and never came back. This would be three strikes at the agency, and they might not want to send any more of their people to us after that.

I turned away. I couldn't worry about Elixabete right then.

I had a poltergeist to go get rid of.

Acknowledgements

This is the part of the book you'll only read if you suspect your name might be in here. There are a lot of people who deserve thanks. So many awesome writers, editors, friends, and family members have helped contribute to the creation of this book.

First of all, my mother, Prisca Crawford, who has always supported and believed in my dreams, no matter how wild and unattainable they might seem. She spent many nights listening to me ramble, offering her insights, letting me read over drafts of this book, and making me tea while I poured over it again and again (even that time I took over the front room of the house after printing the entire book out and spreading every single page on the floor!). You are an amazing mother and I am beyond blessed to have you.

Next up are my younger siblings, William Crawford and Emma Crawford, who have sat through countless readings of this book. They were not "young adults" when I started writing it, but they are now, and there's something very surreal about getting to read a young adult book to the target audience, so thank you for always being there and being willing to listen (and for your shockingly adept insights; you're both brilliant).

Special thank you to my father, Doug Jacob, for encouraging me to keep writing and reading my stories, even when they sometimes made him wonder about my sanity. Your eagerness to see where my words would take me warms my heart.

To my Papa and Mimi, for your support and guidance. I am happy to share this with you.

Huge shout-out to Candice Montgomery, Shiloh Embry, Jason Cantrell, Julia Shaw, and Daevone Molyneux. These are my fellow writers, editors, critique partners, and the members of my #TwitterGroup who beta read, and provided incredibly insightful feedback. They were excited by this book, and eager to read the next one. Thank you all for your time, patience, energy, gentle pushes, and constructive criticism—you helped shape this book into what it is.

My critique group partners, Ann Kimborough and Michael Harley, deserve great thanks. They gave me some of my favorite comments, including "Why didn't you bring more chapters??" and "I can't wait to hear what happens next!" Your enthusiasm for this project, as well as your honesty about where it could be improved, have made me a better writer and person.

Thank you to Matt Davis, for designing an absolutely stunning cover. Cover art has always been hugely important to me, and you helped make my dream a reality, and encase my book in a jacket I'm proud to show to the world.

And lastly, I'd like to thank my very best friend, Mhage, possibly the person I was most excited and nervous to share this book with, and whose love and praise for it has meant the world to me. Thank you for your friendship, encouragement, insistence that my words need to be out in the world, and your general "youness" that makes the world a brighter place.

About the Authors

Jacob Crawford is the pen name for a mother/daughter writing team consisting of E.V. Jacob and P.E. Crawford.

P.E. is a mother of three—E.V. being her eldest—and spends her days philosophizing, studying quantum mechanics, and asking impossible questions. She likes to drink tea and has a habit of overthinking things.

When she's not looking after her family, she can be found watching documentaries, reading articles, and expanding her very eclectic and unique knowledge base.

E.V. is a philosopher some days, a scientist others, and a writer always. It's a wonder that such a scatterbrain ever gets anything done, but based on the existence of this book (and several others in various stages of editing), she can at least jot down some of the ideas bouncing around in her head.

She lives in Las Vegas, where she spends her time planning to take over the world. She is a fan of tea, a hopeless geek, and an Oxford comma enthusiast.

You can find her on Twitter and Instagram @EveyJacob.

www.ingramcontent.com/pod-product-compliance
Lightning Source LLC
Chambersburg PA
CBHW030525310726
48979CB00010B/1801/J

* 9 7 8 0 9 9 9 6 1 0 6 2 6 *